Diary of Sara Hollins

Written By

Hishi Tokou

FOREVER AND A DAY PUBLISHING, LLC

To the extent that the image or images on the cover of this book depict a person or persons, such person or persons are merely models and are not intended to portray any character or characters featured in the book.

This book is a work of fiction. Names, characters, businesses, organizations, places, events, and incidents either are the product of the author's imagination or are used fictitiously. Any resemblance to actual persons, living or dead, and events are entirely coincidental.

Published by Forever and a Day Publishing,
LLC.
Triangle, Virginia 22172

Special book excerpts or customized printings can also be created to fit specific needs. For details, write to the office of the FAAD Sales Manager: faadpublishing@gmail.com The FAAD logo is a trademark of Forever and a Day Publishing, LLC.

ISBN Paperback 979-8-9911703-2-1

10 9 8 7 6 5 4 3 2 1

Printed in the United States of America

Table of Contents

Introduction vii

RECOLLECTION: School Mishaps 1

   Durix 24, 880 2

   Durix 26, 880 6

   Durix 27, 880 9

   Ferix 6, 880 13

   Ferix 7, 880 17

   Ferix 8, 880 21

RECOLLECTION: Wine and Dine 28

   Ferix 9, 880 29

   Ferix 10, 880 41

   Ferix 11, 880 48

   Ferix 12, 880 61

   Ferix 19, 880 66

   Ferix 20, 880 76

   Ferix 21, 880 85

RECOLLECTION: Old Friends, New School 98

   Ferix 22, 880 99

   Ferix 23, 880 105

   Ferix 24, 880 116

   Ferix 25, 880 120

   Ferix 28, 880 124

Ferix 29, 880 131

Ferix 30, 880 141

RECOLLECTION: Settled in for New Discoveries **146**

Ha 28, 880 147

Ha 29, 880 151

Ha 30, 880 158

Ha 31, 880 166

RECOLLECTION: A Royal Break **171**

Mortex 4, 880 172

Mortex 5, 880 176

Mortex 12, 880 192

Mortex 28, 880 196

Mortex 30, 880 220

RECOLLECTION: Vacation **231**

Kirius 7, 880 232

Kirius 14, 880 235

Kirius 15, 880 251

Kirius 16, 880 272

Kirius 18, 880 282

RECOLLECTION: Travel Arc **299**

Niori 4, 881 300

Niori 20, 881 304

Niori 21, 881 330

Kirius 4, 886 342

RECOLLECTION: Graduation **345**

Kirius 5, 886 346

Kirius 10, 886..362

Kirius 12, 886..379

Kirius 13, 886..384

Kirius 19, 886..389

Fori 2, 886..421

RECOLLECTION: I Miss You... **426**

Derix 8, 900..427

Introduction

Hi! You're named "Diary of Sara Hollins", but I bet you want to know who Sara is right? So, I'm here to tell you. Sara is the most beautiful girl in the school, which is pretty great when you're a 12-year-old in a human high school. She has amazing blue eyes, beautifully flowing golden-cream hair, and the voice of an angel. There's only one problem, her ego. Maybe it's because she's a Wolf-Vampire, emphasis on wolf and not werewolf by the way, but Sara is an arrogant, pretentious, know-it-all prick that even her jerk of a jock boyfriend if you could call him that, can't stand. Her father owns a hospital and is a top surgeon and her mother owns an international bank that holds several stocks and companies. To be honest her entire family is, for lack of a better word, richer than God. Now you might be asking, how do I know this? Well because, I'm Sara. Sara Hollins, Wolf-Vampire, nice to meet you. You're my new diary. I may write about school and other stuff of the sort, but you can expect to have some out-of-this-world stuff written in you. Like this one for example: "I stood in the grassy field, dew all around. The power of my bloodline surges forward to attack my foe." See, isn't that interesting?

RECOLLECTION

School Mishaps

The class was so boring. Mr. Anglus, my Calculus teacher, kept waking me up to answer stupid questions.

After I got the tenth question correct, he said, "It seems you understand the information Miss Hollins, but please do not sleep in my class."

I told him I didn't feel well as pathetically as I could and asked to go to the nurse. He stared at me for a second, the look on his face said he was unable to tell if it was an obvious lie or pitiful truth, before saying, "Very well, but can you take the Unit Test before you leave?"

What a pain that was. I took the stupid test, finished all fifty questions in like fifteen minutes, and packed up my stuff. As usual, as I walked towards the door some ignoramuses sneered and glared at me and, like usual, I treated it as positive support for getting through the rest of the day by saying, "Good luck everyone" which aroused more ferocious glares. As I walked to the door, Mr. Anglus' back was turned and one ignoramus thought neither he nor I could see him, as he tried to slingshot a pencil sharpener blade at me. In the blink of an eye, I deflected the attack, catching the blade and then throwing it back with double the force with a quick flash of my perfectly luscious cream-colored tail. Too bad I have to move so fast that no one can see it, otherwise they'd be even more awestruck by my beauty. The boy screamed in surprise as the blade grazed him and bore into his desk. Mr. Anglus quickly turned around to ask what happened then began digging through his desk for a first aid kit when he saw the blood dripping from the boy's fingers.

The class glared at me, but I put on my best-concerned face and said, "My goodness, are you ok!?"

"...Miss Hollins, you didn't happen to see what happened did you?," Mr. Anglus asked while he quickly wrapped a band-aid over the cuts.

"I was about to leave the room when I heard Jared scream."

"...S-she's right. I was fooling around with my pencil sharpener and cut myself." Jared, the ignoramus, said.

After quietly looking around the classroom and seeing no one willing to speak up, Mr. Anglus sighed and asked, "Miss Hollins, since you're going anyway, could you walk Jared to the nurse? I don't want him to do something else stupid." I detested the idea but politely answered yes and Jared and I began walking to the nurse together. The hallway was empty since classes were going on and we walked silently.

"I'll pay you back for making me look like a fool," Jared said after a while.

"Don't worry, I didn't charge you." I mockingly smiled. He scowled but remained quiet. It was strange like he was planning something. As we went down one of the back stairwells, the quickest way to the nurse and which was usually filled with students avoiding class, I noticed it was unusually empty. "Strange," I muttered to myself. As we reached the first-floor landing Jared then shoved me against the wall, put a knife to my neck, and began to laugh.

"I insist you let me pay the bill." he cackled. "Now where should I cut first?"

"How droll, this is going to be over pretty quickly." I sighed. I was pretty irritated since I did really need to get to the nurse. What? Did you think I was going as an excuse? Well, you see vampires drink blood because we need a lot of nutrients, and blood's the fastest route. That said, I'm a special case among vampires, having frequent hypoglycemia while being regular in everything else. This means I must periodically go to the nurse throughout the day to take my medicine...which is basically sugar water.

Anyway, he looked at me and laughed. "That's right, this *will* be over quickly," Jared said. I closed my eyes and took a deep breath. As his cackling faded, my magic began to surge forth. "What's wrong Sara, are you scared?" he laughed.

"You're the one that should be scared!" I growled. In a flash of light, I transformed from a humanoid to a wolf and lunged at him. His screams were quickly silenced as his blood stained the white tiles. After everything went quiet, well as quiet as it can be when you hear teachers rushing to the scene, I transformed back to humanoid before passing out.

Thus, this concludes my first entry. Oh, the nurse is coming to check on me.

"What a pain." I sighed. I had woken up in the hospital with my mother nervously hovering over me and my father arguing with news reporters who wanted my account of the incident. The reporters reluctantly left when officers and hospital staff shooed them away and, after some questions and paperwork, we returned to our mansion which, by the way, is in the middle of our 500-acre land. Unfortunately, that wasn't the end for me since I had an unbelievably painful headache. My father, who had to pass off all his surgeries for the rest of the day, decided to yell at me for my "crude and blatant display of evisceration." My mother, who also passed off her meetings for the day, was more considerate of my woes and let me lay my head on her lap as she tried to calm him. However, after we got home, she got a business call and had to leave, meaning it was just me and Dad.

So, there I was, sitting on my bed, listening to my dad lecture me while I had a throbbing headache, but I must have fallen asleep because I woke up, changed into my pajamas, and tucked in bed. My headache had yet to go away but had lessened. As I sat up to look around, Dad walked in with a mug in his hand.

"How are you feeling?" he asked as he sat on my bed. His hair looked kind of damp, and he smelled like soap, so I guess he had time to take a shower.

I put my hand on my head and groaned as I fell back down thinking, "Great, now I'm going to be lectured about falling asleep during a lecture." Instead of lecturing me, however, Dad handed me his mug, allowing me to smell delicious coffee within, then picked me up and began cradling me as we walked to their room.

In an attempt to gain more sympathy, I whined, "I'm sorry Daddy. I promise I won't do that again."

"Do what again?" he asked in his 'I'm listening' voice.

"Fall asleep while you're lect-, ah, talking," I replied.

"And?" he urged.

"And that Jared got what he deserved." He glared at me and on instinct I mumbled, "Sorry."

When we got to my parent's room, he placed me in the center of the bed by the pillows and laid out a feast on a tray in front of me. I was starving, having not gotten to eat lunch or dinner, but eyed the food suspiciously while I waited for his punishment.

"I'm not going to punish you," he said, sitting down next to me and taking back his mug. "Now eat or you won't regain your strength. I even put hyperglycemic blood in your meal." I didn't wait and devoured the meal. After eating dinner, Dad cleaned up before coming to lie down next to me.

"Thank you, Daddy," I said, snuggling close to him.

"Well I couldn't punish you when you're so down in the dumps," he said as he began stroking my head, "but please try to remember that being a Wolf-Vampire is a secret. You'll be taken away to Kofu if the Hunters feel you're abusing your power against humans. And they already don't like "Half-Breeds" like us. So please, be careful."

"I know Dad. I'm sorry." I sighed. After that, I fell asleep, so I don't remember the rest of his lecture.

Because of the police investigation, the school was closed until further notice. Both my parents were gone, Dad left for work after making me breakfast and Mom had an early meeting. I decided to walk around the park with my "boyfriend" Drake, and the only person crazy enough to be my friend, Shiyu, Shi for short. They were total opposites with Drake being your typical buff football player and Shi being the quiet slender type.

"So Sara, did you see me at yesterday's training?" Drake asked as he put his hand on my hip and pulled me towards him.

"No, I told you I was at the hospital," I replied, moving his hand and putting some distance between us.

Drake continued, "Oh right, that's a shame. I was so amazing too. I darted past these guys who thought they could catch me, but you know I'm the fastest on the team and-".

"Sara, are you sure it's alright for you to be walking outside like this? " Shi whispered.

"Don't worry I'm fine," I smiled back. My headache had left and I felt energized after Dad's breakfast.

"Well, if you say so, just don't push yourself."

9

We walked until we reached the center of the park then Drake spotted some of his football buddies and started playing frisbee with them, leaving me and Shi to sit and talk on a bench.

"So, did you have anything in particular you wanted to do today, or did you just want to walk around? Oh, maybe we could go to your house and play videogames or watch a movie," Shi stated while looking up at the sky. I was about to answer when I caught a frisbee that nearly flew into the back of his head.

"Oops sorry. Did that almost hit you?" Drake's friend, Connor, sneered as he and Drake walked over.

"Hey, be careful! There are other people here," Shi responded as I handed them the frisbee.

"Yeah yeah, whatever. More importantly, I think you're sitting a little too close to my girlfriend," Drake said accusingly as he leaned over the bench next to me.

"We were just talking. Jeez, get over it," I said. They both seemed to ignore me and continued questioning Shi.

"You two looked like you were having fun," Connor sneered. "What were you talking about?"

"Just about what we were going to do today," Shi said, taking a defensive stance against the two jocks who had started to encircle him. "Since Sara's still recovering, I thought we might go to her house and-"

"You hear that," Connor laughed. "The little runt wants to go to Sara's house."

"Yeah I heard him, and I don't think I appreciate a runt like you trying to move in on my girl," Drake said. Connor suddenly grabbed Shi and dragged him from the bench as Drake started revving his fists. "Sounds like it's time to teach him a lesson!"

"H-hey! Let me go," Shi yelled as he tried to break free.

"You think you can do that and get away with it," Drake yelled. "Besides, if we're going to Sara's house, you're not invited. It's going to be just me and Sara, alone."

"Aww come on buddy, don't be like that." Connor laughed.

"You have your own girlfriend."

"Mary'll forgive me for having some fun."

"Sike, no!" I yelled, tired of hearing their crap. I charged Drake and shoved him into Connor, knocking them all down, then grabbed Shi from the pile. "I'm going back home to play video games with Shiyu, and you're not allowed to follow." I ran, dragging Shi with me. We made it out of the park and were able to make it onto a train before Drake and Connor could catch up.

I wonder if I shouldn't have done that though. Drake's definitely going to get the entire football team to beat down Shi once school reopens if he doesn't find and beat him up before then. Then again, Shi's parents are both important to Drake's father's business, so maybe Drake will be smart for once and leave him alone. Oh, I guess I should explain this, but Shi and I are childhood friends, meeting at one of the business parties our parents dragged us. As far as I know, that's the only reason Shi remains my friend, despite the abuse he receives for it. He kind of knows I'm not human, but since it has to be kept secret, I'm not allowed to confirm his suspicion. Anyways, after riding the train for several stops, we decided to walk around town and browse the shops before deciding to eat lunch at one of Shi's parents' cafes. Then we went to my house and played games before deciding to watch movies for the rest of the night. Shi's fallen asleep, but I want to see the ending of this movie tonight.

Mom and Dad must have thought we looked cute, curled up in the home theater together, because when I woke up, Shi's head was resting on my shoulder and a blanket had been draped over us.

"Hey wake up," I exclaimed as I tried shaking him awake.

"What happened," Shi groaned as he slowly sat up and rubbed his eyes.

"You fell asleep on my shoulder."

"What," he exclaimed with his face turning bright red. "I-I-um, s-sorry!"

"Why are you getting so embarrassed? We used to sleep together all the time when we were kids." This only made him turn redder, which I didn't think was possible. I sighed and went upstairs, and he quickly followed. We were greeted by the smell of French toast, pancakes, and coffee.

"Good morning sweeties! Would you like some breakfast?" Mom asked as she placed a plate piled with food in front of Dad.

"Oh, I love your French toast, Mrs. Hollins!" Shi exclaimed as he quickly took his seat at the table.

"Then how about extra French toast with powdered sugar and maple syrup?" She giggled.

"Hey, I didn't get any extra French toast and had to get my own powdered sugar." Dad protested.

"You're neither guest nor daughter," Mom replied.

"You're right, I'm husband as well as father." He retorted.

"A father who needs the entirety of Candy Land inside one cup of coffee." I laughed.

"That's right, we're probably lucky there's even sugar left to put on the toast." Shi joined in. My dad huffed as he took a sip of coffee. We were stuffing our faces while Dad read the newspaper when the doorbell rang. Since Mom was washing dishes, Dad went to answer the door.

"Shouhei! Katherine! How's it going?" I heard him exclaim. There was laughter and talking as they made their way into the kitchen.

"Shiyu, you had better be glad the Hollins gave us a call, otherwise you'd be in big trouble for not coming home!" Shi's mother, Mrs. Hazimi scolded when she rounded the corner.

"Yes, I agree with your moth-Are they feeding you? Gimme." His father said. He reached for a piece of French toast, but Shi quickly picked it up and shoved it into his mouth saying, "Mine."

"Kat, Shou, it's wonderful to see you two again. There's some extra French toast if you'd like." Mom said as she dried her hands.

"Thank you, Helen, but we really only came to pick up Shiyu." Mrs. Hazimi politely smiled.

"Speak for yourself." Mr. Hazimi said as he began stuffing his face. After breakfast, they left, and I took a shower. School was still being postponed, but I had to go to the police station for another interrogation. I waited in the lobby with my Mom but was questioned as a suspect rather than a victim. Of course, considering it was only me and Jared found in that stairwell with no cameras and no viable witness accounts other than myself, I could understand why I was the prime suspect. What helps the least is that I'm actually the one who did it, but oh well. I can't plead self-defense without telling them about being a Wolf-Vampire and they can't prove I did it, so it'll just have to remain an open case.

Jared's parents disagreed, however, and claimed that I was lying, for other reasons, and should be given the death penalty. So even after school started up again a week later, I couldn't go because of all the stupid trials and appeals until finally, the courts forced them to drop all charges. It wasn't so much the missing school part that I found annoying, but having to spend my free day in court. I found it utterly boring and even longed for school after a while. That being said, it's not entirely true that

15

I didn't have school. Since vampires have their own classes they must attend, whether they're full vampires or not, and since I had human school in the day, I had to attend night school in Kofu, our vampiric homeland. It was always dull, and I always longed to go home and take a bath after being in that old dingy building. The only good thing about vampire night school is that most of the students are, like me, half-vampires who take humans or some other school during the day. I'll tell you more about vampire school, but right now I have to get ready to leave.

Vampires have a very strict curriculum because they value education above all else. Well, actually it's so they can hold bragging rights over others, but can't do that if you're stupid. This is even more true for those who take night school though. It's probably the higher-ups' prejudice since they know mostly half-vampires take night school or maybe they really believe that those who take night school need a stricter education, but both result in overwork and stress. The only educational upside I see is that it puts me far ahead of my human curriculum and has allowed me to skip several years.

Oh, and remember how I mentioned that vampire school was better since it had half-vampires like me? Well, that was only a half-truth. Even in this stress-filled environment I flourished and shone like a star at the top of my class, causing the same discontent that I get in the human world. Now with just a little more danger. Though I got a mini-vacation, thanks to the investigation in the human world, we had an actual break coming up next week and I had a 2-week long field trip in Kofu with the whole class year. Students from both the day and night classes would be going together, though we'd be riding in separate train cars. I spent the entire week preparing, between trials, and trying to finish as much work I got from school as I could. By the way, even though I said field trip it's really just a study session. You go to some remote place and do nothing but study and learn 24/7 with very little free time. Then you have to finish a packet they give you at the end of the trip by the next day. I loathe studying, but the scenery is always good when you get to peek at it. Anyways, today's the day of the trip, and Mom and Dad made sure that I had at least one bag, full of my medicine and food, that I was to always have with or near me.

As the train staff loaded our bags on the old-fashioned steam-styled train, everyone got on and sat in little groups so they could talk to their friends. The car had two different types of seats, booths of four where people could sit two across from each other, and booths of two. I sat in the back by myself. Usually, I would read a book, but I was compelled to watch the scenery this year. It was, after all, one of the few times I ever saw Kofu's countryside and it fascinated me how it could look so bleak, but at the same time relaxing. The leaves on the trees glowed an eerie violet and the sun shone as if it were blotted by mist despite the clear skies. Actually, the sky itself is a bleak purplish grey-blue. But for some reason, some strange reason, this bleakness felt like home. Like a treasure that I would never want to be without, glancing around the car and at the people of the villages we passed through, I could tell others felt the same. I felt truly relaxed...until someone threw a balled-up paper at me.

I looked around the car and decided that it was probably the group of boys who kept glancing back and snickering. All the students, while pretending to have not noticed, waited for my reaction, but I gave them no such joy. I moved the paper ball aside and continued to look out the window. We had a ten-hour ride ahead of us and after only 30 minutes all the students had gotten bored and decided to torment me. As paper ball after paper ball was thrown towards the back of the car, I grew to loathe this trip. After another half hour, they grew bored of my dull responses and began to find other, more solid objects, to throw. I cast a spell to create an invisible shield which caught the attention of the teachers, since magic thickens the air within a certain radius and causes a tingle on the skin since when magic is used it influences the air around it, and one came back to ask us if something was wrong. Everyone acted as if nothing was going on, I ignored the question since telling on them would do nothing, and the teacher hesitantly turned to walk back to the front of the car and took his seat.

The students left me alone for a little while after that and I let the spell wear off. However, they started up again after the first rest stop and more ferociously than before. They began to throw paper planes, probably so that I wouldn't use another spell, but I cast them all to the side. This resulted in more paper until there was an overflowing pile of paper planes and balls strewn about the back corner of the car. Fed up with my unresponsiveness the paper stopped and the students started whispering amongst themselves again. I couldn't hear much, what with the roars of the train, but something caught my ear. A spell. They were going to be stupid enough to use a spell to try and hurt me. I sighed at the thought, but since I couldn't hear what spell they were using, I decided it would be a good idea to write everything down and start whispering a barrier incantation. No matter what spell they used the teachers would know, but I'm not sure they'll be able to stop it in time. Actually, just the act of gathering magic to use a spell would have alerted the teachers, so why aren't they doing anything?

I couldn't help but be amazed when I realized what they were doing. What they were saying wasn't a spell, but an incantation, a very strong one. If they finished it my barrier incantation would mean nothing. A glance around showed that all the students were chanting it, with sinister smiles on their faces, which would only make it more powerful. Still, this strong incantation with so many people has made the atmosphere thick with magic, so I was curious why the teachers, or even the train staff at this point, weren't doing anything and glanced to the front of the car. They were under a sleep spell. It was pretty weak, and I could tell they would break it anytime now, but I couldn't be sure if they would break in time. The students, who had been whispering the incantation, chanted louder after seeing I had noticed, and their smiles grew even more sinister.

Since it had come to this there was only one thing I could do. I stopped the incantation I was chanting and began a stronger one, at least I hoped it was stronger. It was in a book titled...um...something Gaōl, that my parents had on the bookshelves in the basement. I was young when I learned it and couldn't actually pronounce the words, but when my parents heard me trying, they immediately stopped me and said it used too much magic for me to perform. I've grown a lot since then and even though I don't really know what will happen, I remember it being around other barrier incantations so at the very least it can't be death. They were nearing the end of their incantation, so I had to hurry if I was to finish it in time. While incantations don't explode in your face like spells do when you mess them up, you do have to start them from the very beginning, and speeding up isn't exactly going to lessen that risk of error. However, since incantations are often used in battle, we are taught how to use them in such high-risk conditions. All I have to do is stay calm. I reached the end of my incantation at the same time they finished theirs, all that was left was to see which was stronger. We each chanted the final words just as the teachers broke the sleep spell and there was a flash of light. I'm not sure what happened after that.

I remember darkness, a hazy figure, and then more darkness. It didn't feel like I was asleep, but it didn't feel like I was awake either. I couldn't tell what my surroundings were, and it felt like I was in a coma. Finally, the haze went away, and I was in a hospital bed. It was impossible for me to move because my body felt like lead, and I had to blink several times to see my dimly lit room.

"I'm glad you're awake." An unfamiliar voice said. I looked in the direction it came from and noticed two men standing next to my bed. One had jet-black hair while the other had grayish-white hair. The black-haired man left and came back with a nurse and a chair, which the white-haired man sat in. They both looked familiar, but my mind was too foggy to tell where I had seen them.

"What happened?" I asked.

"First," the nurse said, "can you remember your name and family rank?"

"Ah yes, my name is Sara Hollins, daughter of Marick and Helen Hollins and my family is first rank nobility." She nodded and continued checking machines and marking them on the clipboard, whispering something to the men each time. It felt awkward. They were watching me like hawks watching prey, but not looking at me. My head started to feel light and the haziness returned. "Um, I don't mean to interrupt," I said, getting their attention. "But is my bag maybe close by?"

"Is there something you need?" the nurse responded with an unnervingly friendly smile. Their eyes were trained on me, burrowing into me in fact, and I wished I hadn't said anything, but I continued.

"Yes, my glucagon medicine and snacks to bring my sugar levels back up," I said. The nurse looked surprised, she probably didn't know about my requirements and quickly bowed before leaving. It was just me and the two men. The white-haired man seemed lost in thought, occasionally looking up to glance at me or whisper to the man standing next to him. It made me uncomfortable, and I tried to avoid eye contact by staring at the ceiling.

Finally, the nurse came back with my bags. They were singed, but otherwise ok, as well as a third man who I presumed was a doctor. He bowed at the two men, gave me my medicine then began talking with them. The white-haired man nodded and dismissed the doctor. A long, awkward silence followed as the nurse helped me sit up so I could eat, and I wished for someone or something to draw their attention away from me. Once I was done, the nurse left to get me a proper meal, and I was once again left alone with the two men. I did have some questions and it seemed they might have the answers, so I tried my luck.

"U-um, Sir," I said. He closed his eyes and sighed, probably deciding that whatever he was pondering couldn't be solved by thought alone.

"Tell us what happened on the train?" He said, "Then we'll see about answering your questions."

"Yes Sir," I told them about how the students were bullying me and had put the teachers to sleep. About the powerful incantation that they had begun and that I began my own to counter it. They seemed most interested in this part. They asked where I had learned it. I told them I read it in a book when I was young, but that I didn't actually know what it did, and they asked why I had used it in the first place. "I remember when I was younger my parents told me that it was too powerful for me. I had thought that meant that until I got older and could control my magic, I shouldn't use it." I said. "It was the strongest incantation I could think of at the time." They were silent, which only enhanced my uncomfortableness. It seemed like he was about to say something when there was a knock at the door.

"Come in." The black-haired man said. A nurse came in holding a tray.

"I have a meal here for Ms. Hollins." She said as she bowed. The white-haired man waved her in, and she placed the tray on a stand above my lap.

"Ms. Hollins, when you finish eating and have regained your strength please come outside. I will answer any questions you have then." The white-haired man said as he stood up.

"Yes, Sir," I said. The nurse and the two men left and I finally felt like I could breathe. A feeling of unease kept me from truly enjoying my food though. When I finished, I put the tray on the bedside table and got dressed before going outside. The sight before me was shocking. Students, teachers, and strangers were lying in makeshift beds, some begging for death, others still like corpses. The place smelled of decay and anguish as many patients were missing limbs and blood-soaked their beds.

"This is what has become of most of the patrons that were on or near the train." I heard one of the men say. The white-haired one walked through the rush of doctors and nurses towards me. "Everyone here is either affected by or under the incantation you chanted."

"They're...under the incantation?" I asked and he nodded. "But wasn't the incantation for a barrier? Not a trance." The stern expression on the man's face didn't change and I couldn't tell if I found his indifference unsettling or comforting.

"In a sense." He said, "An explosion was the first product of the incantation. It blew back everything near you, the caster, to create a barrier-like effect. The second product put assailants in a trance of never-ending pain." Looking at the horror that it had unleashed, it was difficult to say anything. I hadn't known about the trance and despite knowing I shouldn't use magic I didn't understand I did anyway, and people were lying hurt because of it.

"Um Sir, couldn't someone break the incantation?" I finally managed to ask.

"Normally, but the incantation you used wasn't normal." A low growl, indicative of anger was present in his voice, and I could barely choke out an apology as I cast my eyes down. Seeming to have nothing else to say, he left. After that, I was given a bracelet. It looked like a regular identification bracelet, but I could tell that it had a tracker in it, in case I ran away, and I've been locked up in my room until further notice.

RECOLLECTION

Wine and Dine

It was late, I'm not sure of the time, and the moon shone brightly through the window. I couldn't get to sleep at all because of the moans and cries of those outside so I finally gave up sleeping and decided to watch the light coming through the window. It was beautiful and seemed to illuminate everything it touched, but eventually, even the moon got boring. Despite being told to stay in, I was curious about where I was and peeked out of the room. No one was there except the patients and a few sleeping nurses and doctors. I quietly closed the door and snuck past a few beds, making it safely out of the ward and into the hallway. From there I snuck down to the lobby and finally out of the hospital. I sniffed around but didn't smell anything out of the ordinary, though anything smelled better than death so I couldn't be sure. I wandered around for a little bit and noted that despite the late hour there were still quite a few people out. Most were drunk while others were couples enjoying a late-night rendezvous.

I avoided the noisy drunks and pretended not to notice the kissing couples, however, as I walked past one group, they began to harass me shouting things like, "Hey there sweetie, how about you come hang out with us!"

So, I did the logical thing and replied, "No thanks. I'm not in any mood to hang out with roughnecks like you." as I walked faster.

Unfortunately, one grabbed my arm and said, "Hey now don't say that we're not so bad. Just hang with us for a bit and I bet you'll be in all sorts of moods."

"No thanks," I said as I tried to shake him off, however, he tightened his grip to the point where it felt like he was going to crush my arm and I stopped struggling.

"Good girl. You catch on quick." He and his friends laughed. I really wish I hadn't left the hospital at this point. My body was weak and I could barely defend myself as I was pulled into the forest. When he finally stopped, we were in an abandoned building, in a room with only a beat-up mattress.

"Where are we?" I asked in disgust.

"Aww, is the sweet whittle princess afraid there might be a pea under the mattress?" One of them mocked. "We thought you might be sleepy, so we brought you to a nice comfy bed," the one gripping my arm said. He flung me on the repulsive mattress and they all laughed. There were five and they each had a smile on their face that made me sick. I thought up a plan, but it would only work once so if I messed it up it'd be over. I waited until I saw the best opportunity to strike. "Now let's get started." The man laughed. I lunged forward, teeth bared, and heard screams of agony and confusion as I bolted out of the building.

I didn't get very far. Though I executed my plan perfectly, there were two things I didn't factor in. The first was that they had a vast knowledge of the area while I knew virtually nothing. The second was that they were faster runners than me since I was still recovering. "Stupid bitch! We got you now!" They yelled as I was surrounded. Suddenly a man with red-hair appeared and began attacking them. After making sure none of them were going to be getting back up, he cast a spell to protect them and then turned to me.

"Sorry I took so long." he smiled, "Took a while to find such a desolate location using only the hospital bracelet." He held out his hand, but reasonably I hesitated. "Don't worry, I'm not with these animals." He said. He took my hand and pulled me to my feet. "Now, you don't have any problem with me carrying you right? Can't possibly let a queen like you walk around a dank forest like this." Just then the four guys struggled to their feet.

"Who are you calling animals?" One panted.

"Back for another beating?" The redhead asked. "But I already have the maiden, quit being sore losers." They charged towards us, but he quickly swept me off my feet and a gust of wind knocked them back.

31

"Shota get her out of here." I heard someone say. I had no idea where it had come from, but suddenly the two men from the hospital appeared and stood between us and the men.

"Yes, Sir!" Shota said. Before I knew it, we were at a large cottage in the woods. He went up to the door and knocked, probably out of habit, because he didn't wait for a reply before letting himself in. An old woman stood in the foyer. She took one look and ushered us in.

"I already have the bath ready." She said quickly, taking me from his arms. Though she was small and old, she was strong. "Poor girl, poor girl!" She said as she stripped me of my clothes and dumped me in the bath. She began scrubbing my face, body, and hair so hard that I thought my skin might peel off.

"Grandma please be gentle with her," Shota said as he stood in the doorway.

"I am being gentle, but filth needs to be scrubbed so scrub, I will until her skin shines like a diamond!" The old woman yelled. "Besides, what are you doing watching a young girl bathe!"

"I'm a doctor's assistant. I've seen more naked girls than I can count...though they were cut open for surgery."

"Out! Get out now!" The old woman yelled as she threw a soapy sponge at him. He sighed with a shrug then walked away. Once she was done peeling me and drying me off, the old woman began a new torture, brushing my hair.

"OW! Stop!" I yelled as she yanked the brush through my wet hair.

"Oh, stop it! Stop it I say! Quit being such a sensitive drama queen!" She yelled back. When she was finally done, she wrapped me in a towel and led me to a neatly organized room. "Get dressed dear. I'll make a wonderful din-ah, I guess breakfast for you." She smiled and left before I could say anything more.

Alone again, I looked around the room. It felt full even though there was only a bed, nightstand, and dresser in the room, I guess it's what you'd call homely. I went to the dresser and there was a note that read, "You can wear anything you want from here dear." Despite her abrasive nature, that old lady was really nice. I opened the drawers and found an assortment of fabulous clothes. I put on a white shirt, a red sweater over it, and a black skirt when there was a knock on the door.

"May I come in?" Shota asked, though I don't know what for, as he had already opened the door and was looking me up and down before I even said yes. "Yup!" He clapped, "Grandma's clothes fit you perfectly.

But it's missing a few pieces." He went to the dresser and rummaged through it until he found a black ribbon to tie around my neck and a bluish-black jewel to hold it in place. "Perfect!" He said holding his hands out like a camera. I wanted to ask him something, but I couldn't find the words. He looked familiar like I had spent most of my life with him. Maybe sensing my unease, he laughed and sat on the bed. "The name's Shota Martz. I work at the hospital as a doctor's assistant while I get my PhD."

"Oh, I guess that's where I know you from," I mumbled. I couldn't shake the feeling that I knew him for far longer than just the hospital, he even smelled familiar, but I put it aside. "So, you said these were your grandmother's clothes, right?"

"Yeah. I know they look fancy, but they're traditional everyday clothes for Kofu." I looked at his attire. He was wearing a white long-sleeved button-up shirt and blue khakis.

"You don't seem very traditional."

He chuckled and replied, "I guess that's true, but I'm also not entirely from Kofu."

"What does that mean?"

"Nothing important," he said, dismissively waving his hand, "I'll tell you later. Anyways-"

"But I want to know now," I murmured.

"Don't rush your seniors." He laughed as he flicked my forehead.

"Why you-!" I put my hands over the now throbbing spot.

"Unless...Do you like me?" He asked, leaning in close.

"O- of course not!" I blurted, feeling my cheeks turn red. What a stupid question that was.

"You hesitated and you're blushing." He laughed, "You're head-over-heels for me."

"I-I-!" I stuttered. Just then the door swung open and before I knew it, Shota was on the floor looking just as dumbfounded as me.

"How dare you come into this poor girl's room and try to hit on her after everything she's been through!" The old woman yelled as she pounded Shota with her fists.

"Ow! Ow! I wasn't hitting on her grandma! Ow!"

"M-Mrs...., um" I began, dazed.

"You can call me Ms. Mari, dear." She sweetly smiled before going back to pounding Shota.

"Ms. Mari he wasn't hitting on me!"

"Truly?" She asked and I nodded. She looked me hard in the face, then got up. "Fine. You seem like an honest girl. I'll believe you. Now let's go downstairs."

"Ah, grandma!" Shota exclaimed.

"What is it?"

"Actually, I have to get her back to the hospital."

"Hmph, hospital food doesn't have enough nutrients for a growing girl, but fine."

"Thank you for letting me borrow your clothes. I'll be sure to bring them back." I bowed.

"No need, you keep them. I can't fit them anymore anyway." She smiled.

"Then thank you all the same." We left Ms. Mari's cottage and walked down the forest path until I saw the lights of streetlamps.

"Can I ask you something?" Shota asked.

"What is it?" I replied.

"Why did you sneak out of the hospital in the first place?"

"That-Well I wanted to see outside. I've never been to this part of the country and the moon looked so pretty from the window, I just...thought..." He was silent then he mumbled something, grabbed my hand, and began walking slower.

"Right now, we are in Giorgi Park. It has tons of nature and is one of the safest areas to walk around at night...most of the time."

"Um...ok," I said, completely confused.

"And do you know what it's most popular sight is?" We stopped in a rather dark area when suddenly something lit up before us. It was a tree, illuminated by the moon, its leaves sparkled like crystals and its fruit looked like rubies. I was breathless as I stared at its beauty. "The Kokokou Tree. In most cases, only nocturnal animals feast on the tree so it developed a defense mechanism that blinds its predators when it senses movement. Most of us, however, just think it's pretty." He went and took one of the fruits from the tree and handed it to me. "Here, they're safe to eat."

"A-are you sure?" I asked as I looked at the shining fruit.

"Of course!" He laughed. I took a bite and a mix of sweet and sour rushed through my taste buds.

"Delicious!" I swooned.

"I thought you'd like it." He laughed. We sat on a bench as I gobbled down the fruit. Its juice ran down my face and arms, but I was in perfect bliss. When I finished, I jumped up to go get another one, but quickly found myself falling. I closed my eyes, but instead of stone, I felt...warm. I opened my eyes to see a blurry version of Shota. "Are you alright?"

"Y-yes, I think my sugar is low that is all."

"Guess I should have waited for grandma to cook." He sighed. I felt dizzier than usual, probably from fatigue, and couldn't stand even when Shota allowed me to lean on him, so he picked me up and began carrying me. He talked along the way, about Kofu, its different fashions, and other stuff that I wouldn't have learned unless I lived here. It was fun and I enjoyed it, both the wonders of this world and the familiar warmth I felt in his arms. I was barely conscious when we made it back to the hospital though. I knew Shota was talking, but I didn't know what he was saying anymore. The next thing I remember was Shota performing a Bloodth, a process where you take a substance into your fangs then take blood from someone and circulate it in your fangs, before injecting the mixture back into them.

Mom or Dad usually do it when my sugar levels get especially low. There's only one thing I hate about this procedure and that's that it is completely embarrassing. Vampires have several different venoms in their fangs. Most of them are harmless in small amounts except for one that's poisonous. The first is the one that coats our fangs, it completely numbs the area and paralyzes the target on touch while also blocking short-term memory in the brain. It's how vampires take blood without their victims struggling, but it only works on non-vampires. The second is the anticoagulant which makes the blood thinner and easier to drink. The last one, at least for now, is the one that I hate the most. It acts as adrenaline, increasing heart rate and blood pressure, but vampires refer to it as the aphrodisiac venom. Most of these venoms aren't there when a vampire bites you, especially the highly poisonous one, but when they mix the blood in their fangs some of that venom mixes with it and then, as you may have inferred by now, they inject back into you. Blood picks up the adrenaline one easiest which is why I always try to keep my levels from getting this low, but with everything that's happened, that's been impossible. I felt my cheeks flush and tried to squirm away but to no avail. Like I said, the numbing venom only works on non-vampires, so each squirm gave way to a wave of pain.

"L-let me go!" I pleaded. When my tail and ears popped out, I could tell Shota was surprised because he paused, but he started again. Unable to get away I instead closed my eyes and tried to get through it. I would have absolutely died if anyone had seen me at that moment. When he finally finished, I could only think to jump into bed and hide under the blanket.

"Come on Sara I'm done, stop pouting," Shota said.

"Shut up! It's embarrassing!"

He sighed and left the room saying, "Just get some rest. I'll be back later." I decided to stay up and write my frustrations to you, but now I'm getting sleepy, and the sun is coming up so goodnight...or morning.

The next day I was awakened by the noon sun and the smell of Chamomile tea, coffee, and sugar cookies. Without opening my eyes, I reached a hand from under the blanket and took some cookies. As I munched on them under the blanket a familiar voice whispered. "You shouldn't leave crumbs in other's beds." so I peeked my head out and saw my Mom. Filled with joy I jumped out the bed and gave her the biggest hug I could, even my tail couldn't convey how happy I was as it swished side-to-side.

"You certainly are happy." She laughed.

"I've missed you so much! What took so long!" I exclaimed, but my excitement soon faded as a familiar angry voice growled, "Sara, I thought we told you that *Sportagle* was a powerful incantation that you were not to use" I whimpered in response, "I'm sorry Dad, I thought your warning meant for that time. I didn't know you meant ever".

"Oh Marick, stop that! Don't mind him, sweetie, he's just upset at how long it took for them to allow us in." Mom said as Dad scoffed.

"Where's my hug?" he finally begrudgingly asked. I happily went over and hugged him too, then sat on his lap while we ate cookies and coffee while Mom had tea. When we finished, they started to explain the situation I was in.

Apparently, *Sportagle* is the name of that incantation, and it takes a humongous amount of magic from the user and expels it as a shield that then detonates and puts everyone except the user in a trance. However, like with most magic, if the person performing it doesn't have enough magic, it takes as much as it needs from any magic-filled life surrounding the user which causes Magic Deficiency, a fatal condition where magic is used faster than it is regained. It's like overdrawing your bank account with a fatal twist. I was lucky to be alive *and* still be able to use magic without any problems, but some of my classmates and teachers died and the others, as well as some of the civilians who were close by, may never be able to use magic again.

"Sara I've been wondering," Mom said to change the subject, "but where did you get that outfit?"

"Oh! I got it from Ms. Mari. She said she couldn't fit it anymore so that I could have it."

"And who is Ms. Mari?" Dad asked.

"Well she's-"

"She's a crazy old bat who acts before listening or thinking." Shota laughed as he walked in.

"Shota! What a mean thing to say about her! If she ever finds out, she'll knock you to the floor again."

"Aww, I know I know. But she would never mess up her sweet grandson's little face."

"I think she would have no problem."

"You're probably right."

"Sorry to interrupt," Dad growled, "but who might this young man be?"

"Ah! So terribly sorry." Shota bowed. "My name is Shota Zakou. An orphan from the Shirantou Orphanage, no rank."

"What!? Then...Ms. Mari-?" I asked.

"Was the House Mother of the orphanage, until it lost funding and closed down." Mom said.

"How did you know that!?"

"Sara you probably didn't notice, but this is one of my hospitals." She chuckled. Oh, I forgot to mention Mom and Dad have different jobs in Kofu than in the human world. Here, Mom is a doctor, she worked hard to graduate and eventually started her own hospitals, ones that accepted anyone since most hospitals in the country only accept vampires, and Dad...is still a doctor though I think his parents are war heroes.

Anyways Mom continued, "Shota begged to be a doctor so Ms. Mari, an old friend of my grandmother, asked if I would provide a means for him to get to college. Since I'm CEO of this hospital I made a deal with Shota. I'll pay for all his college tuition, books, and housing, and give him an entry-level job once he enters high school if he can keep his PW at a 9.0 until graduation."

"That's...amazing. You're able to keep your PW at a 9.0 even in high school while working?" I asked. I'm a model student and even I have trouble keeping it at 10. By the way, PW stands for Potential Worth. It's kind of like a GPA except if it drops, you'll be publicly humiliated and possibly disowned from your family.

"Nope." she smiled, "He's kept his PW at 18.0, the highest PW in all of the country for someone with his circumstances." I was in awe and Shota giggled at the praise.

"I still don't like him," Dad said, breaking the mood as he put me on the bed and glared daggers at Shota.

"Sir, I promise that I won't tarnish the name of your wife's hospital," Shota said.

"That's not what I care about."

"Tread lightly honey," Mom warned.

"Then may I ask what it is you don't like about me, Sir?" Shota asked.

"You're too close to my daughter," Dad said.

"...Eh?" Shota asked as Mom and I could only sigh at what was about to ensue.

"I said, you're too close to my daughter. Are you trying to date her? I'll have you know that the last person to try and date Sara winded up in the ICU. Would you like to know how?" Dad said, baring his teeth.

"Yes yes, now go sit with our precious daughter," Mom said, elbowing him, "and don't worry Shota. Her real ex-boyfriend is probably back at school playing football." After an awkward check of my vitals, Shota left Mom and I to bicker with Dad since neither of us wanted to give the real name of the one I had been dating. Dad had finally settled down when the two men from before came in.

"My Highness! My Lord!" my parents exclaimed. The white-haired man held up his hand to stop them from bowing and the black-haired man began to speak.

"We came to confirm what happened. We're sure you know that Ms. Hollins used *Sportagle,* but has she told you the context in which she used it and about last night's events?" he asked.

"Yes, my Lord. We have asked her about the first event, but may we inquire what you mean by last night? We are unaware of any event." Mom said. The white-haired man glanced at me, and I shyly looked at my hands.

"Very well." He said, turning back to my parents. They were eerily quiet throughout the conversation and for once I wished I could have left with the two men. Alone with my parents, I shut my eyes and waited for the worst, but instead, nothing happened, and I opened my eyes. My parents both stared at me, expressionless.

"I-I'm sorry for disobeying." I whimpered, looking back at my hands. "And I'm sorry for not telling you sooner. A-and I promise-"

"Is that all you think we care about?" Mom said as she and Dad wrapped me in their arms.

"You're safe. And alive. That's all we care about." Dad said. Their tears and hugs felt warm, and I couldn't help but start crying too. I know my parents love me, but it's moments like these that make me feel so happy. Once we had all calmed down, I remembered the burning question I'd been meaning to ask.

"By the way, who are those two men?" They looked at me in surprise.

"Y-you didn't know!?" Mom exclaimed.

"King Nexus Moritier the IV and Lord Aster Fidelie. You should have learned about them in your history and politics classes." Dad said. I was dumbfounded. I had been talking to the King and highest Lord of the land. Have I said anything disrespectful? Have I shown proper respect? Just thinking about it is making my head spin.

I fell back asleep after a while and woke up to a strangely familiar room. I wasn't in the hospital, that I could tell. The room was dark since it was early morning and the sun had only just begun to rise, but I could make out walls painted maroon with a black vine-like design on them. My bed had a canopy and it, along with the sheets, was pretty white. I slowly sat up and found I was no longer in the outfit Ms. Mari had given me, but a plain bluish-white nightgown. Spotting the door, I crept out into the hallway. There was a faint light coming from downstairs, so I went to the banister. The light was coming from a closed door, and I crept down the stairs. I heard mumbles, but couldn't make out what they were saying, however, as I crept closer the voices seemed to stop. As I was about to peek into the room, someone came out. Startled, I jumped back, tripping, but the person caught me and picked me up.

"You're so much trouble if no one watches you." They sighed.

"Dad!" I excitedly exclaimed.

"You should be asleep." He sighed. I rubbed my head under his chin and with a "Humph", he carried me into the room with Mom and two glasses of wine, crackers, and ham.

"Sara, good morning." Mom said. Dad sat down with me on his lap.

"Where are we?" I asked.

"Our house in the country."

"We have a house in the country!?"

"We never told you?" Dad asked.

"No! I would have remembered having a house in the country!"

"Oops! Oh well." Mom laughed.

"To be more specific," Dad said, "this house belongs to my grandfather. It's the house he built to be close to the winery."

"The winery? We have enough land to own a house near it?" I asked.

"Hmm, I guess we never told you. Your grandparents, and great-grandparents, on your father's side own Hedieli Winery." Mom said.

"What!? That's the biggest wine company in Kofu!" I knew he inherited a winery, but I didn't think it was the most famous wine company in the country!

"Exactly, so more than enough land. Guess I should tell you your father's the CEO too."

"What!?"

"Enough." Dad sighed, sipping his wine.

"...So, since you brought me in here can I have a small taste?" I asked. Despite apparently owning a wine company, Mom and Dad keep very little wine in the house back home, so I was curious about what it tasted like.

"Sara-"

"O-only a small taste, please! It just looks so pretty and smells so sweet."

"No." Mom said.

"Ok." I sighed, having lost the battle.

"If you really want, you can have some crackers." She said, holding up the plate for me to take a few and munch on. The time flew by and before we knew it, the sound of a grandfather clock rang throughout the house. "I guess we should get to bed."

"But I haven't been up that long," I said.

"Well, we've been up for several hours and are tired," Dad said.

"Then...can I sleep with you two?"

"Sara, you're a big girl." Mom laughed.

"Please."

"...How about this?" Dad said as he sipped from his glass, leaving a little less than half, then put a cracker in what was left, "Once that cracker has absorbed most of the wine, you can eat it and that'll be your taste. In exchange, you sleep in your room."

"Ok!" I said enthusiastically as I guzzled the cracker and wine.

"Marick." I heard Mom growl.

"It's not enough to give her a hangover...I think." I heard Dad say before I quickly fell asleep.

I woke up with a headache. Someone opened the curtains, allowing the room to be flooded with light and forcing me to retreat under the covers which were quickly pulled off. So I tried to throw the pillow over my head.

"Sara, get up," Dad said.

"I don't want to," I whined.

"But there's breakfast, I even made you coffee." He said, handing me the cup. I sat up and took a sip.

"It's sweet."

"I put extra sugar. Was it too much?"

I shook my head, "No, it's fine."

"Good, now take a shower, get dressed, and come downstairs when you finish." He said, tussling my hair.

"Daddy, I don't know where anything in this house is." He sighed and started to think.

"Ok," He said finally, "I'll take you to the bathroom, and when you finish, just come to the room we were in last night." I quickly finished my coffee, and he led me to the bathroom before going downstairs. When I opened the door to the bathroom, I was amazed to see a huge room even though there was only a sink, toilet, and hamper in it and another door leading to the shower and bathtub. I took a shower and was surprised to find a new outfit folded up in the hamper. I put on a sky-blue, ruffled dress, a traditional dress of the wolf country, Brexior. I looked at myself in the mirror and twirled around, gleefully laughing as the dress rose and twirled with me. I skipped down the stairs and found the room I was in last night. I went to push open the door but stopped when I heard unfamiliar voices inside. Putting my ear to the door I tried to listen and figure out who they were, but I found it hard to hear through. The best I could make out was muffled voices. Before I could realize the voices had stopped or the footsteps that were coming, the door opened. The person I fell into was just over my height, had blond hair, and wore a maid-like outfit. She looked at me as I frantically tried to pretend I wasn't eavesdropping, and smiled.

"Glad to see you, Ms. Sara. Please take your seat." She said warmly. She led me into the room, which was now decorated with lavish flowers of various colors. In the center of the room was an oval table with seven seats.

I was led to the empty seat on my dad's left. Across from me was a kind-looking woman and next to me, at the head, was a very tall, gruff-looking man. In front of my Dad sat another gruff-looking man and at the other table head, by my Mom, sat a quiet lady. The atmosphere was awkward since I could tell that they were all looking at me, so I tried to keep my head down and stared at the utensils placed neatly out in front of me. The maid and several other people dressed as servants placed plates in front of us before beginning to place the food in the center of the table. They set out biscuits, cinnamon rolls, blueberry muffins, pancakes, cheddar cheese grits casserole, waffles benedict, scrambled eggs, lemon-blueberry quinoa porridge, hot water, various types of tea, coffee, sugar, and cream. My mouth watered looking at all the delicious food set out before me, and I had to check to make sure I wasn't drooling. The food was passed around so everyone could get some and before I knew it, my plate overflowed with food. I completely forgot about the thick atmosphere that surrounded us and happily stuffed my face until I felt I would pop. I poured myself a cup of coffee and decided to drink it black since Dad had already brought me a cup with extra sugar.

"You sure you want to drink that black, Cream Puff?" The man sitting next to me asked.

"Ah, y-yes, Sir." He looked to Dad, who saved me from having to give the explanation.

"She only drinks coffee with sugar to raise her levels."

"And?" The man asked.

"I have already given her a cup with extra sugar this morning, Sir." From their conversation, I assumed the man next to me was to be highly revered and I was sure the women and other men were to be too. I realized the room seemed to have become very quiet. The rest of breakfast went by with an intense atmosphere that made it hard for me to swallow my coffee.

After breakfast, Mom and Dad said they needed to have a private conversation with the people, giving me the perfect excuse to slip away and explore. The house was humongous and was styled like a late 1800s-early 1900s plantation house with a few modern rooms here and there. There was a large door that I suspected led to a library. I was going to go in, but I heard voices and decided against it. There was a door that led to a large kitchen with many more doors around the room and, going through the door across from the one I entered through, opened to a hallway that led to an annex house which was really two houses, one for the maids and the other for the butlers. There I learned that the blonde I had run into was the head of the maids and her name was Katheli. I must say that even though they are servants and live in a separate house, the house itself is just as big and lavish if not more than the main house and they wear clothing just as pretty.

The servants, though I just met them, seemed to know me very well and talked about how cute I was when I was little. They invited me to have tea, but I told them I wanted to explore a little more first, to which they giggled and remarked how I always loved to explore. After leaving the house through the front door, I found myself in a beautiful grassy field. There were at least 100 acres of land as far as the eye could see. It was also the perfect day for a run, with the grass flowing in the wind, so I transformed into a wolf. As I bounded about the field, I made out a grape wall in the distance, rows upon rows of them, and headed for it. Transforming back, I took a big purple grape, as big as an apple, from the vine and ate it. It was sour and made my mouth go numb with flavor as the juice rolled down my face and stained my dress. I went to reach for another when I heard a growl behind me and turned to see three wolves.

"Don't you dare touch another!" They snarled.

"I-I'm sorry. I didn't know that I couldn't," I whimpered. In hindsight, it makes sense that I wouldn't be allowed to eat the grapes of a winery. Regardless, I put my ears back and sat on the ground.

"Take her in!" One of them said.

"Wait!" A voice said. They turned around and moved to the side to show a beautiful creamish-gold wolf.

"Lady Zoria." The first three bowed. "We found this trespasser. She was trying to steal the grapes used for the winery."

"Dunken don't tell me you don't recognize her?" The beautiful wolf asked. She transformed into the kind-looking woman I had seen at breakfast. The wolf named Dunken, a silverish-black wolf looked up and judged my face.

"Well I'll be," he gasped, "if it isn't the little troublemaker herself!"

"Eh?" I cocked my head.

"It's been a long time since she's seen you. I doubt she remembers." The one called Zoria laughed.

"Well, I'll never forget her." Dunken laughed. "It's alright boys. This child is the Master's great-grandchild."

"Eh!?" The other two wolves exclaimed.

"Come on Cream Puff." Lady Zoria smiled, "I'll explain while we walk." She motioned for me to follow her down through the rest of the garden. "We haven't seen you since you were three."

Which I guess is why I can't remember being here. "You used to love taking the biggest grapes from the vines and shoving them into your mouth and pockets, resulting in you being a sticky juicy mess."

"D-did I really?" I asked, looking down at my purple-stained dress.

"Yes, whenever you came into the garden your parents had to give you a bath. Usually, two or three because you'd come right back for more." I had a vague memory of someone trying to rub my face and hands with a rag as I laughed and giggled.

"Um, did you ever clean my face when I came in covered in juice?"

"I never got to clean your face because of the two who would hog you to themselves."

"Who are they? I want to remember."

She laughed, "Well one was my husband, the one who sat next to me. We're your grandparents on your mother's side. We happened to be visiting at the same time, so we get to meet again."

"Hm, so you don't own this winery?"

She shook her head, "The person who owns this winery is your great-grandfather. He's-"

"Huh? Hey!" I exclaimed as someone covered my ears. I broke away from the person and turned to see Lady, or I guess Grandmom's, husband.

"She can figure it out by herself." He said.

"You never change." she sighed then she smiled at me, "This is your stubborn Granddad, Decus."

"Ah! Um, pleased to meet you." I bowed. He made no move, just stared at me with an angry face. "Um..." I mumbled and glanced at Grandmom who just sighed and shook her head. He then walked up to me and started smelling me, a common thing that wolves do when they meet someone. It's meant to show both parties trust each other since their teeth are usually near vital parts like the neck or wrists. He circled around me several times before standing next to Grandmom.

"Her dress definitely suits her...even if she did already ruin it." He finally said.

"Um, I was wondering, are you two half-wolves as well?" I asked. Most vampires stand at around seven or eight feet, but these two were just shy of six, which is customary for wolves. Of course, everyone is different, so I didn't want to assume.

"Oh yes, we forgot to tell you." Grandmom smiled.

"We didn't forget." Granddad scolded, "At your age, you should at least be able to tell if someone is Vampire, Wolf, or both."

"I'm sorry. I never learned how." I whimpered.

"Excuses." He puffed. With nothing to say to that, I hung my head.

"Decus look what you've done!" Grandmom scolded. "You only just reunited and you're already scolding her!" She wrapped her arms around my shoulders and began petting my head, bringing a familiar warmth. "Don't be sad Sweetie. I know he's scary, but he means well."

"You're scarier," Granddad mumbled.

"What was that?" Grandmom growled. He walked up to us and looked up at the sky, then at the ground, and then at me.

"I didn't mean to make you sad." He said, then quickly turned and started walking down the aisle of grapes.

"That man. Why can't he ever say how he feels?" Grandmom sighed.

"Hurry up or we won't make it to the facilities until tomorrow," Granddad yelled.

"I know I know, we're coming!" Grandmom called back, and took my hand, "Come on Cream Puff." We caught up to Granddad and explored the winery together.

The next day I woke up a half hour before the sun. Since no one else was up this time, I decided to go down to the room I hadn't explored. I slowly creaked open the door and inside were billions of books, maybe even trillions. They covered the walls of the room, which had little light except for a few candles here and there. I twirled around, wishing I could stay forever. A particular book caught my eye, it had an ancient-looking brown spine and was written in a language I didn't know, but it was particularly high up and I didn't see a ladder. There was a short stool, but it didn't come close to helping me reach it, so I looked at some of the other books around. Most were really old, but some looked newer. I stacked the newer-looking thick books as high as I could on the stool, but it still didn't look close to reaching the book. Not to mention that if it had, it would probably have been too unstable to let me climb up, and even if I jumped to the top, it would have probably fallen immediately. As I tried to think of another way to reach the book, the books I had stacked began to glow in a faint blue light and soon floated back to their places. The book I had been trying to reach also removed itself from the shelf and began floating down. Since it was old, I thought it might be an ancient spell book, those books are notorious for having minds of their own, but instead of coming to me, the book floated just out of my reach and began going to the center of the room.

"Wait, come back!" I yelled as I chased after it. I stopped, seeing the person it had begun to go too. In the center of the room, arguably the darkest part since it was furthest from the candles, there was a group of chairs and lamps. One of the lamps was on, next to a chair with the gruff-looking man from yesterday morning sitting in it. The book rested in his hand as I wondered how I could miss a lamp being on in such a dark room. "I-I'm sorry, Sir. I didn't realize anyone was in here and had no intention of disturbing your reading."

"Come here," he said. I shamefully walked to the side of his chair with my ears back and my head hung low. "You're not in trouble," he said, though his tone spoke otherwise. Not sure which was true, I kept my ears back but slightly raised my head. An irritated sigh left his lips and I quickly put my head back down and heard him suppress another sigh. "Do you fear me?"

"I...am not sure who you are, but I know you are to be respected," I replied. He sighed again.

"Is this the book that you were trying to get?" He asked and I nodded. "May I ask why?"

I thought for a moment then said, "I...I just thought it looked interesting."

"Interesting?"

"Yes, Sir. The book looks very old, and I find old books interesting, so I thought..." The man was silent, very silent. I thought he was angry. A random stranger snooping around my books just because they thought they were interesting would make anyone upset. Then he started laughing. It was a deep gravelly laugh that bellowed and shook the room.

"Here child! Come here!" He laughed. He pulled me onto his lap. Sitting there, his laugh felt like an earthquake. "I used to sit you on my knee all the time when I read to you."

"You used to read to me?"

"You don't remember me, but I remember you." He said, settling down. "You tried to come in here every chance you got to read even though you couldn't even spell your own name. Ah, I loved teaching you the different words and letters."

"I did, Sir?" I smiled. I didn't remember it at all, but it still made me happy.

"That's Grandfather for you, got it. I'm your Great-Grandfather and I'll tickle you 'till your eyes water if you ever forget again." My smile widened at that thought.

"Oh? What was that? I don't think I quite remember you yet."

"You little Cream Puff!" He laughed as he began poking my ribs. When we finished our fun, he picked up the book and used magic to get another book, a note pad, and a pencil.

"So that was a spell that put the books away?" I asked.

"Yes, you should be learning spells like that in school." He replied.

"I have low grades in that section, better than my classmates, but I can't understand what the teacher means by, "You'll be able to tell.""

"Let me ask then, how do you imagine magic?"

"Imagine? I guess I imagine it as…um…I don't know…a light or water maybe."

"Then how about this Cream Puff, since you imagine magic as light, imagine its source like a lighthouse, and the beam of magic you see should lead you to it." I closed my eyes and tried to imagine what he said. Focusing on his magic, I followed it from the book to him and nearly every book in the library. Some paths were faint like it had been quite a while since they were made, others shone brightly.

"I think I did it," I said happily. "Grandfather, how did you know that would help me?"

"I had the same problem in that class, so I hoped what helped me would help you." He laughed.

"Thanks." I giggled, hugging him.

"Now a test. What am I?"

"Hm?"

"Based on my magic, am I a vampire, wolf, or both?" I thought hard about it, focusing on his magic as well.

Dad said that both his parents and grandparents were Wolf-Vampire, so I excitedly exclaimed, "Both!"

"Explanation."

"Because Dad said that his ancestors were Wolf-Vampires so you must be as well."

"Wrong! I'm a vampire, through and through. And I asked you to use my magic to determine what I was not in your memories. Next question-" The test went on for a while, I got question after question wrong and had failed by the end, but it was a ton of fun.

The final week of my 2-week study vacation and break from school. I've been having so much fun sitting in the library with Grandfather and running around the winery. It was early in the morning and the sun still had three hours to get up, so it was pretty dark in the house. Since even Grandfather wasn't up at this time, I decided to wander around the garden. In the far back, past what I learned was called the vineyard, I galloped to the barn that Katheli told me about, and was the only building I had yet to explore. Transforming into a humanoid, I creaked open the barn door. It was dark, not a trickle of light could be seen and despite my night vision, I bumped into several things while looking for a lamp. I finally found one after six ouches, eight bumps, and two falls. It was an old oil lamp instead of the modern magic crystal one though. This barn was used rather often so the lamp was filled with oil, meaning I had to painstakingly control my fire magic to ensure I didn't blow the whole thing up. Using the light to look around, I was able to see countless cows, horses, pigs, and other farm animals, all staring at me as if I were some kind of show.

"U-umm...hi?" I said nervously. The animals continued to stare, then one horse tapped its foot against the wood floor. There was a clutter of noises as if whispering. The horse who tapped its hoof was now the only animal staring at me. Entranced by its stare I walked up to it without realizing I was moving my feet. "Have we...met before?" The horse blinked as if answering my question. The other animals had quieted down and stared on. Up close the horse had a beautiful grayish-blue coat. "I'm sorry, but I can't seem to remember." She shook her head, as if to say, "No problem", and licked my face. Her big tongue tickled, and I giggled as it moved across my face.

"Seems the old girl remembers you." a voice said. I looked at the door but saw no one there. "Up here." The voice said. I looked up, but the light didn't reach so I found the ladder and went up to the hay loft.

"Dunken!" I exclaimed as the light shined on his face. The two from before, still in wolf form, were also up here. They each opened one eye and then went back to sleep.

"You remembered me?"

"No, I just figured from your reaction when we met, that we used to be good friends."

"That's a shame, real shame. I got my hopes up thinking we could go back to old times. Anyways, you weren't wrong to get the vibe that we used to be buddies. You even used to tell your dad that if he wouldn't give you what you want, you'd marry me instead. The look on his face was priceless and you always got yourself a cookie or treat after that."

"I guess I was a little devil back then."

"You sure were! But enough about that for now. What are you doing out here in the barn so early in the morning? If it weren't for your loud tripping and falling, we would've attacked you as an intruder." I glanced at the two who were comfortably sleeping without a care in the world then back at Dunken. "Ok, I would have attacked you and these two would have continued sleeping, but I'm ferocious so tell me why you're here."

"Katheli told me that the barn was here and since it's the only place I have yet to explore and I woke up early with nothing to do, I decided to come here."

"That Katheli, well I reckon she just wanted to surprise you."

"She knew you'd be here?"

"Well, this is where we live, of course, she'd know we're here."

"You live...in the barn?"

"There's a problem with that?"

"Why not live in one of the annexes? I bet Grandfather would even build a guardhouse if you asked."

Dunken shook his head and said, "Every year the master asks us if we want him to build a guardhouse and every year, we say no. After taking us in and paying us more than any guard should get paid, we couldn't possibly ask him for more." I couldn't help but feel there was more to this story than Dunken let on, but it also didn't seem like I would be getting any answers from him.

"Alright fine. Then is there anything I can do to help?"

"Well, if you're deadest on helping, then why don't you try getting the food for the animals so we can leave a little early this morning."

"Yes, Sir," I said, quickly going down the ladder and nearly falling. I heard Dunken laugh as I got fresh hay for the animals and helped him, and the others, clean the barn and feed the animals. Afterward, I ran to the winery and took some grapes before heading back to the house for breakfast. I decided to take a nap around lunch time.

When I woke up the sky was dyed red as the sun set. I stirred only to wish I hadn't moved. My body hurt from helping at the barn and I didn't feel like getting out of bed, so I snuggled a little further under the covers.

"Humph." Someone said, prompting me to open my eyes again. I couldn't see anyone by the door and there wasn't anyone near the window behind me.

"You're pretty relaxed for a girl on the run." Someone else said into my ear.

"What!?" I said, turning my head. There was a red-headed boy hovering inches from my face and I had no idea where he came from because the window was closed!

"Maybe she thought she got away." the first someone said. I turned back to the door and saw another red head. They looked about the same age as me and were twins, but that wasn't the problem. Since I had been training with Grandfather, I tried to follow their magic to see where they got in, but it was basically non-existent since they were pure Brexiorian.

"Reg." The one near the door said.

"Yes, Rag?" Reg, still inches from my face, he said.

"Why don't we do that thing that Katheli does for Dunken whenever she wants him to do something? No one's here right now so it'd be perfect."

"That's a great idea. Then maybe she'll come back and do more barn work for us." They each climbed onto the bed, their tails swished from side-to-side, their faces giddy with joy.

"Wait," I said trying to get hold of the situation, "where did everyone go?"

"To town," Rag said.

"Why?"

"Because they wanted to get a surprise," Reg said as they started to take the covers off me.

"Wait."

"We can't answer any more of your questions about everyone's whereabouts."

"Ok. Then...umm...are you two twins?"

"I guess," Rag said.

"In a way," Reg replied. "We have only slight differences in our fur colors." He was right about it being slight. Reg's fur was orangish-red, while Rag's fur was reddish-orange.

"You're right I hadn't noticed." I laughed.

"Most don't." Rag said as they started moving towards me.

"Wait!"

"No more waiting. The longer this takes the sooner Dunken will notice we're gone." Reg said.

"Wait or I scream for Dunken right now." Which caused both to stop.

"Scream?" Reg cocked his head.

"In a house with no people?" Rag cocked his head in the opposite direction.

"No Rag that's not the problem."

"What is it then?"

"Lady Sara, what do you think we're trying to do?" Reg turned to me and asked.

"What any sensible girl would think when two strange boys climb into her bed!" I replied. They both looked at each other.

"Rag, I think she believes we were trying to sex her."

"Is that true?" Rag asked, drawing close to my face.

"Yeah, please say I'm wrong," Reg said, doing the same thing.

"Y-yes now get off!" I yelled, pushing them back. They looked at each other, then me, then down to the bed as their faces turned red.

"I mean, you are beautiful," Rag said shyly.

"But we would never dare to go behind the master's back like that." Reg finished.

"Yeah, we just wanted to give you a massage, so you'd come do our work for us again. Please, forgive us!" Rag exclaimed as they bowed down.

"Ugh...fine, just get off my bed!" I exclaimed.

"This is your fault," Reg said, turning to Rag.

"Mine? You were the first one in here so if anything, it's your fault!" Rag said. The two started bickering, with me in the middle when suddenly a booming voice roared, "Off the bed NOW!" We turned to see Dunken in the doorway holding a tray and Katheli behind him.

"Attention!" He boomed and both boys quickly got in line. "Now I'm going to ask each of you a question and I'm only asking once! What are you boys doing? Reg!"

"Rag and I were trying to help Lady Sara feel better, Sir!"

"Rag!"

"It is as Reg said, Sir!" Dunken walked past them and up to me.

"What's your report?" He asked.

"Eh? Oh, well Reg and Rag were trying to give me a massage to help me, but I misunderstood, but then we got it cleared up and...."

I had hoped to keep the bickering part out, but Dunken knows them too well because he said, "Then they started bickering."

"...Y-yes, Sir." He sighed and started pacing in front of the two. After several minutes of him saying nothing, I could tell the boys were getting agitated and so was I.

"If you wait too long, her porridge will get cold," Katheli said as if to no one.

"Alright, I hear ya." Dunken sighed. He turned to Reg and said, "You're going to work an extra shift and clean all the bathrooms on the property as punishment.", then to Rag and said, "You are going to work an extra shift and clean all the dining rooms on the property."

"Yes, Sir." They both sighed.

It seemed like Dunken wanted to say something about their lack of enthusiasm, but let it go with a simple, "...Dismissed." The two quickly exited, leaving me, Katheli, and Dunken together though Katheli also left soon after.

"Here," Dunken said holding up a spoonful of porridge. "Katheli was right when she said that'll get cold soon. Eat while it's hot."

"Thank you, Dunken." I smiled. After letting him feed me the porridge, I decided to head back to sleep.

The next morning my sore muscles had disappeared. I energetically jumped out of bed and skipped down to the dining room.

"You're in a good mood." Mom laughed when I hugged her.

"I feel great." I laughed alongside her.

"I'm glad Katheli's porridge made you feel better." Dad smiled. We had breakfast then I went to the barn, however, the group on break said that Dunken was on guard duty, along with the others, so I went down to the vineyard instead. I looked all over the garden but couldn't find a hide or hare of any of them.

"Where could they have gone? The wolves at the barn said it was their shift." I mumbled to myself.

"And what did we do to earn the little miss's attention?" Dunken laughed. I spun around and saw Dunken, Reg, and Rag.

"There you are! I just wanted to spend some time with you guys."

"Aww well that's fine and all, but as you know we're on duty so maybe-"

"I know you're on duty that's why I want to spend time with you. It'll be fun."

Dunken stared at me then after a while sighed and said, "Fine, you can tag along on our rounds, just one rule."

"Yes?" I said, transforming into my wolf form.

"Never interrupt me when I'm talkin' unless it's an emergency." I nodded and off we went. Even though we only covered a small section of the land, I was still exhausted by the time I bid them farewell for lunch.

"Did you have a fun morning?" Grandfather asked.

"Mmhm." I nodded with a mouth full of food.

"That's good because we have a surprise for you." Grandmother said. I didn't write about it, but we talked a lot during my time visiting them. I learned that she was a purebred wolf, so my family lineage started with my great-grandparents on my father's side. Most of the clothes I had been wearing during my stay came from her teenage years.

Anyways, I started to ask what it was but began choking as a biscuit went down my throat.

"Cream Puff I know you're half-wolf but chew your food more." Grandfather sighed. I nodded as Dad patted my back. After lunch, I was taken to a waiting carriage driven by Dunken with Reg and Rag as bellboys. They bowed and helped me into the carriage, and I sat next to the window as everyone else got in. Once we were settled, the carriage

77

began its two-and-a-half-hour journey to town. I took a deep breath as I jumped out of the carriage to breathe in the crisp fresh air.

"It's finally over!" I exhaled happily then saw Dad whispering something to Mom. "What? What'chya talking about?"

"Oh, it's nothing." Mom giggled.

"So where are we going?" I asked, too excited to press further.

"Wherever you want, so long as it's in town." Grandmother said.

"Sara you'll be spending the day with your great-grandparents." Mom smiled.

"Yay!" I waved bye to my parents and explored the town with Grandfather and Grandmother. They took me to several different sightseeing places and shops. In every store, I found something, sometimes things that I just had to have. In return for buying me all the different outfits and trinkets, my grandparents only asked that we go to a particular dress shop. Grandmother and I went inside while grandfather waited and wandered around outside. The sparkling dresses inside glittered with hues of red, blue, and any other color you could think of along with a multitude of designs and I was told to pick just one. After much indecisiveness, Grandmother finally decided to pick for me. They made me a royal blue tulle dress with a closed back and matching gloves.

The band on the midsection was sky blue and had a dark blue design of roses and vines. I was given 15 minutes to choose shoes and picked royal blue flats. After finalizing the dress, the staff took my measurements and said that it would be done by evening. Then, after doing some more shopping and sightseeing, we stopped at a little cafe for an early dinner. "Today was so fun!"

"We know, your tail says it all." Grandfather chuckled.

"I'm glad we could have fun like this today and, just so you know, there's still one more surprise left." Grandmother said.

"There is! What is it!" I asked. She slowly took a sip of tea and gently placed the cup down.

"You'll see. Now dear, please sit properly."

"Yes, Ma'am." I smiled as I laid my tail beside me, but I couldn't hide my happiness and it was soon back to swishing back and forth.

"Sweetie..."

"Aw let her be darling. If you weren't focusing so hard, you'd be wagging your tail alongside hers." Grandfather smiled, "In fact, Cream Puff ignore your grandmother and let your excitement show! If there's a vampire here bold enough to have a problem with it, I'll take care of them!"

"Dear, stop it, you'll draw attention." she scolded, "And Sweetie don't listen to this crazy old man."

"Crazy old man, huh? Then you won't question if I do this!" he smiled and quickly started poking at her ribs. Having no time to defend, Grandmother couldn't hide her tail and ears as she was tickled to tears. Seeing this, I couldn't hold in my laughter and together we laughed, creating such a commotion that anyone's eyes not being on us would be strange. When we finally settled down, our teas had been knocked over and spilled.

"L-look what you've done!" Grandmother scolded as she tried to hide her laughter.

"I'll go get some napkins." I giggled.

"There's no need." Grandfather said, "Watch closely." He held his hand over his and Grandmother's spilled tea and cast a spell. The spilled tea rose and went back into the cup.

"Woah!"

"This is a Time Reverse Magic. Like all Time Magic, it takes a while to learn, but I've taught you the basics so try it out."

"Y-you want me to try?" The spell he wanted me to perform was a basic restoration spell that we've been practicing in class for a while, but

Time Magic is no joke since even the slightest error can result in things going from ok to horrible in a split second, not to mention the other issues. The side effect changes depending on the type of spell you use and how far back you want things to go, but it's basically an explosion. Not one as big as the train one, but if you fail using Time Magic then the spell blows up in your face and sends a stabbing feeling through your veins.

Fearfully, I put my hand over the spilled tea and concentrated. Within seconds, my magic faltered making me lose concentration, and my spell would have caved in on itself if Grandfather hadn't added his magic to stabilize it. Depressed by my failure, I hung my head and folded my ears back.

"Don't be depressed Cream Puff. It's not your fault." he said, "Like I said, Time Magic is a tricky thing to learn."

"...I'm going to the bathroom." I pouted. This was an old-fashioned cafe, so the bathroom wasn't attached to the building, but instead a small building a little ways away from the backdoor. I splashed water on my face and looked in the mirror, I had to pull myself together. I nodded to myself and shook off the water.

"Oh, look at the little puppy shake." Someone from behind said. I looked up and saw two girls walking in, I believe they were doing a double date at the cafe. I wanted to ignore them, but they were blocking the exit.

"Do you need something?"

"Just need to put a dog back in her place." The second girl laughed. If we were back at my middle school I would have screamed, but we were too far for anyone at the cafe to hear and any passersby that might have helped would have refused after finding out I'm half-wolf thanks to that stupid war.

"What's wrong little puppy, aren't ya gonna scream?" The first girl asked as if reading my mind. If I took long enough, I figured Grandmother would come to check on me, so I began to step back to buy time.

"Aww, you scared?" The second girl asked. I could have tried attacking them, but with the damage I've already done that doesn't seem like a good idea. With my back against the wall and the girls' inches from my face, I was out of options. "I have an idea, why don't we rip out her fangs?"

"Great idea." The first agreed.

"Excuse me, but do you need something from my granddaughter?" I was overjoyed seeing Grandmother walk in to help me.

"Oh um, we saw her trying to perform that restoration spell in the cafe and, as her elders, thought we could give her some advice." The first girl said with a big smile. I dashed past them while they were distracted and hid behind Grandmother.

"Well, I thank you, but she has plenty of elders at home to help her." Grandmother smiled. She turned me around and started to push me out the door before suddenly grabbing me and jumping to the side as a magic whip struck the air where we were.

"We didn't say you could leave you Brexiorian bitch!" The second girl yelled. They had sinister smiles on their faces just like the students on the train.

"You think that just because you marry a vampire and have disgusting half-breed children you're welcome in this country!? Don't make me laugh!" The first girl said, "It's foreigners like you that make me sick!"

Grandmother pushed me behind her and stood tall against the girls, "I apologize for any hatred you feel. The war has taken a heavy toll on everyone. However, you should know that I fought in the war as an independent medical officer, so I'm no stranger to combat. I wouldn't recommend ruining your dates fighting me." The girls didn't look deterred in the least and jumped toward Grandmother but were quickly flipped and landed hard on the ground. I didn't even see what Grandmother had done before it was over. "Let's go, Sara. Our tea is getting cold." she smiled as we left before the girls could recover.

After that, we left the cafe and met up with Mom and Dad at the carriage. When they asked me about my day, I told them all about the shops, sights, and trinkets I had bought, but Grandfather nudged me when I was about to tell them what happened at the cafe. At home, Katheli and the other servants made us a big dinner and I enjoyed the time we were spending together and loathed that there were only two days left of my vacation.

That night, my parents asked me to put on the dress Grandmother had made for me at the shop. I had completely forgotten about it, but apparently, Grandfather had gone to get it early that morning. When I finished putting it on, I was put in a carriage and taken to the ballroom, which was in a separate building connected to the main house by a canopied long cobble stone path.

"W-what is all of this?" I gasped upon seeing all the people dancing.

"This is your surprise." Grandmother smiled as she came up to me.

"My...surprise?"

"We thought you might like it. One night as the second richest vampire." Grandfather said.

"And you get to dance with whoever you want without interference from us." Grandmom smiled. Just then, Reg and Rag ran up to me in the most formal attire I had ever seen them wear.

Rag spoke first, "C-can I-?"

"No! I want to dance with her first!" Reg interrupted as he tried to push Rag out of the way.

"No fair! I won the rock-paper-scissors tournament!"

"You hesitated, that means I get to ask her!"

"You're both idiots." Dunken sighed as he walked over.

"You're just saying that because you got last place!" They both yelled. Dunken sighed then, seeing something behind me, walked away mumbling, "I don't want any part of this." Rag and Reg were about to start arguing again when I heard a familiar throat clear. We looked over to see Dad, Granddad, and Grandfather glaring at the boys.

"Wait a minute! I thought you said you wouldn't interfere!" I protested, though I was glad they stopped the fight.

"Well, most of us." Mom sighed.

"But I can't pick if they scare off everyone!"

"Then I'll pick for you." A familiar voice called. I felt someone grab my hand and I was pulled to the dance floor by none other than Shota.

"No fair! You weren't in the tournament at all!" Rag yelled.

"Sorry boys, but I'm an opportunist!" Shota laughed as we disappeared into the crowd.

"You know those guys are going to hate you, right?" I giggled.

"They'll get over it." He chuckled. We were dancing hand in hand to a medium-paced song.

"And what about the males in my family?"

"I'll...deal with them somehow.... or your mom will deal with them for me." We laughed together and continued dancing as the tempo of the song slowed down, then Shota suddenly stopped.

"What is it?"

"I-um...May I...Would you mind if I put my hand on your waist?" There were a few giggles from the surrounding dancers and my face turned red.

"I-idiot!" I whispered.

"Sorry." He nervously chuckled. I let go of his hand and he placed his on the upper part of my waist while I tried to put mine on his shoulder, but even though he was only a year and a half older than me, he was far taller.

"Complete idiot."

"T-thank you." We danced for a little while longer, helping my embarrassment to slip away, and then we decided to take a break and sit down.

"That was so much fun!"

"Mm."

"What's wrong? Are you upset that I called you an idiot?"

"No." He sighed, "Just thinking about something. Why don't you go walk around for a little?"

"Ok, but don't be upset if someone else asks me for a dance." I decided to go outside since, with most people dancing or drinking, it was fairly quiet on the balcony. I let the night air brush past my face and leaned against the rail. After a while, I heard footsteps and then Shota leaned on the rail next to me.

"I've made my decision and have come to ask you for your answer."

"Decision? Answer? What are you talking about all of a sudden?"

He stood up straight and turned to me, "Sara I...I like you. I think you're strong, confident, a bit of a troublemaker, and very cute and I would be honored if you would c-consider...going out with me."

I couldn't hide my ears or tail and I felt my face turn bright red as I mumbled, "I...um..." I couldn't figure out where to start.

"Um, on second thought, you don't have to answer right this second. I know I kinda sprung this on you. In fact, I think I'm going to head back inside and-"

"Stop talking, you silver-tongued...I just needed to organize my thoughts." I sighed, "Shota I...I like you too. You can be a pain, with your constantly cheery attitude, sly moves, and caring demeanor, but I like you. It's just...I like someone else too and...I think he may like me also and since I've known him a lot longer, I want to give him a chance."

Shota didn't say anything, he just leaned against the rail and stared out over the grassy field. After a while, he took my hand and chuckled, "Come on. Those scary males are probably looking for you." We went back into the hall and were greeted by Mom in seconds.

"There you are!"

"Sorry, just wanted some fresh air." I chuckled, not quite sure how to react just yet.

"Well, that's understandable. Being around a bunch of stuck-up nobles is draining," she said loudly, warranting some scoffs from the eavesdropping crowd, "but this is a party in your honor. A chance for you to rub their noses in your half-wolf wealth."

"Truth is some nobles said a pretty nasty thing about Wolf-Vampires and your Mom wants you to put them in their place," Dad said as he came through the crowd.

"That doesn't seem very nice, Ma'am." Shota laughed like usual. It was like nothing had happened on the balcony and it made me feel better that things between us hadn't changed.

"Yeah yeah, just go Sara." Mom said as she separated us and dragged me away. For the next few hours, I was dragged from one person to the next, exchanging fake smiles and formalities. Many of the nobles were old and many I hadn't met until the moment Mom brought me to them. When we were finally through with the "Rub Your Wealth in Their Face" tour, I sat down at one of the tables. My great-grandparents were checking on everything, and my grandparents and parents were dancing. Shota got called away for an emergency at the hospital and doubted Dunken or the boys were going to try asking me to dance again, so I was left all alone, sipping my champagne-colored Apple Cider as I looked at all the people dancing.

"My, you are beautiful!" A voice said. I turned to see a tall man with golden brown hair dressed in very formal attire. Next to him was another man though he looked like a boy.

"If only I were several years younger, maybe a thousand and one, I could ask for your lovely hand in marriage."

As if this was routine, the boy stepped forward and said, "What he means is, it's a pleasure to meet you."

"Oh, t-thank you," I said.

"May we sit and have a conversation?" The man asked.

"I don't mind." I nodded as they took the seats across from me. Despite this man's weird approach, I felt like I should be most forthcoming with my formalities, but at the same time, I felt I could lower my guard.

"You are such a lovely girl, why are you sitting alone?"

"My family is dancing, and my friend had to leave due to an emergency at his workplace."

"He has a job so important that it could take him away from such a beautiful maiden?"

"Indeed, he does."

"Then it must be a very good job indeed."

"Indeed, it is."

"Then," The man got up and politely reached out a hand to me, "since you are alone and have nothing to do, why not dance with me?"

"I'm afraid I have many who wouldn't be very fond of that."

"Oh, but I am nearly half a million years old! Surely, they would have no concern with that." The boy at his side stifled a scoffed, likely because the man was far older.

Though I was tired from all the dancing and running around, it is seen as uncouth to be by yourself at these noble parties, so I smiled and took his hand. He told the boy to sit and wait unless a beautiful girl asked him to dance, and we went to the floor and had a wonderful time as we talked. Throughout the dance I could always feel eyes on us, some surprised, some disgusted, but they would quickly disappear as soon as the man glanced up. It was strange since normally, taking your eyes off your partner would make people comment more, but when he did it, it felt like people were afraid to comment.

During the last song we were dancing together, he asked me a question, "By the way, Sweet Plum," a name he had decided to call me, "may I ask for your name and if you know mine?"

"You may. My name is Sara Hollins and, though it pains me to say, I do not know yours."

"Oh, how dreadful! This pains me so!" He exclaimed with an exaggerated flourish, "Oh well, allow me to enlighten you. My name is Todo Vicer." The song stopped as my body froze.

"T-Todo...Vicer?" Just so you know, Todo Vicer is a world-renowned, illustrious author of all kinds of books, but is also known for many other high-ranking jobs across multiple nations. He is often asked to be an ambassador, sit on political councils, and even teach, making him one of the highest-ranking nobles in the country. Though, most Kofuians only know him for his stance on the country's current isolation, adherence to tradition, and treatment of non- and half-vampires. He hosts two major parties a year as charity events, one for vampires and the other for non-vampires, but you can only get in through a special invitation and you must stay on your best behavior. Despite his wealth and accomplishments, Mr. Vicer is a vampire-dragon and so there are those who oppose his wealth and fame. And to think I actually talked to him, danced with him! That explained why there were so many eyes on us!

After making our way back to the table Mr. Vicer said, "I'm sure you know my assistant's name."

"A-ah, yes! It's a pleasure to meet you, Mr. Hidakari!" I said, snapping out of my paralysis while trying to hide my surprise. Tomo

Hidakari, he's a half-Lyconian who has been Mr. Vicer's attendant for many years, which gives Mr. Vicer's unique nature, is no easy task.

"Oh, don't be so tense. I just want to talk." Mr. Vicer smiled.

"Aha, I'm sorry it's just that, I never thought I would meet someone as famous and renowned as you, at a simple garden party." It was always important to downplay a party's significance with nobles to make it seem like you were just having some frivolous fun. If you let on you actually put in effort then the guests would find fault with everything, and I felt that now that Mr. Vicer was here that was doubly true.

"Oh, I love parties! When your great-grandfather invited me, I was thrilled and honored to get the chance to dance with such a magnificent person as yourself."

"Oh, you tease."

"Ah, could this be modesty? Or do you really not know your own beauty? Well whatever it may be, the fact will never change. Now then, dancing is not the only reason for my being here."

Mr. Vicer, who had been flighty and carefree for most of the night, suddenly became very serious, "Ms. Sara, would you like to make a deal with me?"

"What type of deal?"

"I will take on all debts and charges for the spell misconduct case, as well as be your lawyer, and in exchange I would like for you to attend Adestria Vigdrore Boarding School."

"W-what do you mean, spell misconduct case?"

Some nobles who had been eavesdropping started mumbling, "Ah she didn't know? No wonder she was so happy.", "Well, ignorance is bliss.", "More like stupidity. Is she really going to be an heiress?", "Not a chance. There'll be nothing left to inherit once the case is over."

I couldn't believe it, a spell misconduct case...Mom, Dad, everyone would lose their wealth and status. I mean, I know they technically wouldn't care, but they earned everything through years of work, and it would all be ruined because of me. Tears began to form as Mr. Vicer glared at the whispering crowd, and they immediately scattered away.

"Sara let's go outside." Mr. Hidakari said as he took my hand. He looked toward Mr. Vicer who nodded and started talking to my family who were making their way through the crowd. I didn't hear what they were discussing as I was led outside, but it seemed he was scolding them and saying things like, "Can't protect forever." Once outside, Mr. Hidakari sat me in a chair where no one could see me and left to get me an orange drink with bubbles in it. "I have to go, but please don't worry. Todo will definitely win the case for you." He said before leaving.

"Don't worry?" I muttered, my tears dropping into the drink. After crying for, who knows how long, I finally came to a decision. Whether I accepted Mr. Vicer's help or not I still had a case against me and since I didn't have any friends at vampire school, transferring wasn't a big deal. The real issue was the human school since Adestria was a boarding school in the magic world, and more importantly, Shiyu. I don't want to leave him, especially since he's always stood as my friend despite being bullied for it. I'd feel like I'm betraying him if I were to just up and leave.

"That won't be a problem." Mr. Vicer said, interrupting my thoughts as he handed me a handkerchief to wipe my tears.

"What do you mean?" I asked.

"You'll see." He smiled. Wait, now that I think about it, how did he know what I was thinking?

Anyways, after that he said, "So I take it you'll accept, correct? Wonderful! Then I'll make sure to get everything ready and sent to your house. Oh, and keep the handkerchief. I have more." Then he disappeared. The party lasted well into the early morning and I'm fairly certain we're leaving today so I think it's time I go to bed.

RECOLLECTION

Old Friends, New School

I only got a few hours of sleep, as expected, before being stirred awake by Dad. I refused to get up, of course, and tucked myself further under the covers. I heard a sigh and before long was being carried down the stairs in my pajamas. I was kissed by my family as they said goodbye and was laid down in a carriage where I quickly went back to sleep. When I awoke again, it was to the orange light of the evening sun and the sweet smell of Autumn Pancakes, pancakes with autumn colors, fruits, and spices that Mom makes especially for me. In fact, there was a pancake for each season. I got up and stretched before laying down once more, then jumped up and skipped down the stairs.

"Good morning!" I excitedly exclaimed.

"It's evening," Dad said. He was sitting on the couch reading a book while sipping a cup of coffee. He glanced up for a moment to look at me and said, "Sara why don't you get dressed before having...whatever it is you're having."

"No thanks, it's just breakfast!" I said skipping along.

"Except it isn't." I heard him mumble as I went into the kitchen.

"Good morning!" I yelled to Mom.

"Good morning my little sunflower!" She said as she gave me a big hug. Her face was covered in pancake batter, which I happily licked off. "Did you ask your father if he needed more coffee?"

"No. I'll go ask now." I zipped out of the kitchen and plopped down next to Dad. I sat there and smiled at him, wagging my tail, while he pretended not to notice. I bumped his arm with my head, rubbed against his chin, and even took his coffee and sat between his face and the book so he had to see me, but he still pretended to read his book, so I puffed out my cheeks and drank the rest of his coffee in one gulp. Like always, I truly regretted it. If I had low levels when waking up, they were definitely up now. "Why do you use so much sugar?" I gagged.

"Next time don't take my coffee." he replied while patting my back, "Are you ok?" I nodded and he said, "Then go get me another cup.", as he playfully pushed me from his lap.

"Keh! The universe will run out of sugar if I get you another cup!" I went to fix him another cup and noticed that the coffee was his specially brewed Autumn coffee. It was just like my mom's pancakes, different autumn colors floating all around, except without the fruit and it had a cinnamon stick in it. I fixed us both a cup and ran out of the kitchen to give him his and a kiss. "So, any news?" I asked as I sipped my coffee.

"Well, that Drake kid that used to hang around you got arrested again for beating up a referee and several players, both on his and the opposing team, because they called him up for misconduct."

"Oh, that reminds me that I have to find a way to break up with him."

"Wait, he's your previous boyfriend! Oh, come on Sara at least give me a challenge!" I silently sipped my coffee as Dad ranted, kicking myself for letting that slip. "I could kill him, then my little girl wouldn't have to worry about breaking up anymore." He said after a while, pulling me into a hug and ruffling my hair.

"Dad!" I whined, "You're making me spill my coffee!" He laughed and continued to pester me.

"Hey, you two, evening breakfast is almost ready." Mom popped in and said before turning to me. "Sara, go upstairs and wash up. We have a special guest coming."

"Yes ma'am" After I finished washing up and getting dressed, I came back down and found Mr. Vicer and Mr. Hidakari. "Mr. Vicer, Mr. Hidakari, it's wonderful to see you again."

"Sara, always wonderful to see you as well." Mr. Vicer smiled. Mr. Hidakari just nodded.

"They'll be joining us for break-ahem dinner." Mom said. I heard Dad chuckle and Mom sent him a glare before going back to smiling. "The food is ready if you're ready to eat."

"Wonderful!" Mr. Vicer said as he and Mr. Hidakari followed her into the kitchen.

"Pancakes...for dinner?" Mr. Hidakari said when he saw the plates before him.

"Lovely! A little randomness never hurt anyone." Mr. Vicer laughed. He took a huge bite and then said, "My, you simply must give me your recipe!"

"Todo please chew and swallow your food before talking." Mr. Hidakari sighed. Dinner went on without much issue and afterward, we sat on the couch, but as they had been away for so long, Mom and Dad had to make a few calls. Mr. Vicer sat in the chair across from me and Mr. Hidakari stood beside him.

He smiled at me and said, "Don't worry, I'll make sure you win the case." I had no doubt that Mr. Vicer would win the case for my family, my concerns were what to do when I went back to school in three days since I might have to say goodbye to my only friend. "I understand your feelings Sara and I'm sorry that we gave you such a short time to make your decision."

"Oh, I doubt time would have made things any better." I smiled.

"Hmm, true. Too much time gives you the chance to second guess." He sighed, "But like I said, I don't think you have to worry about Shiyu." Just like last night, it felt like Mr. Vicer could read my thoughts. Actually, how did he know my friend's name was Shiyu? W-was he actually reading my thoughts?

Ok, so I went to get a book that talked about the abilities of various species, and apparently dragons have the ability to telepathically communicate, whether their recipients know they're communicating or not!

"Indeed, and because dragons are so powerful, I retain that ability as a vampire-dragon. It's quite handy for long-distance communication too." He chuckled...in my head...just now! I can almost see the smile he's making right now, and it irks me so much! "By the way," he has the audacity to continue, "I prefer not to be so formal. Mr. Todo is fine and "Mr. Hidakari" prefers to be called Tomo."

"G-get out of my head!" I, out loud and telepathically, yelled at him. Mom and Dad probably think I'm going crazy if they heard that.

"Ouch not so loud. I have sensitive hearing."

"Don't give me that, it's creepy!"

"You know if you throw thoughts at me, I can't not hear them. Anyways, just think of me if you have any questions, but for now, I'll let you get back to writing your diary."

Ugh alright, I think he's actually gone now. Going back to his visit this evening, I glanced over and noticed that Mr. Hida-well Tomo, looked sick and Mr. Todo noticed as well as he let out a sigh and got up.

"Looks like I'll have to cut this visit short. Tomo's stomach doesn't seem to be doing well." I hadn't remembered at the time, but Tomo is half-Lyconian. Lyconians' have sensitive digestive systems, as do vampires. As a half-wolf though, I don't have to deal with any issues, so I can only imagine the extreme agony Tomo was going through.

"Tell your mom...that her pancakes...were nice." He managed to get out before collapsing to the ground.

"Right so, I left a package for you on the chair over there. Have a wonderful day...or night." Mr. Todo said as he and Tomo disappeared.

"I wonder how much longer I have?" I sighed while walking to school. I still felt conflicted about what to do with Shiyu. Mr. Todo said not to worry, but I couldn't help but wonder if he'd really be ok.

"How much longer for what?" Shiyu asked as he popped up in front of me. I had been so absorbed in my thoughts that I hadn't noticed he was walking beside me.

"Oh um...nothing." He looked at me like he wanted to press further then smiled and looked to the sky.

"Well so long as you're ok. Oh, look Sara it's a bunny rabbit!"

"Really! Where?" I asked, looking around before realizing he meant the clouds.

"By the way Sara, there's a new ice cream stand in the park. Want to go check it out after school?"

"Sure." As we laughed together, I realized just how much I didn't want to give him up. Shi was talking about something, but all I could think about was how much I would miss him.

"Sara." He said, snapping my attention back.

"Mmhm, the arcade sounds great." He silently stared at me, and I thought maybe I had said the wrong thing.

He sighed, looking back to the sky, and said, "Hey Sara, if you ever got an amazing-looking letter for an amazing-sounding place, would you leave your current life to be there?"

"No, it sounds too good to be true so it's probably a scam. Besides, I would want to stay with my friends and family."

"Even if it meant passing the opportunity of a lifetime?"

"Shi, are you getting scammed by someone right now? Show me the letter, I'll have someone verify it."

"I'm not being scammed Sara, and what could your investigation group dig up that mine's can't." He burst out laughing, "But...I would go. I wouldn't want to pass it up and I know that no matter where I go, my friends and family will always be there for me."

"Shi," I murmured as I felt tears welling up. He smiled and patted me on the head.

He then ran off laughing, "Let's get going or we'll be late for school." After a quick moment, I wiped my tears and chased after him.

Despite the touching morning, the day was a total blunder. Everyone blamed me for Drake getting arrested, even the coach and some of the teachers, and tried to give me a horrible time. They were even more upset when I completed their challenges with ease and some even started taking it out on Shiyu by not doing anything to stop the students from bullying him and when they did step in, they took their time. By twelve our parents had been called, since I had sent half the students and a teacher, by accident, to the hospital when they started outright beating him, and we were sent home. After telling them what happened the school decided not to press charges. Since we were out of school for the rest of the day, and Shi's wounds were light, thanks to my intervening, Shi and I went to the arcade and that new ice cream stand he was talking about. After, we went to his house and played games until I had to leave to get ready for my night school.

It wasn't much better there either. The few students and teachers who survived kept a distance from me or were angry that they could no longer use magic and passive-aggressively took it out on me. After an hour or two I just decided to bail and went back home. Since I was by myself, I decided to finally look at the package Mr. Todo had left. Inside was my uniform which was a crimson red blazer and skirt with golden trim, some papers asking for my medical information and anything that would be important to know, and some maps, school brochures, and stuff of that sort.

"Your parents will have to fill out the medical papers, but everything else is for you." I heard Mr. Todo say. "And don't yell, "Get out of my head!", I have a headache."

"Fine. So, this is everything?"

"Yes. I've sent a special gift to you as well, but you won't see it for another day or two I think." I tried to question him further, but it seemed like he was ignoring me. Bored, I texted Shi and asked if he wanted to go to the arcade again. He was concerned that I was skipping tutoring, the lie most vampires tell when they go to vampire school but agreed.

"Sara is something wrong? You never skip tutoring." He asked as soon as I ran up to him.

"I'm fine, just a little tired of dealing with everyone there." After brushing off any further concerns, we went inside and stayed until it closed at twelve. We decided to walk around the park, but it was strange. Even though it was late, the park was unusually empty.

"Hey Sara," Shi said, "there's something I've been really meaning to ask you."

"What is it?"

"Well, um, I wanted-" he stuttered, but was suddenly cut off by a bright red light.

"Hello, Sara!" I heard someone sing and as the light dissipated, found Shota standing in front of me.

"What are you doing here!?" I exclaimed.

"Todo sent me. He said he wanted to give you a special gift." Shota laughed.

"Todo you bastard!"

"E-excuse me, but who are you and how did you appear out of nowhere!?" Shi yelled.

"Oh, I should introduce myself, shouldn't I? My name is Shota Martz and I'm Sara's friend from Kofu. As for appearing out of nowhere, well, you're the ones walking around inside a barrier."

"Wait we're in a barrier? No wonder it's so eerily empty!" I chuckled but quickly stopped. Shota's sudden arrival had made me completely forget that Shi knew nothing of the magic world. I quickly turned to him to try and explain, but soon realized a bigger problem. "Shi, are you ok?"

"I...I don't know." He muttered. His skin had gone pale, and he was sweating bullets as he looked ready to keel over. "I think...I think I should go home."

"Unless your home is a hospital, I don't that's a good idea," Shota said. As he touched Shi's forehead, though, he recoiled, and they both collapsed.

"W-what's going on!? Are you ok?" I panicked.

"I..he..." Shi stammered.

"...It...it can't be..." Shota muttered. He and Shi stared at each other while I tried to figure out what to do. Suddenly Shota stood up and walked over to Shi. "Hey Sara, I'll...we'll explain everything, but for now can you get us home once we're done."

"Once you're done? Done what!"

Neither of them cared to explain this sudden understanding they had between each other, as Shota knelt down and Shi took his hand. There was a flash of light, an influx of magic, and a nagging feeling of Mr. Todo giving off, "I told you so" vibes, then everything settled, and in front of me laid a single unconscious boy who was neither Shiyu nor Shota. Not knowing what else to do, I carried him home. As expected, the Hazimis weren't too happy to see me carrying an unconscious boy who sort of looked like their son.

I told them that I wasn't sure what happened and that Shi said he was really tired before immediately falling asleep. They didn't really believe me but didn't ask further and allowed me to stay until he woke up. After waiting for several hours, I fell asleep on the couch.

"Wakey wakey sleepyhead." I heard as I was poked in the cheek.

"What? I rubbed my eyes and looked around. Both my parents and the Hazimis were sitting and waiting. "Um, what's going on?"

"Now that everyone is here, it's time to explain." The Shi/Shota hybrid said as he sat down next to me. Seeing him in the light, he had Shota's red hair, but Shiyu's face. "I've enlisted the help of Mr. and Mrs. Hollins, but to begin, I'm a Dimensional meaning my existence is split across different dimensions."

"Different dimensions?" Mrs. Hazimi asked.

"It's a bit complicated to explain," Dad sighed, "but basically think of the world as a shattered mirror. Every choice creates cracks, which create shards known as dimensions. Sometimes we call them worlds, but they're all part of the same mirror."

"And Shiyu is a being who exists in multiple dimensions at the same time? And because he met his other self, they merged?"

"Yes and no. With a few exceptions, everyone exists twice in the world. One being who is similar to your soul and one who's similar to your body. In the case of Shiyu though, only one of him exists, but it's been broken and scattered across the dimensions."

"And I have no idea how many parts I have or where they are." Shi/Shota added.

Mr. Hazimi broke the long silence that followed, "So, you're Shiyu, but not Shiyu?"

"Yes."

"And you're still our son?"

"He is most definitely still your son," Dad said.

"Um, but how?" I asked. "If everything Dad and Shi/Shota are saying is true, then Shiyu wasn't born."

"Indeed, he's adopted." Mrs. Hazimi said.

"...Huh?"

"A young woman gave him to us while we were out one night. Her body was thin enough that we could even see her heart beating. We tried to get her help, but she handed us her baby, smiled, then faded away. Shiyu is the only confirmation we have that she wasn't a ghost."

"I...you never told me that part." Shi/Shota said.

"We weren't sure you'd believe us."

"...Fair."

Everyone sat silently, unsure of what more to say, until once again, Mr. Hazimi broke the silence, "I have another question. Why did Shiyu call you two to help him explain?"

"Um well," Dad said, "We may or may not be from this dimension."

"May or may not?"

"We're...Wolf-Vampires." Mom said and awkward silence fell over the room again.

"So that's the secret you've been hiding from us this entire time?" Mr. Hazimi finally said.

"Um, yes."

"And you didn't tell us because?" Mrs. Hazimi questioned.

"We didn't want to concern you if anything happened," Dad responded.

"Nonsense! Do you know how many people want you two to fall? At least if we know you're not human we don't have to worry about human things killing you."

"We're sorry." Mom and Dad sighed.

"You too Sara. How could you keep such a secret from us?" she scolded.

"Sorry," I said as Shi/Shota giggled beside me.

"And Shota!" Mr. Hazimi scolded.

"Y-yes Sir!" He responded, quickly sitting up straight.

"You're grounded. Do you have any idea how worried we were when Sara brought you home unconscious? You even had her lie for you!"

"Yes Sir."

After getting scolded by the Hazimis a bit longer, they took us out for dinner where we discussed that I would be transferring to a new school. I also learned that Mr. Todo had told Shi/Shota that he could attend the school with me, but it would mean giving up his job at the hospital until graduation. He talked it over with Mom and the Hazimis and decided that if Shi/Shota was ok with it, he could attend the school. Mr. Todo, who as always is listening, ahem get out ahem, chimed in and said he would have everything sent to Shi/Shota by early tomorrow morning. After an awkward explanation of how Mr. Todo was able to use telepathy, which he conveniently made himself scarce for, we finished dinner and went back to the Hazimi's house to help Shi/Shota prepare for Shoyu's the name and teasing Sara is my game! I didn't know you cataloged our time together. It's touching.

...Shi/Shota, who would like to be called Shoyu now, just stole my diary and the only reason I'm not erasing what he wrote is because he also stole my eraser!

We were up late last night talking about Adestria, and trying to get my eraser back, that I fell asleep on the Hazimi's couch again, this time with a fuzzy blanket and a marshmallow soft pillow under my head.

"Good morning, Sara." Mrs. Hazimi smiled.

"Good morning." I yawned.

"Would you like a cup of coffee?"

"With some sugar." She nodded and I heard Mr. Hazimi take a sip of his coffee as she went to go make mine.

"Thanks for helping Shiyu. We really appreciate it." He said.

"No need to thank me, he's my friend."

"Speaking of which," Mrs. Hazimi said as she set down my coffee, "I heard you had a big dance in, Kofu was it, and that Shota asked you out." Ugh, I found out later that Reg and Rag were eavesdropping when we were on the balcony, in the hopes of siccing Dad on Shota.

"Y-yes, but as Mom no doubt told you, I rejected him."

"She did! She said it was because you liked someone else. Someone you'd known for a long time."

"Yeah," I said, bracing myself.

"Well, I was just thinking, since the two people in question are now one person, maybe you could reconsider."

"Well even though they're physically one person, they're still sort of, mixing and matching their mental state so..."

"Oh, but that won't be too much of a bother. Helen says it'll only take a few days." We went back and forth for a bit, with Mr. Hazimi occasionally trying to help only to get shut down by the "Think of the grandkids" line until finally Shoyu came down and dragged me away to the escape.

"Sorry about that. You know how Mom is. Well...this mom." Shoyu sighed as we walked around his manor's grounds.

"Don't worry about it." I chuckled. We walked a little further, the awkward silence settling between us. Gah even just writing this down makes me feel the awkwardness all over again! Look we wandered for like thirty minutes until we asked each other out, ok!

"Well, um, I guess this means we're dating now." Shoyu nervously chuckled.

"Yeah..."

"Um, are we supposed to do anything different now that we're dating?"

117

"Why would I know?"

"Well, you dated that Drake guy for like...geez six months. So, I thought you might know."

"I wouldn't really call our relationship dating. His dad needed dirt on Mom and Drake thought he could get it by hanging out with me and telling everyone we were dating. I just didn't care enough to actually stop him."

"Fair enough I guess."

"...I guess we could...keep being friends, but maybe...hold hands?"

"You don't sound very confident." He teased.

"Do you want to hold my hand or not?"

"Yes please." He smiled, quickly taking mine. It was warm and before long I could feel myself smiling and the awkwardness slipping away.

"Aw, young love." An annoyingly familiar voice sang. Mr. Todo soon appeared right after. "It's so adorable how innocent you both are."

"Why are you here?" I sighed.

"Oh my, we've barely seen each other and yet you sound exasperated by my presence already. Oh well, I just wanted to let you two newlywed lovebirds know, that there are strict dating rules what with it being a boarding school and all. So, try not to let your love get in the way of your learning. Toodles!"

"We are not newlywed lovebirds!" I yelled as he disappeared. After calming down, we continued our walk for a bit until I went home.

The next day, Shoyu suggested we practice magic together. It seemed like a good idea since he was technically new at magic and a partner was better than alone. So, I cast a barrier spell so no one could interrupt us and a spell that would keep us from getting seriously hurt, then learned that I was wrong about it being a "good idea". Despite this being Shoyu's first time using magic, he was adept at using spells and incantations and dodged them just as perfectly, though, if I had to guess, I'd say we were around the same level.

"Humph, you're good Sara."

"Well, I have been practicing this far longer than you."

"We'll see if your experience can help you survive my next barrage!" Jumping into the air he used a spell of light to try and blind me.

"Nice try, but I know that's a faint!" I shouted as I deflected a knife made of magic.

"Ha! Guess I'll just use brute force!" He aced his landing and then charged head-on towards me.

"We're equal in magic, but I have the upper hand in physical strength, and you know it!" I got ready to counter, but just as he closed in, he used another light spell. I turned to stop his attack from the side, thinking the front was fake, but felt no connection. From the front, he emerged from the light and plunged a magic knife into my stomach, so I fell backward onto the ground.

"O-oh my gosh! Sara are you alright!? I-I thought you would have dodged-"

"Fooled ya," I smirked as I used my hind legs-er well I was in human form so just legs, to launch him into the edge of the barrier, a good fifty or so meters away. The no-damage spell added a point, meaning it successfully prevented a fatal blow, and I cheered, "That's a win for me! Did you think I was out of magic, or did you really forget that vampires have auto-heal spells?"

"That's...that's dirty Sara. I thought you were actually hurt." He coughed as the spell repaired his body.

"Oh come on. All's fair in a magical war." He didn't say anything, just sat there and pouted, so eventually I walked over and held out my hand. "Alright fine, I'm sorry."

"Hmph," He smiled, taking my hand, then stabbed me in the heart with a magic sword, "all's fair in a magical war." He triumphantly looked over to the point counter, but nothing happened. "Wait didn't I gain a-Ow! Ow! Ow!"

"Again," I smiled as I crushed his hand, "did you think I was out of magic, or did you really forget vampires have auto-heal spells." Then I successfully secured another point. By the end of our training, we were both exhausted from using more magic than I had planned too, and Shoyu from constantly running away and being on the defensive.

"Well, that was certainly a good practice!" A cheery half-dragon chimed as we lay on the grass. I wanted to ask when he made it through the barrier and how but figured he wouldn't tell me. "Yes, none of that is important!" He said, answering my unasked questions, "What is important is the good tidings I bring to you."

"And what good tidings are those?" I asked.

He smiled, gearing up for a dramatic reveal, then said, "Sara Hollins and Shoyu Hazimi-Martz, in regard to your admissions into Adestria Vigdrore you are...accepted!"

"Wait, really!" Shoyu exclaimed. Even the exhaustion couldn't hide the joy on his face.

"Is it really that much of a surprise? I did give you brochures and uniforms and I invited you."

"But the brochures said even an invitation doesn't guarantee acceptance."

"Really? I should change that."

"Does this mean you came to pick us up?" I asked.

"No. I simply came to tell you so that you'd start packing, and to hand you these letters for your parents. Now, any questions?" We both shook our heads, fighting the urge to tear open the letters and read them ourselves. "Well then, I'll be taking my leave. Be sure to be at the train station specified in your letters in three days." After he left, Shoyu and I immediately went to tell our parents and they had a banquet to celebrate our acceptance.

The next days were filled with packing everything I would need and taking out things I wouldn't. I constantly had to go through my bag to take out things that Mom insisted on putting in. To be honest, though, there really wasn't much to pack since Adestria Vigdrore was a strict academy. There wouldn't be many times I could wear anything but the uniform so the only things I really needed to bring were undergarments, toiletries, and some medicine in case the school didn't have it for the first few days.

On the day of my departure, I woke up alongside the rising sun. Mom and Dad were already up and had probably snuck several things into my bag already as I took a shower and got dressed. Checking my bag, I immediately saw a ton of different clothes I wouldn't be able to wear. I sighed but couldn't help but giggle at how much effort they put into picking these, so I decided to keep the two outfits I liked most then went downstairs for a fabulous "Going Away" breakfast and coffee. After that, we drove to the train station where we met up with Shoyu and his parents. The train came right on time and from the window we waved goodbye to our parents. I even felt tears form as I realized this would be the last I would see of them, and this town, for a while.

"Don't worry." Shoyu smiled as he took my hand, "We'll be back for a break."

I wiped tears and nodded, reassuring myself with, "Yeah, they'll still be here when we get back." The train's whistle blew, and our long journey began.

The letter that told us what train to get on said that it would be a two-day trip to get to the academy, so I had guessed that this was a special train, one that went between the different dimensions. The car we were in was a super fancy sleeper car, with separate rooms, a lounge/dining room, and a shared bathroom all big enough to be considered part of a hotel. This was thanks to a super complicated spatial spell and honestly, it was awesome. For the duration of our trip, we had an attendant who was to be our guardian and if we ever needed anything, we just needed to push the call button. We explored the train car and then the rest of the train, because we got bored, then, after dinner, went to our rooms and fell asleep. Despite the fancy car, there was nothing to do on the train, so we slept until the afternoon when the attendant came to wake us. She said we were coming up to the dimensional shift and that the train would be stopping just before and right after for maintenance. It would take an hour and a half each time so if we wanted to get off and walk around, we could. We decided to take her up on the offer and bought a few books and souvenirs for ourselves and to mail back home. I thought going through the rift on a train would be a bumpy ride, but it turns out the rifts are pretty calm. Still a chance we could veer off into the never-ending abyss, but calm.

The attendant woke us up again around 6 am and told us that we should get everything ready and check that we had all our belongings. We were passing through somewhere's countryside and saw open fields as far as the eye could see. Behind us, far in the distance, I could see Kofu Forest, and, on the horizon, I could make out Brexior's mountain peaks. Ahead of us, looking out over such a beautiful landscape, was a huge building that took the beauty of the landscape and added it to its own, creating a breathtaking scene...until the train pulled into the station and obscured our view. As the attendant guided us to the exit, I couldn't help but feel an unbelievable amount of gratitude towards Mr. Todo for allowing us to experience this, and anticipation for the school year that lay ahead.

After dropping us off, the attendant told us to wait until someone came to pick us up and it didn't take long for a carriage to drive up. A man with black hair and in butler attire stepped out and bowed, asking if we were the new students.

"Wonderful! My name is Dube Marque. I'm the head butler for Adestria Vigdrore and I shall be taking you to the academy. You may ask me any questions you like and if you ever need anything during your stay, please feel free to find me or one of the staff."

"Thank you very much." We bowed before getting into the carriage.

Once at the academy, he led us into what I assumed was the main hall and said, "Though you missed getting a proper tour with the other first years, I hope this will provide you with the information you need. Currently, we are in the office building where the principal's and teachers' offices reside."

"Other first years? I thought we were starting in the middle of the semester." Shoyu asked.

"Oh not at all, in fact, you came at a very good time. The new year has just started so you won't have to worry about catching up." Perhaps we still looked confused because he continued, "Adestria runs on a slightly different schedule than most human or vampire schools and is instead more similar to the Brexiorian school schedule, at least in some regards. You'll learn more about such things during your stay." We reached the principal's office on the second floor and a familiar voice told us to come in when Mr. Marque knocked on the door. "Here are the students you requested, Sir."

"Thank you, Marque. You're a big help." Mr. Todo said staring out the window overlooking the grounds.

"Always glad to be of service, Sir. Well then, I shall take my leave." Mr. Todo nodded, and Mr. Marque bowed before leaving.

"Now then," Mr. Todo sighed, "how was your trip?"

"Fine. Though there wasn't much to do." I said.

"We slept for most of it." Shoyu chuckled.

"I figured as much. You both have a terrible case of bedhead." Mr. Todo laughed.

"What really!" We both exclaimed as we tried to fix our hair.

"Relax, relax." he laughed. "Here are your schedules. I'll take you both to your rooms so you can get situated and take a shower if you want." The room had its own bathroom, but the showers were in a side building connected to the main dorms. When I came out and went back to the room Mr. Todo was waiting.

"You certainly took your time."

"I like being clean." I puffed.

"I don't take long in showers and I'm still clean." he boasted.

"Why are you here?" I asked so we could get to the point.

"I came to let you know that you don't have any roommates, so if you get lonely you can come to me."

"Really? Why not?"

"Well with your personality I couldn't find anyone that'd be a good fit."

"What do you mean, "my personality"?" I growled.

"Easy easy. That was only one reason I couldn't find a roommate. The other is, I know you've never shared a room before so I thought it would be better if, for the first year, you stayed on your own."

"Hmph."

"Don't be mad, I just don't know how your personality will mesh with the other students yet!" We talked for a little while longer, about who I should talk to when I needed refills for my medicine and such, then he left.

After getting dressed and unpacking my things, I laid down on the bed and took out my phone to see several texts from Mom and Dad asking if I got to school ok and a text from Shoyu saying hi. I texted my parents to let them know I was settling in fine and asked Shoyu what room he was in since Mr. Todo had taken me to my room first. He texted back, giving me his room number, and asked what my schedule was.

Unfortunately, since Shoyu was in high school, and I was in middle school, we only really had lunch periods together. He asked if I wanted to come over and talk face-to-face one last time, since with the curriculum we had, we probably wouldn't be seeing each other much anymore.

The next day, school started at 6 am with the entire girls' dormitory going outside in our PE clothes and doing stretches and laps. I, along with several other girls were extremely tired and got yelled at several times by our drill sergeant of an instructor. After taking a shower we put on our uniforms and left to start class at seven in the main school building. Since I hadn't been given a tour like the other first years, I was completely lost in finding my classes. The final bell was about to ring, and I felt completely hopeless when someone had the nerve to shove me.

"Move it first year!" a rough-looking girl said. She had two people who I assumed were her friends laughing beside her.

"She looks so totally helpless." One laughed.

"Poor thing." The other said. They pushed past me and continued on to their class. As I sighed to myself, lamenting my situation, someone tapped me on the shoulder.

"Don't mind them. They're mean to everyone." a cheerful-looking girl smiled. She had dark brown hair and brown eyes, which were cat-like. "More importantly, how about I help you find your class? I didn't see you at the orientation or tour, so I bet you're totally lost."

"T-thank you," I said, basking in this bastion of hope.

"No problem. I was a first year just like you not too long ago." She continued to smile. As she looked at my schedule, her face lit up even more. "Oh, how wonderful! Showing you to your classes will be easier than I thought." She grabbed my hand and led me to my classroom, having me sit at a desk before sitting down next to me.

"Um, don't you have to go to class?"

She gave me a triumphant smile. "This is my class."

"Oh? So that's why you smiled when you looked at my schedule."

"That and look." She said, handing me her schedule which looked identical to mine.

"We have the same classes together!"

"I was surprised too." she smiled, "My name's Keri Hadanel. What's yours?"

"I'm Sara Hollins. It's nice to meet you." We shook hands and couldn't help but giggle.

"Well, I think this is the start of a beautiful friendship!" Keri exclaimed.

The class had other plans. Aside from the pace being faster than what I was used to, those girls I had met in the hall were also in my classes and kept bugging me by passing notes. Keri noticed though and mentioned it to the teacher who took them outside to have a talk. It was...weird. I'm used to having to protect myself, so it was new to not only have a friend help me but to have teachers who actually cared as well. Anyway, the rest of the day went mostly the same. At lunch, I introduced Keri to Shoyu, and he introduced us to his roommate, Gene Hadelimf. He had light brown hair and green eyes and was sweet, cheerful, smart, and great at tutoring people. He even let Keri, Shoyu, and I ask him about the teachers and classes we were yet to see. Lunch flew by, so we decided to make plans to go to the school cafe after classes ended at four, to study.

While studying we also decided to learn more about each other. Keri has been at Adestria since she started middle school three years ago, and Gene started high school two years ago. Gene is Brexiorian and Keri is Nekolian, so they always rode the same train together, but this was technically the first time they actually met. Immediately upon hearing that Shoyu and I were childhood friends, they started pressing us on our relationship status.

"Oooh, I love it! Childhood friendship turned white hot love! It just oozes romance!" Keri swooned.

"Guess that means Sara's off limits." Gene sighed.

"Same for Shoyu." Keri mimicked.

"But," they said, the passion burning in their eyes, "we now have a target to embarrass!"

"D-don't you guys! That's not cool." Shoyu protested.

"Y-yeah. You don't want to tease us, it'd be boring." I agreed.

"Ha! Looks like we're going to have a fun year." Keri giggled. She and Gene both started laughing while Shoyu and I contemplated our situation.

"What's with all this stupid laughter?" The girl from this morning scoffed as she and her friends walked over to our table.

"Who's that?" Shoyu whispered.

"The girl I told you about," I whispered back. I guess trouble follows me no matter where I go.

"Hey! I hate stupid people who stupidly whisper!" She shouted then looked to Shoyu. "So, first-year has a boyfriend? Looks pretty cute."

"So cute we might have to steal him." Her friend snickered. The girls walked over and pushed me aside as they surrounded Shoyu.

"Hey, my name's Hadesia and these are my friends Lucia and Satania, but you can call us Lust. Why don't you ditch your loser girlfriend and come spend the night with us?"

"I thank you, I guess, for the...kind offer, but I'll have to pass," Shoyu said, begging me for help out of this situation.

"Oooh, really?" They said crawling all over him.

"Really." He said, pushing them off. "I'm dedicated to my girlfriend.

"Well, how you like that!" Keri laughed. "You couple breakers have been turned down by the power of true love!"

"Shut up!" Hadesia snapped.

"Looks like the princess isn't happy that she couldn't get her way." Gene chimed in.

"Shut up!"

"If you don't mind, my boyfriend said to get off him so if you could leave," I said. She glared at me and then turned to Shoyu who was wriggling to escape.

"It's them, isn't it? You want to keep your "good image" don't you? Well I understand, just come by tonight." She smiled.

"He said he doesn't like you, get over it and stop trying to be a boyfriend stealer."

"Shut! Up!"

"That's quite enough!" someone shouted as a dark cloud that smelled of sweet...pastries maybe, descended on us.

"Yes, I would hate for my uniforms to get damaged after just one day." another said. The cloud made it impossible to see or feel anything, but once it receded, we found ourselves sitting on the floor. "Are you ok?" the person, now right above us, asked. I looked up and saw Ms. Girda, our sewing teacher, standing above us.

"Ah, yes we're alright," I said.

"Not you, my uniforms. Ugh, I can't believe Marque would put my beautiful creations on the floor like...like...like trash!" she said.

"Oh, um yeah. I don't think they got ripped..." Ms. Girda is a bird-like creature, I forget the name, with brown feathers and a black beak and talons on her hands and feet. Unlike Tengus, or that ancient bird race, her wings and arms are one and the same, like a wyvern, and the only thing really humanoid about her is that, despite her feathers, she wears clothes. She adores creating outfits, and is the one responsible for the school uniforms, but, as you might have guessed, sometimes cares more about her creations than the people wearing them.

"Lady Girda, I'd appreciate it if you cared for our students." The black cloud said as it took shape and revealed itself to be Mr. Marque.

"...I guess I'm glad you're alright too." She sighed, helping us to our feet.

"Now, Hadesia, Satania, Lucia," Mr. Marque said, "I do believe you have already been told many times to stop your advances toward the staff and students. If you continue this behavior, you will be sent home, do you understand?" Lust, as the three of them like to be called, glared toward me, but Mr. Marque quickly stood in their path and repeated, "Do you understand?"

"Yes Sir." They scowled before leaving the cafe. By now a group of bystanders were watching us, so I asked, "Mr. Marque is there anywhere else we could go?"

"Of course." He nodded and Girda wrapped us in a light and teleported us to Mr. Marque's office.

"Jeez, guess it'll be a while before we can sit in the school cafe without being stared at." Keri sighed.

"I hope we won't have to deal with Hadesia tomorrow. Class is hard enough without having to deal with her and her friends." I sighed as well.

"She'll probably be suspended for this." Mr. Marque said as he handed us our stuff.

"Geez those girls." Ms. Girda sighed. "How long do they plan on staying here? I'm tired of making uniforms for them."

"How long has she and her friends been here?" I asked. Even though Lust was in Keri and I's middle school classes, it was clear that they were full-grown high schoolers.

"Last year, the year before, maybe since birth." Gene chuckled.

"Now now, speaking ill of another is to speak ill of oneself." Ms. Girda sighed. "By the way, Keri dear since you're always such a big help, do you mind coming with me to buy some fabric for tomorrow's class?"

"I would love to!" Keri said.

"Wonderful! Because of those girls, all my fabrics got destroyed. I'm so glad Master said that if they don't pass this year, he's kicking them out."

"That sounds terrible," I said though based on what I've seen, I was already glad, "how come?"

"Because of things like this." Mr. Marque sighed. "Picking fights, stealing boyfriends, we've even had to fire quite a few teachers over the years because they fell for the girls' seduction. They even tried to seduce Master."

"Yes, oh, but look at us! Telling the students not to speak ill then speaking ill ourselves!" Ms. Girda exclaimed. "Oh well, I'm certain you are all the talk of the school now. Please let us know if you have any problems."

We nodded and Keri chimed, "No need to worry! As the Middle School Victorian and Student Council President, nothing bad can befall us without my say-so!" We laughed at her enthusiasm and went back to our rooms to finish our studies.

So, I was about to go to sleep, but I realized there were some things I talked about that you might not know, precious diary. First, Nekolians or basically, cat people. Their home island was destroyed centuries ago so most Nekolians live in Crexior, a territory within Brexior. There are different tribes based on the type of cat, with the main two being the Homemakers and the Hunters tribes. Even though Keri looks closer to a Homemaker Nekolian, she's actually a mix which is why she tends to have so much energy while other Homemakers are content to lounge in the sun.

The other thing is about how school works. Most schools in the magic world work similarly to the ones in the human world, we just start one year earlier and stay one year later. For instance, middle school for most human world schools ends in three years and starts at the age of eleven. In the magic world, it's five years and starts at age ten. So, you may have thought that I was close to graduating from middle school soon, but I still have two more years after this one. Oh, and high school is also five years, though the fifth year is fewer classes and more like a gap year where you figure out basic life things like hobbies and such.

Now that that's explained, time for a sincere good night! ...Ugh I looked at my schedule one last time and it's going to be a long day tomorrow.

The next day we got up and did our morning exercises and showered, before going to the classroom, whose atmosphere was totally awkward. Everyone whispered and eyed us suspiciously and to make matters worse, Lust didn't show up, so people thought we had gotten them expelled.

"Don't let it get you down," Keri whispered. "We've got each other. Nothing will beat us!"

Her enthusiasm made me smile so I nodded, "Right. There's no need to worry." We laughed and began talking like usual, ignoring the whispers around us, until the teacher came in to begin class. The bell rang at four to signify the glorious end of an academically torturous day. "I never thought I'd wish to go back to those boring schools." I sighed.

"Hehe, yeah the curriculum here can be pretty daunting when you first come, but you'll get used to it." Keri giggled. Shoyu and Gene had gotten roped into helping Ms. Girda shop today so Keri and I were sitting in an empty classroom, just talking.

"I hope so. Do you think you could help me study? I need some help on some of the material."

"Wish I could, but I have a council meeting with the headmaster and other Victorians, I can come by your room when I'm done, and we can study then."

"Ok." I pouted. She headed off and I began to pack my bag. I was using the duffle bag I had brought all my things in as a school bag. Of all the things I didn't think about when packing, a backpack had to be it. "I wonder when the weekend is." I sighed. Since Adestria is so strict, we get almost no breaks and only one day for the weekend, and from what I heard, it's usually spent going to tutoring sessions. I picked up my bag and headed out the door.

"You're not going to win." A voice said from behind me. I turned and saw Hadesia glaring at me. I decided to ignore her and continued walking down the hall. "Didn't you hear me? I said I won't lose." I continued walking, but Lucia and Satania appeared from around the corner, blocking my path.

"I have someone waiting for me, so please move."

"Listen to me! I'm going to steal your boyfriend one way or another, then we'll see who's so tough!"

"I'm afraid my boyfriend isn't as easily swayed as you think. Now please move."

"Humph, we'll see about that. They all say they can't be swayed until they find themselves pleasantly enjoying every moment, we give them." Hadesia and her friends laughed.

"I'm afraid that won't be happening," Shoyu said as he casually walked in from around the corner that Satania and Lucia were blocking and moved them out of the way. "I went through far too much trouble and pain to get her. I wouldn't let her go even if my life depended on it."

"Shoyu! I thought you were still shopping with Girda." I said.

"A little birdie, or in this case giant dragon, told us what was happening, so she let me leave to come to rescue my fair maiden."

"Fair...maiden?"

"Well you are beautiful and I've known you long enough to know that you are, indeed, a female." He laughed.

"Hey!" Hadesia yelled, then more seductively said, "Shoyu darling, don't say such confusing things."

"Butt out." Shoyu scowled.

"What a mean thing to say," Satania said.

"Looks like we'll have to punish this naughty boy." Lucia swooned.

"I wouldn't touch hags like you no matter how long the pole." He said.

"How dare you!" They growled.

He took my hand and bowed like a prince. "Shall we be off malady?" He asked, kissing my hand.

"I-I guess." I blushed. He suddenly picked me up and as he jumped out the window, Hadesia yelled that she would get her revenge.

We hung out in Shoyu's room until Keri's meeting was over, then met at the school café, which had few people since it was so late, and I told them about what happened.

"Jeez, I should have left with you instead of leaving you alone." Keri sighed.

"Well at least now you know you're Lust's number one enemy, so you can stay on your guard," Gene said.

"I guess, but that's going to be so annoying." I sighed.

"Don't worry. We're here for you and to be honest, the headmaster is probably keeping an eye on you too." Keri said.

"I've been meaning to ask, by headmaster do you mean Mr. Todo?"

"Yeah, he tends to, well, read people's minds. Though since you had to interview with him to get in, I bet you already knew that."

"Interview? Oh, Mr. Todo invited us, so we didn't have to interview."

"What, but that was the hardest part!" Gene exclaimed.

"I bet Sara would have aced it anyway." Keri laughed. "But...maybe don't mention that to anyone else." After finishing up at the cafe Shoyu and Gene walked Keri and me back to our dorms saying it was a man's duty then Keri and I went and took a shower and studied in my room while drinking fruit milk until curfew.

RECOLLECTION

Settled in for New Discoveries

The next weeks went by relatively the same. We would go to the cafe after school or to each other's room to study. Once a week Shoyu and I would use our dorm kitchens to make lunch for each other and then would hide behind a tree to eat together, though, that was more so we could test each other's dishes for culinary class. Hadesia and her friends bothered me from time to time, but they've become more cautious. Shoyu became the star of the school after acing in a tournament in PE class and girls would always ask him out, but he turned them down telling them that I was his girlfriend. It made me happy, but also anxious. Rumors about me started cropping up and I started receiving threatening letters demanding I break up with him, but with Keri and Gene's constant support, occasional teasing, and Shoyu purposely doing PDA, like hugging and hand holding, whenever other girls were around, they slowly stopped. I had an inkling that Mr. Todo, Mr. Marque, and the rest of the staff may have also helped, but they all denied it.

Finally, a weekend where I was actually free came around. I had been studying very hard and, thanks to the teachers not giving me a lot of homework, I managed to finish all my work in one night and could finally go into town and get a new bag. Since it was our first weekend, Keri and Gene volunteered to show me and Shoyu around. I was happily getting ready for the next morning when I came to a horrible revelation, I didn't bring any money. I had only thought of the train ride and didn't bring any more than was necessary. As I lamented my predicament, I noticed that I hadn't checked one of my bag pockets and that it had something in it. When I opened it, I found a gold-colored credit card, well really a gold family sigil that acts like a credit card in this world, with a note from Mom that read, "I know you don't think you'll need it, but it's always good to have money." I'll have to write her a letter soon. There was a knock at my door, and I wondered who it could be since it was after curfew, but before I could go peek through the hole, Mr. Todo teleported in.

"Wha-! Why are you here!?"

"Quiet now quiet. You'll alarm everyone."

"Then leave."

"Aww, but I came to give you this." He said, handing me a card. It was similar to what Mom had given me, except it was the school sigil. On the back, it also had my name and class. "It's your student ID. With this, you can buy whatever you want so long as you put money into it. You'll even get discounts at the stores in town."

"Thanks, but you know I just found the credit card my mom left for me."

"I know, but I wanted to give it to you anyway. Keri has something to give you tomorrow as well."

"Really? I wonder what it is...do you ever not eavesdrop on people's minds?"

"Well let's move on then." He laughed.

"No matter what I say, or do you'll keep doing it, won't you?"

"Come Sara let's sit on the bed and chat." He continued to ignore me and plopped himself on my bed. I sighed and sat next to him. "How has school life treated you? Are you used to the curriculum yet?"

"Good, I guess. I made a few friends, so we study together."

"A few friends, and a number of enemies."

"Well, that's not my fault."

"I know you don't try to make enemies, but somehow, they seem to find you. I'm worried, I don't want to see you hurt."

"Hmph, you sound like my parents."

"Well your parents did charge me with protecting you and I can't do that if I don't act like one," he said. After a moment of silence, he changed the subject, "So, have you gotten used to the long days and early morning routine?"

"I'm used to being at school until midnight so that's not a problem, but the early rise thing...even in the human world I didn't have to wake up until 7."

"I figured as much. Even I can't get up at that time." he chuckled.

"Then why do you make us?"

"Marque likes doing things early. Really early. This is a compromise I made with him. You should be glad you're not waking up at three in the morning. Anyway, I should let you get some rest. Have a fun weekend." He got up to leave, but instead of teleporting out, he went through the door and ran straight into Mrs. Berseria, our PE teacher who happens to also be a former military commander for some war-heavy country. Apparently one of the girls heard me yell and she was coming to check on me.

The minute she saw Mr. Todo, she turned red with anger and asked what was going on. Mr. Todo, who was greatly flustered, tried to calm her down by saying he was listening to my thoughts and, since I was alone, thought he'd drop by but, not surprisingly, that made her angrier and she yanked him by the ear to her office. Come to think of it, I guess this means Mr. Todo's mind reading isn't on all the time.

I was sleeping in, since for once I didn't need to wake up early, but was forced out of bed when Mrs. Berseria knocked on the door and asked if I was still in. Sleepy and sluggish, I opened the door, and she asked how I was doing and if I wanted to talk. I told her I was fine, and she looked at me up and down then told me to go take a shower and get ready for the day. I did as she said and since it was a weekend, I decided to wear one of the outfits Mom gave me. I put on a red skirt, one that had a typical Scottish pattern, a white shirt with three buttons on the top, and a light blue hoodie. When I got back to my room, Mrs. Berseria appeared, seemingly out of nowhere, so I invited her in. Once inside, she looked around my room.

"Aside from the clothes on the floor you keep your room very neat, especially the desk area," she said.

"Is that strange, Ma'am?" I asked.

"You'd be surprised what a pig stein the other rooms are. The only room cleaner than this is Keri's."

"Really? I figured with all that she does, she didn't really have time to clean."

"Yup, she's a special one that girl. But I have a question for you so I'm going to cut to the chase. I read your record, you got a lot going on and a lot has happened to you, so I wanted to know...do you have any formal combat training?"

"Eh?" I was expecting her to ask about Mr. Todo, but so this took me by surprise.

"I said, "Do you have any formal combat training?"

"I...um...no Ma'am. I've only gotten spell cast and incantation training at school and some magic detection from my great-grandfather."

"Hmph." She sighed. "Well, I have to go. Take care on your day off. I saw Keri, Gene, and your boyfriend over at the Student Meeting building." She walked to the door and as she put her hand on the handle said, "Oh and..." She swung the door open and revealed a horde of girls that looked ready to pull a giant prank only on me, "If I hear that any of you hurt Sara, you're going to be having a nice long talk with me, the headmaster, and your parents!" They quickly scattered and ran back to their rooms. "Be safe now Sugar Puff," she said before leaving. Sugar Puff? That's close to Cream Puff, but only Grandfather calls me that. Actually, why does everyone keep coming up with a nickname that has "Puff" in it?

Anyway, I made my way towards the Student Meeting building. Keri and the others weren't outside so I figured they must have gone to the council room. I knocked on the door and opened it when I heard Keri cheerfully say, "Come in!" Inside was a mess of papers and books that made me wish I was in the wrong room.

"Oh Sara, good morning!" Keri said cheerfully from the buried desk.

"Um...what happened here?"

"We're trying to clean out and organize old papers while Keri works on the new ones," Gene said from under a pile of papers.

"We?"

"Well Shoyu was here, but we sent him on a delivery."

"Oh." I had only looked at the mess and was already completely exhausted.

"I'm sorry Sara, we promised to show you around town, didn't we?" Keri said. "I can always finish this later, let's go while it's still daylight."

"No that's fine!" I quickly declined. "Even though it looks like a lot of work, I'll help out! So, what do you need me to do?"

"Really!?" Keri exclaimed.

"Then if you could help file the papers and books in alphabetical order that'd be great," Gene said.

"Alright!" I yelled, pumping myself up. I figured if I was going to do work then I might as well be chipper about it. Shoyu came back a few minutes later and with all four of us working, it only took until sunset to clean up the entire office. We all collapsed on the ground and sighed.

"Done. We're finally done!" Gene exclaimed.

"That took forever!" Shoyu sighed.

"Yeah," Keri said, "but you all stuck it out with me even though you didn't have to so, thanks. I'll buy us dinner. Sorry, we couldn't walk around town though."

"No problem. After all, we're friends." I said.

"And we can always try to go next weekend," Shoyu said.

"Yeah and if worst comes to worst, I could always ask my Mom to send me some stuff."

"Well well look at all of my precious students!" A voice rang as the door swung open.

"Hi, Headmaster. We finished organizing all the documents you needed." Keri smiled, handing him the one ton of papers.

"I can't help but feel that this was punishment for something," I said.

"Now whatever do you mean?" Mr. Todo smiled.

"It's your fault you got in trouble." I scoffed.

"What are they talking about?" Shoyu whispered.

"Beats me," Gene whispered back.

"Knowing the Headmaster, it probably has something to do with eavesdropping," Keri whispered. Mr. Todo cleared his throat, and they quickly gave him innocent smiles.

"Anyways," he said, "because of all your hard work, and not at all because I was scolded for making up said work, just this once I will allow you four to stay in town until all the stores close."

"Really!? Sara that means we can get you everything you need!" Keri cheered.

"It'll be fun! Thank you, Mr. Todo!" I smiled.

"Of course. Just remember that I know when the last store closes." The stores in town close around ten so that meant we'd have to be back at school at least half an hour after that so we grabbed our stuff and hurried out. We went to several stores, and I bought some school supplies I needed and a cute light blue messenger bag. We also got several accessories to wear with our uniforms. Despite the number of stores we went to, however, we finished our shopping an hour and a half early.

"Oh, we have so much time left before ten," Keri whined.

"If we go back now, Todo will have a field day complaining about giving us the extra time." Gene sighed.

"Hmm, I have an idea." I said, "Why don't we have dinner at that restaurant and then go to the bathhouse?"

"Hmm, good idea. After all that work and walking around, I'm sweaty and hungry." Shoyu said.

"Sounds great to me." Gene agreed.

"I'm in! So, it's settled, let's go!" Keri exclaimed. We had a great dinner at the restaurant and then soaked at the bathhouse.

"Aah, this feels great!" Keri sighed.

"Yeah, after a long day of running around, a nice hot bath really hits the spot." I stretched.

When it was time to get out, the bathhouse provided yukatas for us, and put our clothes in a bag to take home. The boys came out a few minutes later. Gene had gotten a nosebleed and passed out from the heat, but once he woke up, we got some fruit milk and headed back to the school.

"Aaah, the night air feels great on your skin after a bath!" I exclaimed. I stretched my arms and tail and let the air wrap around me.

"Hehe right?" Keri giggled as she mimicked me.

"...You guys, your yukatas are opening," Shoyu said shyly.

"Eh!? D-don't look!" I yelled as I frantically closed it.

"Y-yeah! That's totally rude!" Keri agreed.

"At least we told you," Gene mumbled.

"What was that?" I growled.

"Um...nothing." After that, Keri and I walked in front of them and made sure our yukatas were properly tied before we let them walk beside us.

When we woke up the next day, we felt exuberated about classes, but that quickly changed. We had a joint workout with the boy's dorm, but Mrs. Berseria seemed to want more effort from me, Keri, and the boys. The same was true with Mrs. Henendez, our school nurse and health teacher as well as our language teacher. By the time school was over, yesterday felt like a dream.

I sighed as we collapsed in the café chairs after school.

"Today was a nightmare." Gene sighed.

"Why did Mrs. Berseria want us to do everything so perfectly?" Keri whined.

"Same with Mrs. Henendez. She refused to let me mispronounce a word or make even one mistake on the patient dummy." Shoyu complained.

"Same. It's like they were trying to punish us for something." Gene said.

"But what? We didn't do anything wrong. The headmaster gave us permission to stay out longer." Keri whined. Just then I smelled something sweet and soon after Mr. Marque appeared.

"I am glad I found you all." he said, "Master asks that you come to the front gate. We will likely be gone for the night so please make sure you pack a small bag."

"What? Did we do something?" I asked.

"Not at all, not at all, in fact, I would say it's something extraordinarily good." After we packed, we went to the front gate and found Mr. Marque waiting by a carriage. He drove through town and to a dirt highway that ran alongside the train tracks, then, after three hours, turned off onto another dirt road covered on both sides by thick vegetation. After twenty minutes, the road changed to paved and we came up to a white mansion. Mr. Marque led us inside and took us to a lavishly decorated room then told us we could sit and wait on the couch while he went and made tea. Shoyu and Gene curled into balls and rested their heads on my and Keri's laps while Keri and I leaned against each other's shoulders, and we immediately went to sleep. We were awoken by the sound of a camera shutter and Mr. Marque setting down our tea.

"What's going on?" Shoyu said sluggishly. I sat up straight and Keri woke up before she fell. We all yawned and rubbed our eyes.

"Oh yay, I'm glad I got the picture before you all woke up." A voice chimed. I looked across the table and saw a woman with grayish-white hair.

"Am I seeing things? Maybe I should go back to sleep." I mumbled.

"Now now everyone. It's time to wake up." Mr. Marque said. He woke up Gene who slowly got up and asked, "What's going on?" as he rubbed his eyes. "Now that you are all awake, let me introduce the Lady of Kofu, Princess Moritier."

"Oh, good morning." I yawned.

"It's evening." She giggled.

"Sorry," Shoyu said.

"Not at all. You're all tired after such a long trip. Honestly, I was taking a nap upstairs before you came."

"By the way," I said pointing to the camera, "where did you get that, I haven't heard of cameras being created in this dimension yet, and what were you doing with it?"

"This?" she giggled. "Cameras are really expensive here. Only the press uses them, so I understand why you'd think they don't exist, and I was taking pictures of my precious students' sleep."

"Oh?" we said. "Wait what!"

"Y-you mean you took a picture of us sleeping!"

"Creepy, but ok," Gene said.

"W-why would you do such a thing?!" Keri asked.

"Delete them!" I yelled.

"Pretty please!" Keri pleaded.

"Hmmm...nope." Lady Moritier smiled.

"Hey, what's the problem? It's just a few photos?" Shoyu said.

"Yeah, aside from the lady being a creeper, there's no problem," Gene said.

"D-don't you remember how we slept?" Keri asked as her face turned red. Gene and Shota closed their eyes as they thought back.

"Delete them." They said simultaneously.

"Nah I'm good." Lady Moritier smiled.

"Then you shall forever be known to us as Creeper," Gene said.

"Awww! But worth it."

"This is too much stress after I just woke up." I sighed as I took a sip of tea.

"Then I am glad I made Chamomile to relax you all." Mr. Marque said. "By the way, you all did hear me when I said, "Princess", right?" We paused as we processed what he said.

"P-princess!" We all exclaimed as she giggled and calmly sipped her tea.

"W-we were just joking when we said we'd call you Creeper!" Gene stuttered.

"Y-yeah and you can keep the pictures! In fact, print them out!" Keri exclaimed.

"I prefer "Lady" if I must have a title and relax. I'd prefer we all stand on equal footing as teacher and student than royalty and peasant." Lady Moritier laughed.

"Teacher? Does that mean you'll be working at the school?" I asked.

"Yes, as training for her teaching program. In fact, you four are going to be Lady Moritier's first students." Mr. Marque said.

"I think I need more time to process this," Shoyu said.

"You and me both." I sighed. After having tea and cookies and a casual conversation while trying to suggest the photos get deleted, we asked about the reason we were brought here.

"Yes, of course, let's get to the main reason." Lady Moritier said. "But first, Mr. Marque would you mind starting dinner?"

"Not at all." He bowed before leaving.

"So, the reason I brought you here." She said as she took a sip of tea. "First, did you enjoy today?"

"Yes. It's been rather fun." We all nodded.

"Good." She smiled, "So about the class, I can't tell you anything about it, but I must warn you that the curriculum will be extremely different and more difficult than what you're used to at the academy, so it is your choice if you want to accept or decline my offer."

"Can we get a trial run maybe?" Gene asked.

"I'm afraid not."

"May we ask why we were chosen?" Keri asked.

"Certainly, you may ask anything." We patiently waited as she sipped her tea.

"Um, so I guess you're saying we can ask, but that won't mean we get an answer."

Lady Moritier chuckled, "Sorry, you're all so easy to tease. The reason you were chosen is because out of all the students, you all would

gain the most benefit from these new classes that Todo is trying out."
Everyone was silent as we glanced at each other.

"Well, I'm in," I said.

"It sounds interesting and fun, I'm in too." Keri smiled.

"It can't hurt," Shoyu said.

"Hopefully." Gene sighed.

"So... all four of you accept?" Lady Moritier asked.

"Of course!" we said.

"Oh, thank goodness." she sighed. After we accepted, she said the class started immediately once we got back to school so she'd tell us more about it then. At dinner, we were all surprised as she downed six bottles of wine. After that, we had a bath and got dressed for bed while Mr. Marque dragged Lady Moritier back to her room. The next morning, we had a wonderful breakfast despite the fact it was three in the morning. I honestly thought Mr. Todo was joking about that.

"Why?" Lady Moritier whined. "Why? Why? Why? What point does getting up so early in the morning serve?"

"We have to be back before school starts. We would have left last night, but you had too much to drink." Mr. Marque said. Once breakfast was done, we packed our things.

"Oh, I forgot," Lady Moritier said after we got in the carriage, "Here's the room number for the class."

"It's in the old wing of the school. I'll show you the way when we get there." Mr. Marque said. Now then, everyone's asleep so I decided to let you know how things are going while we ride back, but it's now time for me to join them in getting some rest.

When we got back, Lady Moritier disappeared with a "Toodles!", and we went to our rooms to drop our stuff off. Mr. Marque then showed us to the old building wing but was apparently told, by our dear headmaster, not to help us any further, so we walked through the halls of this seemingly abandoned part of the school until we came across the room and knocked on the door.

"Come in." Lady Mortimer called then firmly said, "Take a seat.", when we entered and since there was no one else in the class, we all sat in the first row. Gene sat next to the window, then it was me and Shoyu in the center, and Keri closest to the door. After we had gotten situated, she passed out some papers that we were to lay on our desks face down. "Now then, I know all of you, but let me formally introduce myself. So, the elephant in the room, I am Princess Kavlika Moritier of Kofu, but so that titles and formalities don't get in the way of our classes, you will address me as you would any other teacher. I am your new teacher, but also a new teacher. I have taught day classes at Kofu's Royal Academy, but only for a few hundred years, so I hope you understand if I make mistakes. Now then, turn over the paper I gave you." We turned over the paper and moaned at what we saw. "You have thirty minutes to complete this test. Please don't cheat and do your best."

"But Instructor Kavlika we just got here. Couldn't we take notes before testing?" Gene asked.

"Now now, it's only five questions, one for each subject." They were the five hardest questions of my life. Aside from the fact that they were probably meant for college students, we hadn't even learned about the things she was asking. The first one was an English question, the second was science. I skipped the third one for last because it was magic, the fourth was history, and the final was math. The English and history ones were actually easy for me because I love to read, especially about historical battles and commanders. The science one was easy for a similar reason, though it took me some time. The math and magic ones had me at a complete disadvantage. The math one asked me to find an answer from several different letters, I've done "X equals" before, but X was usually the only letter, and then it asked me to find the type of graph the numbers made and give the points of said graph. The magic one asked me to tell what happened when the spell *Kieroug* was used which...I didn't even know what that spell was. By the time the half-hour was up, I hadn't even been able to write something down for them. We woefully passed up our papers and waited for the crushing results.

"Instructor Kavlika," Gene said.

"Yes, Gene." She replied without looking up from grading.

"That math problem, was it some of that rocket science that humans use?" Instructor Kavlika stopped grading and stared at the ceiling then got up and began writing something on the board.

"W-what the heck?" We gasped.

"This, Gene, is the formula used in rocket science," Instructor Kavlika said, "and this is the answer. Working together, I want you to figure out how I got this answer."

"B-but Instructor!" Keri exclaimed.

"We don't understand this formula at all!" I finished.

"Just try your best. You have until I finish grading." She smiled. Even working together, none of us knew how to start it and just stared at the board. "And...done! Did you guys make any progress?"

"Of course not!" Shoyu exclaimed.

"Well that's too bad, but expected. I wrote the formula wrong." She laughed.

"Yeah. That's the reason we couldn't solve it." I sighed. She passed back our papers and we cringed to turn them over.

"Huh?" I said as I looked at the grade.

"An... A?" Shoyu said.

"But of course!" Instructor smiled. "I never said it was an important test."

"Cruel." Keri pouted.

"I think I need to lay down after that." Gene sighed.

"I'll join you." I concurred.

"Now don't be upset!" she laughed.

"Just cruel," Keri repeated. For the rest of the class, the Instructor taught us various things. She wasn't kidding when she said the curriculum would be harder, but because there were only four of us, she was able to help each of us individually. The most interesting thing about this class was that it acted like a tutoring session, helping us understand what we learned in other classes while also building on them to teach new things. The worst thing was that after class, we had to hurry back to the main building for our other classes, with Keri and mine being PE.

"First, Sara! Keri! You're both getting new gym clothes." Mrs. Berseria said as she handed them to us. "Girda found a fabric that's supposed to be more durable, so we need to stress test how much it can take and you two are the lucky winners for the girl's dorm. This fabric might even be used for new military uniforms if it's good, so make sure to go all out."

The new gym clothes looked much like our old ones, except Girda put a gold embroidery of the school's sigil on the top left and it felt heavier. After we changed, we began our strenuous workout. The class was broken up into groups, with Keri being the captain of one half and me being the captain of the other. Our goal was to stagger Mrs. Berseria at least once to pass and, though it was a competition, we could choose to have our platoons work together or individually. We tried our hardest, but by the end of class, we were exhausted and had failed. We took a shower, changed back to our regular uniforms, and dragged ourselves to Mrs. Henendez's class for health where she had us learn several different healing spells. By the end of the day, we were completely exhausted. You're lucky I decided to even write to you.

RECOLLECTION

A Royal Break

Sup, it's been, what, a month since I last wrote to you? Well, the new fabric uniforms were also given to two members of the boy's dorm, and Shoyu and Gene were the lucky ones, no surprise since the decision was made by Mr. Todo, and the months continued. Kavlika gradually quickened the pace of her teaching, but we always got help. Even though I know I agreed to this offer, I began to terribly regret it. Also, we haven't staggered Mrs. Berseria even once so I'm sure we're failing PE. Winter break was coming up, meaning it was time for students to go home and give their parents their report cards. Because of my failing grades, I'm sure Mom and Dad are going to be less than happy to see me, so I decided to send a letter telling them I was going to stay over the break to help a friend. I had convinced Shoyu to go home without me and put in the paperwork with Mr. Marque, who looked like he wanted to say something but didn't. After school, the day before break started, I was strolling around campus, taking in the quiet since most of the students had left already.

"Hello, Sara!" A cheerful voice chimed.

"Oh, hello Instructor," I said as Instructor Kavlika came up beside me. She was bundled up in a scarf and jacket and holding a coffee.

"Oooh, it's so cold out! How can you walk around like that?" I was wearing a blue dress, one of the outfits Mom packed, and a scarf I bought from one of the stores.

"Wolf's blood I guess."

"I'm so jealous!" she pouted. "Well even though I'm obviously the only one cold, why don't we go to the cafe where it's warm, and talk?" I agreed and we made our way to the cafe. "So, I saw that you put in to stay on-campus during the break, any reason why?"

"Not really, I just don't feel like going home. Plus, I thought I'd give my parents time to be happy I was gone."

"Are you sure it doesn't have anything to do with giving them your report card?"

"Why would I care about that?" I huffed.

"Good because report cards are mailed to parents," she said, taking a sip of coffee.

"What?!" I exclaimed. She gave me a disapproving look and, seeing the grave I dug for myself, I put my head on the table.

"Sara your grades aren't that bad."

"Says you," I said from the table. "I haven't gotten a C since kindergarten."

She was quiet, then I heard her place her empty cup down and sigh, "Since you're staying here anyway, why not come with me to my home?"

"Why? What good would going to your home do?"

"Just come. It'll be fun, promise." And so, by noon I was on a train with Instructor Kavlika to her house in Kiori, the capital of Kofu. It took one day since we went by magic train, which is like a bullet train, and an hour by carriage to get to her home, the royal manor, which was a little ways away from town, in the woods, so it was night by the time we arrived. Even with Kofu Forest's natural glow, the only thing visible were the lights from the manor and the ones atop the carriage. "Sara, I know you're tired, but could you bring the bags in for me?" she asked.

"Ok, but you still haven't told me why I'm here." She giggled and quickly went inside. The carriage driver had taken the bags off the top, so all I had to do was bring them into the manor which I learned was a complete chore. My bags were easy, of course, but the Instructor's own were heavy as lead. "What do you have in this bag?!" I heaved after I dragged the first one in.

"Oh, nothing much. Just books, papers, and maybe I cast a spell of heaviness on them."

"Why?!"

"Because." she giggled. "Now come on. I'll show you to your room and let you get some sleep." Ugh, my arms still hurt from carrying her bags.

The morning rays streamed into the room and rested on my eyes. As I searched for something familiar, I remembered that I had gone to the Instructor's home. The bed was so comfy that I must have fallen asleep immediately after placing my head on the pillow because you were still in my hand, pencil and all. It was so comfy, in fact, I decided to stay in it a bit longer.

I went to turn over and that's when I heard, "Haven't you slept enough?" I looked over and saw the Instructor standing in the doorway.

"No such thing," I mumbled.

"Just make sure to come down by noon or I'll punish you." After sleeping a while longer, I finally got up, took a shower, and then went downstairs to the sitting room. "Oh, Sara your tail is so pretty!" Instructor exclaimed as I was drying my ears.

"Thank you," I said sleepily.

"By the way, you forgot to get dressed. You might want to do that."

"Ok...wait." I looked down and realized that I had let my sleep impede my thought process and forgot to get dressed. It's pretty normal for wolves and other animal-centric species to do, and usually isn't a problem. It happened with a lot of the girls at the dorm too, so Mrs. Berseria always stood by the exit of the showers during busy hours to remind us. Since I was at someone else's house, though, I ran upstairs and quickly got dressed.

"So, can I put barrettes and tie flowers and ribbons in your fur?" Instructor asked.

"No."

"Aww, but why?" she whined.

"I get the feeling you have terrible taste."

"Aww mean! But I still want to put something in your fur so, ta-da!" She showed me a fancy silver hairpin with black jewels made to look like a family crest. "I got this from my mom and I'm sure she would love for it to be in such pretty hair."

"Really?" I asked as she used it to slip my hair back.

"Yup, and it looks perfect. Actually, I bet I can make it better by waiting here," she said before rushing upstairs. The look on her face looked very sad, but I didn't know why.

"Maybe I should take it off. It seems important to her." I mumbled to myself.

"Everything of Ce'Ra's is very important to us, but...it does look nice on you Miss Hollins." Someone said. Startled, I searched around the room but saw no one. "Right here," they said. I heard someone tap on the table, then saw Lord Moritier standing in front of me.

"Eh?! King Moritier! Um, I'm sorry I didn't notice you had come in." I frantically bowed.

"Raise your head. I was using magic to hide, so you weren't supposed to notice."

"Y-yes, Sir," I said, raising my head, but I couldn't bring myself to look him in the eyes considering last we spoke, he wasn't a fan of mine. Plus, he had just said he was purposely hiding from me.

We sat in awkward silence until he sighed and got up to leave, saying, "There's breakfast. So, why don't you go to the dining room before it gets cold."

"Yes, Sir," I said. It looked like he stared at me from the corner of his eye, but he didn't say anything. Just sighed before going through one of the doors. After a few minutes of recomposing myself, I got up to go to the dining room, which, in most Kofuian-style homes, also counted as the kitchen and foyer. To be honest, though, I've never been in a Kofuian-style home, so I didn't know where exactly that was, but using my knowledge of where I was, how the layouts usually work, and the smell of food, I finally found myself standing in the kitchen. When we came in last night, I was too tired to look around, but seeing it in the daylight, it really was modest for a royal manor. In front of the stove was a man with brownish-gold hair and in a similarly colored suit, wearing a pink apron over top of it, and cooking breakfast. I was hesitating on whether to say hello or not when he looked up.

"Oh hello. You must be Sara." he smiled.

"Oh! Um, yes. Hello." I said shyly.

"No need to be nervous, though I know it can't be helped. My name's Yama'Ori Fidelie-Moritier. I'm almost done with breakfast so you can sit down and get comfortable while you wait."

"Thank you." I bowed as I took a seat.

"No need to bow." he laughed. His last name was Moritier, but since Kofu only has one heir, I guessed he must be Instructor's husband, which makes him Lord Fidelie's son. He's really nice and friendly and good at cooking, which Shoyu is not. I was thinking about how it would have been nice if I had brought Shoyu to learn something when a plate was placed in front of me. "Here you go, one serving of breakfast!"

"Ah, thank you." He smiled and went out to the stairs.

"Kavlika! Mr. Moritier! Breakfast is ready!" I heard him call. "Sara," He said coming back to the dining room, "my dads are going to be joining us as well. I hope you don't mind."

"Of course not, I'm only a guest."

"Still," he sighed as he began making the other plates. "I know they can be...intimidating."

"Good morning my delectable husband!" Instructor chimed as she burst in and gave him a peck. "And good morning again to my delicious student!" She wrapped her arms around me and nuzzled her face in my neck.

"Hey stop, that tickles!" I giggled.

"Mmm Sara, your skin smells so nice! I bet you have the best blood inside you, maybe even better than Yama'Ori's cooking."

"Hey, I take offense to that!" Yama'Ori said. "But if you like it so much, maybe I'll just have to take a sample or two to mix with the food."

"Hey, no way!" I laughed as they both began tickling me. They were mercilessly teasing me so much that I didn't even notice when King Moritier came and opened the front door.

"Good morning, Aster." King Moritier said as he sat down.

"Good morning, Nexus. What took you all so long to answer the door?" Lord Fidelie said.

"Sorry Dad, didn't hear you knock." Yama'Ori laughed.

"We were too busy teasing Sara!" Instructor giggled. Lord Fidelie stared in my direction without changing expression.

"G-good morning, Sir!" I quickly bowed as I tried to recompose myself. He continued to stare then turned to King Moritier.

"I need to talk to you." he said then turned to Yama'Ori, "We'll have breakfast later, so save some for us." After they left, there was an awkward silence.

"Maybe it'd be better if I stayed at the academy," I mumbled.

"Nuh huh." Instructor said.

"Don't worry Sara. Something probably happened at the Affairs Building and they need to discuss it. It's not anything you did." Yama'Ori smiled as he sat down.

"Knowing those two, it's probably not even that." The instructor said, her mouth now full of food. "They probably have to go to some noble's house for a breakfast meeting, where it is socially unacceptable to eat the food before you."

"Really?" I asked, picking at my food.

"Yeah. It happens all the time. Keeping up appearances and everything is important. So, do you feel a little better?" Yama'Ori smiled.

"A little," I said.

"Good, now eat or I'll eat it for you!" The instructor said, her plate empty.

"No, this is my food!" I protested, fighting away her fork. I quickly learned that food was a precious commodity with her around and that I could never leave it unguarded, but thanks to my wolf half, and to Yama'Ori's joy and dismay, I was able to eat more than enough to show her who's boss. After breakfast, I lay on my bed and stared at the ceiling. "I should really go downstairs," I mumbled as I forced myself to get off the comfy bed and explore the house a bit. I looked for Instructor Kavlika or Yama'Ori but couldn't find them and got lost. I finally found my way to the kitchen and saw a note on the table that read, "Sara, we're going to town to get a few things. If you need anything ask one of our dads. They should be in either the office or the big dining room, both are on the first floor."

Well, there was no way that was going to happen. I couldn't even bring myself to be in the same room as them, much less interrupt whatever important conversation they were having to ask for a tour of the house. With no options left to me, and not wanting to go someplace I shouldn't, I decided to take a walk outside. The town was far enough away that I could transform and still not have to worry about being spotted. In my wolf form, I walked around for a little bit, found a nice sunny spot, and laid down, however, having too much energy to take a nap, I decided to run through the surrounding forest instead. Unfortunately, I got lost and was scratched mercilessly by branches and thorns. I couldn't even use my sense of smell because everything smelled the same. I finally made it out of the forest, after hours of walking, only to find that I was in a random open field. Exhausted from my long trek and the various cuts and bruises swelling up on my body, I collapsed on the ground and curled up. The twilight looked very pretty with the stars sparkling in the orange and purple sky. I closed my eyes and began drifting to sleep when I felt a hand petting my snout. I opened my eyes a little, but they were blurry, so I tried smelling them. The person smelled familiar, but the exhaustion and smell of the forest surrounding us made it difficult for me to tell who.

"Sara, do you think you could transform to a suitable size?" they asked.

"Transform? Well, I can try, but I doubt it'll make me feel better." I thought. Still, I figured it couldn't hurt and transformed back into my human form. I felt a shooting pain as I was picked up. Whining, I tried to wriggle out, but the pain only increased so I stopped.

"Let's go back home." they sighed. "I already called the doctor." I think I fell asleep after that or passed out. Either way, I woke up to whispering, their voices going in and out.

"Sweetie don't be mad at them. They couldn't have known."

"Couldn't have known!? They were following her!"

"We didn't think she would appreciate us walking with her."

"Appreciate! I bet she would have appreciated not being lost and running through thorns too!"

"That's...true."

"Sweetie please, you're being loud. You'll wake her."

"That's tru-Hey! Where do you think you're going? I'm not done lecturing you!"

"She's awake. I'm going to get the doctor."

"What? Oh Sara, thank goodness." They said as I felt someone hug me, causing my body to hurt.

"Mmm," I whined as I tried to pull away.

"Oh sorry."

"Sara, can you open your eyes?" I believe Yama'Ori asked.

"Don't want to...body hurts," I mumbled.

"I know, but please. So, we can make sure you're really ok."

"Not ok...body hurts."

"Leave her be." a new voice said. "Her body's trying to counter the poison."

"Yes, doctor." I believe Lord Fidelie said.

"Sara if you need anything, I'll be right here so don't hesitate to ask, ok?" I believe the Instructor said.

"Mmhm," I said, drifting back to sleep. I woke up again and opened my eyes a little. I was in my room and outside I could see it was dark, but there were little peeks of sunlight coming over the horizon. My body still hurt, and I couldn't move very much. "Instructor," I mumbled as I slowly tried to get up, "can I have my medicine and some sugar?"

"Where's your medicine?" the person asked.

"In my bag." I flopped back down as my vision went black.

"You aren't in good enough shape to give this to yourself," they said. After a few seconds of listening to them fumble with the needles, I felt a prick in my arm.

"You were supposed to sterilize the spot first," I mumbled.

"Oh...sorry."

"I didn't tell you so it's fine." Once they were done, I heard them leave and a few minutes later, come back with several other footsteps.

"Miss Hollins how are you?" the one called doctor asked.

"Still in pain and can't move."

"Understandable," he replied. "Miss Hollins the plants you were stuck with were Nexior plants. Nexiors are vine-like carnivorous plants with beautiful flowers of various colors on them. They have developed a poison that coats its thorns which is helpful for medical purposes, but lethal when taken in pure form due to the swelling it causes. It is honestly a miracle that you're alive after taking such large amounts of it. That said, the antidote doesn't seem to be working on you, and keeping the poison in your body too long can cause permanent damage. Do you have any medical deficiencies I should know about?"

"My body uses up sugar very quickly."

"Oh? That's probably the reason. Which medicine do you take to combat this?"

"Mom and Dad pick it up for me, so I don't know, but I was just given it a few minutes ago."

"I see. Any others?"

"No."

"Very well. Well, unfortunately, as it stands the poison has been in your body too long and must be manually removed. It may hurt, but I ask you to bear with it. Once that's done, I can give you the antidote to get rid of whatever remnants remain."

"Can we skip that and go to the antidote part?" I moaned.

"No, though I am glad to hear you're well enough to make comments like that." After eating some sugar, to help boost my levels further, the doctor started taking out the poison. Like he said, it hurt like crazy and I'm pretty sure I passed out several times. When I woke up again the pain was finally gone, and I was being gently swayed. Everything was hazy and there was a cool wet rag covering my eyes. The rest of my body was extremely hot and itchy, and I felt like I might vomit if I moved.

"Oh Sara, you're awake thank goodness!" Instructor said.

"Instructor Kavlika?" I mumbled, feeling shooting pain even from that.

"Shh, don't try to talk." She said, putting a finger on my lips. She took the rag off my eyes and replaced it with a new one. "I'm sure you're not feeling very well." I felt a pinch on my arm and suddenly felt very sleepy. "Just rest for now. Everything will be better soon." I woke up again in complete darkness.

"You're awake again? Do you feel any better?" I heard a deep voice ask. I opened my eyes a little to try and see, but my eyes were covered by a cold rag. "You still need this...probably."

"King Moritier?" I asked.

"...Yes."

"Um, thank you for taking care of me, but I think I should be fine now, and I don't want to take up your time so-" He sighed loudly like he was irritated. "Um, King Moritier?"

"It's nothing. What were you saying?" Just then I heard the door open, and the bedside lamp was turned on. "Doctor, how are you?"

"Better than you, your Highness." the doctor replied. "You're fifteen minutes late for your medicine. I know you want to make sure she's ok, and I can assure you that you and Lord Fidelie took out all the poison in her system, but if you don't take your medicine on time then the Nexior poison will rot your fangs."

"Yes, doctor." King Moritier sighed. He and the doctor left the room and then came back a few minutes later. The cold rag was removed from my eyes, and I tried to block the lamp light.

"Ah right, sorry." the doctor said as the lamp light went out. "You're going to be ok Miss Hollins. The poison was completely removed. Right now, you're feeling the side effects of light sensitivity, nausea, vomiting, body aches, and pains. I ask that you take one of these pills every four hours until you run out and to call for me if you feel your symptoms are too much."

"Um, ok," I said. He smiled and patted my head.

"I know, a lot of information. Just remember to take your pills. I'll be in to check on you whenever it's time." After that, he left, and it was just me and King Moritier in awkward silence.

"Um, thank you for taking the poison out," I said to try and break the silence.

"Mmhm," he replied.

"Um, and for taking care of me."

"Yeah."

"Oh, and can you tell Lord Fidelie I said thank you as well? Or maybe I'll tell him myself later." He sighed. "Um, I'm sorry if I'm bothering you, your Highness."

"We didn't help you to be thanked." he sighed. "It was our fault for allowing you to get into this predicament. We were simply being responsible adults."

"Um, but even so I should still thank you." He sighed again then turned to the window and we returned to awkward silence.

"Do you want anything?" he suddenly asked.

"Oh um, well I'm a little hungry and maybe thirsty." He got up and left and when the door opened again, it was Yama'Ori.

"Hey Sara, I brought you some food." he smiled.

"Lord Yama'Ori, thank you, but what happened to King Moritier?" I asked as I sat up.

"Don't call me "Lord" I hate that," he said as he sat down and placed the tray on my lap. "And Mr. Moritier...isn't feeling well. The doctor has put him on bed rest."

"What? But he was just in here."

"I know, but Nexior poison can be very complex and take a heavy toll on a person in a short amount of time, so don't blame yourself, ok."

"Right." I sighed.

"Really. He'd be upset if he found out you were pouting."

"Ok." I sighed again.

"Come on Sara don't be so down. Let's eat then you can rest some more. After that, I'll take you to his room so you can see he's totally fine."

"Thanks." I giggled as he bopped my nose. After eating, I read a book for a little bit, since getting out of bed was difficult. The pills the doctor gave were bitter and I hated taking them, but they did make me feel better. Yama'Ori and Instructor would come in to entertain me and occasionally King Moritier and Lord Fidelie as well, though usually in very short bursts. After a week we got better and everything was back to normal, but now I wasn't afraid of King Moritier and Lord Fidelie.

My days did not get any easier after I got better. Instructor Kavlika used the time to teach me all sorts of things. Most were academic and difficult for me to understand, but with her working one-on-one with me, I finally figured them out. Others were more life lessons, like how to not teach cooking in a way that annoys Yama'Ori. Also, he taught me a lot about cooking. The last, and honestly most confusing, was the stuff I couldn't figure out a use for, like how to sneak into and pick the lock for, the wine cellar, undetected. Why would I ever need to know that? The hardest of the lessons were the combat ones she had me do whenever I failed or got something incorrect. I thought Mrs. Berseria's class was difficult, but the Instructor's is so much worse. She would have me practice spells and incantations then have me use them in battle. She would also have me fight hand-to-hand, which I am not the best at, resulting in many failures. Worst of all, she had me fighting the King and Lord, both of whom had trained battle experience. By the end of the first day of this grueling winter school, I was exhausted and didn't even want to take a shower before going to bed.

Unfortunately, I was refused the pleasure anyway, but it wasn't so bad I guess since it was dinner. Yama'Ori made soup, but I was too tired and beaten to pick up the spoon, so I sat with my head on the table, patiently watching the wisps of steam.

"Sara if you don't eat it now, it'll get cold," Yama'Ori said.

"I'm waiting for it to get below 98 degrees."

"How come?" The instructor asked as she put a spoonful in her mouth. She quickly took it out and fanned her tongue.

"That's why. I don't want to burn my teeth so I'm waiting."

"If it's too hot I'll blow on it for you." Yama'Ori chuckled.

"No. I'm waiting for all of my soup to cool down, not just a spoonful."

"Aww, but why?" Instructor asked.

"My arms hurt too much to want to pick up a spoon." I moaned.

"Aww, but why?" I glared at her and she gave me an innocent smile. After a few more minutes, I used my tongue to check the soup. It seemed to have cooled down enough, so I began to drink it. "Sara, I know our teeth are for blood and other liquids, but...don't you think you could try to pick up the spoon?"

"Hm? What was that, Mrs. Torturer?" I growled as I glared at her, receiving a chuckle in response.

"Now now, don't name call." Yama'Ori laughed. I went back to drinking my soup and finished it in a minute or so. Then I used my tongue to get out the vegetables and meat.

"Sara." Instructor sighed.

"I wouldn't have to do this if you hadn't beaten me to death, Mrs. Torturer," I mumbled.

"Sara, I said no name-calling." Yama'Ori scolded. I puffed out my cheeks and continued eating until I had licked the bowl clean.

"May I have seconds?"

"Will you eat it like a lady?"

"I'll eat it like a Wolf-Vampire lady."

"Then no." Lord Fidelie said, taking my bowl. I puffed my cheeks again and laid my face on the table.

"Sara if you're not careful, you'll get splinters." Instructor said.

"I can't get splinters from a tablecloth," I mumbled.

"...Fine just pick up your face." she sighed as Lord Fidelie placed the bowl back in front of me, full of more soup.

"Yay," I said as I began eating the soup as I did before. The rest of the night we had a wonderful time talking about Instructor's and Yama'Ori's school days, at their expense of course.

The rest of the break was fun. Instructor Kavlika worked me half to death with her chores, worksheets, and punishment programs and I barely squeezed out of the mock battles, but with each one, I was able to learn and better my skills. I always had fun being with everyone and the Instructor would let me borrow something to wear from her mother every day. Since this was the King's house, though, tons of politicians came to have meetings and discussions. In my third week, the council that has been in charge of advising the Moritier family since the beginning of King Nexus Moritier the Third's reign ten thousand or so years ago came over. Yama'Ori was at work, so I was told to stay in my room as much as possible so as not to disturb them. The reason for which, I understood when I left to get something to drink and snack on.

I figured since they were important figures, they'd be using the main stairs and since the main kitchen was in front of the main door, I went to the secondary one. What I forgot to count on is that they might use the back hallway to get to the office. There is nothing more stressful than meeting the nine members of the council, especially since I was stuffing my face while walking with arms full of food and drink. I had read about them and seen their pictures in my textbooks, but up close they were so intimidating that I could barely keep from crumbling to the ground when they spoke to me.

"My what do we have here? An adorable little wolf girl." Councilman of Accounting, Rafeas smiled.

"G-good morning, Sir!" I exclaimed, quickly swallowing my food, and nearly choking while bowing and dropping everything I had. "Ah, I'm terribly sorry, I'll move this out of your way!"

"Now now," he said bending down to help me pick everything up, "No need to be so nervous. I won't bite, unless, of course, you want me to, right Dex?"

Councilman of Law, Dexrious began helping in the pickup and said, "Does your womanizing know no bounds? Thirty children with only two in college, a stunning wife who puts up with your wandering, and who knows how many mistresses, and you still hit on this girl? She doesn't even look like a high schooler."

"Tisk tisk." Councilman Rafeas waggled his finger. "I have fifty mistresses remember, and I'm not womanizing. Simply showing my love and affection for women."

"The women can do without it." Councilman of the Census, Herius said.

"I'm sure they'd love to be without it." Councilman of New Technology and Transportation, Beas laughed.

"Enough of your prattling. We have a meeting." Councilman of Taxes, Dreis said. He went inside the office and Councilmans Kear, Vince, and Nu, in charge of Weapons, Culture, and Press, respectively, followed, only giving me a passing glance.

"Don't mind them." Councilman Rafeas smiled, placing my last dropped item on top of the pile in my arms before a giant monster moved him out of the way and stood in front of me. It was Councilman of War, General Bradely and even though I've seen him in pictures, they did not capture just how huge he was. Standing at ten feet tall, the top of his head nearly touched the ceiling and it felt like I was in the sights of a giant monster bear, ready to swallow me whole.

"So, this is what you were talking about," he grunted.

"Ah, n-nice to meet you, Sir." I quickly bowed, making sure to not drop my stuff again.

"Girl! Raise your head," he said in a gruff, booming voice.

"Y-yes, Sir."

"What was that!" he bellowed.

"Yes, Sir!" He towered over me, and I felt ready to bolt at the first chance I could. He got on one knee and bent down, taking my pea-sized head in his humongous hand, and turning it every which way.

"Oye Moritier, is this brat a half-breed?"

"Yes, she is half-Brexiorian." King Moritier said. He looked ready to intervene at a moment's notice.

"And? where'd you get her?"

"She's from Adestria Vigdrore and one of my students, so please stop referring to her as an item." Instructor Kavlika said.

"Hmph, a nice school...even if it's full of foreigners and half breeds," he grunted, continuing to look me over and grabbing my arm to look at my hand, causing me to re-drop most of my stuff, when something caught his eye. "Oye Moritier, isn't this Ce'Ra's dress? Why is a half-breed wearing our late queen's clothes?"

"Ce'Ra's clothes look nice on her, so I gave her them to wear." King Moritier said.

"Heh, I guess it can't hurt to make 'em think they're pretty." He pulled me up into the air to check the dress more thoroughly and it felt like my arm would be ripped off.

"General I would appreciate it if you didn't harm my students." Instructor said. She was smiling, but it was easy to tell that she was ready to break his arm.

"Ah sorry sorry, forgot I was dealing with your pet," he said as he dropped me on the floor.

"Bradley there's no reason to be so rude." Councilman Rafeas said as he walked around him. "She is a lady, first and foremost, and of high societal breed. If you treat her wrongfully, you may soon regret it." He then kneeled down and took my hand. "I'm sorry for my friend's rudeness, Lady Hollins. Please accept my deepest apologies on his behalf." He kissed the back of my hand and then helped me up.

"N-no it's-" I abruptly stopped as he gave me a quick glare. "I mean...apology accepted."

"Wonderful." he smiled. "Well then, I do want this meeting over in time for my children's birthday party...whichever of them is getting older, so let's go, General." General Bradely scoffed and they all made their way into the meeting room. Lord Fidelie helped me pick up all my stuff again then walked me back to my room, I think to make sure I didn't get into any more trouble. I was working on an essay the Instructor asked me to look over it when I heard a bell from the maid belt, a strip on the wall that had several small pipes to talk through. Usually, one of the staff answers it, but due to the meeting, only one was scheduled for today and she called out due to illness. I went to the check and saw that it was coming from the large meeting room and, hoping it was a mistake, I answered.

"Sara hooray you answered!" The instructor's cheerful voice chimed through.

"Yes," I said suspiciously.

"I was wondering if you could bring thirteen cups of tea and a bunch of cookies."

"Sure." I sighed. If you're thinking, "Why would Sara not question thirteen cups of tea?", it's because I know Instructor has the stomach to drink all eleven by herself and still have room to steal the other two, and I was hoping that since it had been several hours, the meeting was over. Since she'd be coming out of a stressful meeting, I figured Chamomile would be the best choice for relaxation. After pouring the tea and setting up the cookies, I went to the meeting room and knocked on the door. "Here's the tea and cookies you wanted." I said after hearing, "Come in." I froze seeing the sight before me.

"That was very kind of you, Miss Sara." Councilman Rafeas smiled as all Council Members' eyes turned to me.

"Sara you can place the tray down in the center of the table and, I hate to ask, but could you pass out the tea?" Instructor smiled.

"Vile women, you tricked me!" I wanted to say as I placed the tray down and did as she asked.

"Oh, German Chamomile, as the humans call it! You certainly know exactly what tea to bring to a stressed mind." Lord Rafeas said.

"Thank you," I said.

"Humph, the kind that makes you relax?" General Bradely grunted as he took a sip.

"Yes."

"Has a strong taste."

"Forgive me, I left the leaves in for an extra minute." He glared at me. "Is something else the matter?"

"Admit it!" he yelled. "You gave us this tea so we'd let our guard down, didn't you? And that, "leaving the leaves in an extra minute", that's so we wouldn't taste whatever poison you put in isn't it!"

"General Bradely, please calm yourself." King Moritier sighed. "Miss Hollins is not a spy. She's the daughter of our country's head medical facilities creator, heir to many companies that help shape and fund this country, and the great-granddaughter to the founders of the country's best wine company, Hedieli."

"Tch. So that old man really did go and fall for a wolf's manipulation. He was such a great general too." General Bradely scoffed.

"Now now, let's not ruin the mood set by Sara, I hope you don't mind me going on a first-name basis. wonderful tea with bickering." Councilman Rafeas said.

"Shut up you half-wit!" General Bradely yelled.

"My, it seems we're still upset about my proposal to cut some funding for the military." Councilman Rafeas said as he sipped his tea. General Bradely slammed his hands on the table and bolted up.

"A womanizing pencil pusher like you wouldn't understand! Those wolves, hell any country on this continent, can attack us at any time and you, you dimwits, want to cut funding for the military!"

"General, please calm down." Councilman Drexious sighed.

"Calm down? Calm down! They have spies all over the country waiting to ambush us, and you tell me to calm down!" He glared over at me as I set the last cup down next to Instructor and I really wish I had just thrown it and ran. "You! Why are you still here!"

"Ah! Well um-!" I hesitated.

"She's a spy!" he bellowed. "You all want to cut off military funding, how do I know you're not being controlled by this she-devil?

How do any of us know we're not being controlled? Instead of cutting funding we should be bolstering our military and taking these devils to war before they can attack us!" I was quickly making my way to the door and had almost made it out when the General caught sight and grabbed me back by the neck. "And where do you think you're going, spy!?"

"General put her down!" King Moritier snarled.

"I'll make her talk one way or another! I bet you were off to go tell your little pack about our meeting, weren't you?" His grip around my neck was growing tighter and more painful. I was doing pretty well hiding my tail and ears so far, but I couldn't continue to hide them in these conditions. I flailed, kicked, and dug my claws into the General's hand, but nothing affected him.

"I'm not a spy, I'm a student!" I yelled.

"Tch, a student? I'm sure that's your cover, but what's your real aim? Our national budget? Foreign relations? I bet you little devils are working up a plan to take us down as we speak through your telepathy, aren't you!" He roared.

"General put her down now!" King Moritier warned. Lord Fidelie was already in stance to attack, as was Instructor.

"I'm trying to help you! This demon has invaded your home and polluted your minds." The General yelled. "If you won't release them from your tricks on your own, then I'll help convince you." He began tightening his grip faster and air became scarce. No matter how much I fought I couldn't break free, and I began to panic as death by this lunatic's hand seemed more inevitable.

"Please...let me...go." I pleaded between breaths.

"Tch, so you decided to beg for mercy? That won't work!" I couldn't tell what was going on as my vision got blurrier, but it sounded like yelling and fighting. I guess he put up a shield, but I can't be sure. As panic and a lunatic, gripped me, my mind let go of reason and my instincts took over. Everything blurred after that. There were several screams and gasps and it sounded like there was an explosion. I had transformed and was running, but I didn't know where to. I finally settled underneath something. It was dark, but I felt safe there. From my hiding place, I could see the manor and all its annexes, completely destroyed on one side, but the people running in and out were too far. A carriage pulled up and someone quickly rushed in to help carry a man to it. He was screaming things like, "That bitch!" and "I'll kill her!", so it must have been General Bradely. With the wind blowing towards me, I could smell the blood, even from this distance. Several other carriages came and went, but nobody else was put in one.

After everything looked settled down, and waiting for what felt like a century, I finally began to feel myself relax...then I heard footsteps. I had hoped they were aimless, but they walked right to my hiding spot and stopped. I was ready to attack, but then they started moving again and finally faded away. Relaxing again, I fell asleep and when I woke up it was evening. I stretched and finally looked around my hiding place. I had been hiding under a tree, a really big tree with a rather small entrance, so I wondered how I had gotten in since I was as big as a one-story house in this particular wolf form. The tree was on a mountain, overlooking the Moritier house, which was now repaired, and part of the town. I heard footsteps approaching again and tried to figure out what to do when they stopped, a little further away this time, and placed something on the ground before walking away again. They didn't go very far, but they were far enough that if I left, I could quickly run back in, so I tried to smell what they had placed on the ground.

As a breeze blew towards me, I could smell vegetables and rice covered in spices in it. I was suspicious but also hungry. I decided to inch out and smell for threats, keeping an eye on the direction I last heard the footsteps. The plate was small compared to me, if I wasn't careful, I'd swallow the whole thing, so I transformed to the size of a normal wolf, by human standards, and smelled the plate again. I looked around for more threats then began eating, licking the plate clean after just a few seconds, before running back under the tree. The footsteps came back and picked up the plate, leaving and coming back to place a full plate down again. We did this several times until I was full. The sun had set, and the moon was sparkling on the cold plate of food outside. The footsteps came, picked up the plate, then came back and squatted in front of the tree. The instructor's face suddenly peeked into the hole.

"Sara, sweetie, come here," she said. I whimpered and backed away. I felt safe here and didn't want to come out. Seeing that I wouldn't move she began squeezing her way in. I growled and she said, "Relax Sara, it's only me. Since you're too afraid to come out, I'm going to come in." After getting through the hole, she crawled over to me and began stroking my head. "See nothing to be afraid of." Her voice was soothing, and her hand was gentle and slow. Eventually, she coaxed me out from under the tree, both of us covered in dirt and moss. Back outside, I saw King Moritier and Lord Fidelie waiting.

King Moritier sighed after seeing I was alright then bowed saying, "Sara, I am truly sorry for the General's actions and for my inaction."

"We all are." Lord Fidelie bowed as well.

"It's...alright. It's not your fault." I said, transforming back to human form. "And I'm sorry for attacking General Bradely. Um...what is my punishment?"

"I would never punish any citizen for protecting themselves." King Moritier said.

"No one's going to hold you accountable for what happened Sara, so don't worry." The instructor said as she knelt down and patted my head. Some dirt fell from her hair and caused me to sneeze. The flurry of dirt that flew off me caused her to sneeze and a chain reaction of sneezes ensued among the four of us.

"Maybe we should go back so you two can get in the bath." King Moritier coughed. As we walked down the mountain, they picked up containers of rice and soup, and the plate of cold food, along the way back to the house. Yama'Ori was in the kitchen washing dishes when we walked in and smiled at us.

"Sara are you feeling better?" he asked.

"Yes," I said.

"I'm glad. Oh, did you enjoy the curry? I know you like a lot of spices, so I let myself be a little heavy-handed."

"Ah really? Thank you, it was wonderful."

"Good. I drew baths for you all, so you can go ahead and go upstairs. Once you're done you can come down and have some dessert. It's chocolate cake with a vanilla ice cream center."

"Thanks, sweetie." The instructor said as she led me upstairs. I told her that I could take a bath by myself, but she refused and scrubbed me from top to bottom. Maybe I didn't do a very good job at hiding it or she just knew, but I was glad that she stayed, it made me feel more comfortable. Once she was done with me, I helped make sure she was clean then we went downstairs and had some of the cake Yama'Ori made. It was delicious and melted onto my tongue and eventually, King Moritier and Lord Fidelie joined us before Lord Fidelie returned home. Full of ice cream and cake, we sat in the sitting room and Instructor petted my head while I rested it on her lap, and I fell asleep. I woke up the next morning in my bed with the Instructor sleeping beside me. "Good morning, Sara." she yawned.

"Good morning." There was a knock on the door before Yama'Ori came in.

"Oh, good you're both up," he said.

"You didn't even wait for an answer." Instructor yawned.

"No, well, I was expecting you two to still be asleep. Anyways, breakfast is almost ready so brush your teeth and get dressed."

"Yes, Sir." we yawned. After getting up, we went downstairs and had pancakes and French toast.

"How did you know this was my favorite?" I asked as I sat down and devoured the plate before me.

"A little birdie told us two weeks ago when we were in town." Instructor giggled.

"Little birdie?"

"A little birdie who's a little upset that you didn't come home for break."

"And who's going to be really upset if they read today's newspaper." Yama'Ori sighed.

"Wait, you met my parents!?" I exclaimed.

"Well, it didn't seem right to keep you at my house without their permission and we needed to do some shopping for your giant appetite." Instructor giggled.

"Why didn't you tell me, I would have stopped you!"

"I know, that's why."

"Um, but why would they be upset if they read the paper?"

"Oh, well..."

"Just tell her. She'll find out eventually." Yama'Ori said. I waited patiently for the Instructor to tell me when King Moritier and Lord Fidelie came in.

"What are we talking about?" King Moritier asked as he sat down next to Instructor.

"Good morning. Lord Fidelie, how come you don't just stay over if you're going to be here first thing in the morning?" I asked.

"And we're telling Sara what's in the paper," Yama'Ori added.

"I leave because I like the comfort of my own bed and why not just let her read it." Lord Fidelie replied.

"Fine, after breakfast." Instructor sighed. Once done, King Moritier brought me the paper and I understood why Mom and Dad would be upset.

On the front page were giant bold letters that read, "General and Councilman of War to the Royal Family Gravely Injured During Monthly Meeting!" The article under it read, "During the monthly Council Meeting, held at the Moritier Royal Manor, General Bradely was gravely injured. While others present declined to speak, the King and Princess kindly gave us their accounts, stating that the Princess had brought a charge, a middle school student from Adestria Vigdore, to spend winter break with her. During the meeting, she asked the charge to bring tea as the maid-on-duty had called out sick. Upset that the military budget was getting cut, the King stated that the General lashed out at the youth, grabbing them by the throat and choking them. In a panic, the youth defended themselves, resulting in the General's severe injuries. The General has lost his right arm and left eye and scars have been left across his face and body. Doctors say that the bite marks on his shoulder and claw marks on his face and chest will never heal and even though the claws narrowly missed his right eye, they still damaged it enough that he is partially blind and can no longer work as an acting General. Whether he remains a Councilman is up to the royal family."

"Well," I said after reading it, "at least we know my parents haven't read it yet."

"How are you so certain?" Yama'Ori asked.

"Because they would already be here at your throats if they had." I did feel bad that I had hurt the General so severely, but I also didn't. I was terrified and had no idea what to do.

"Well now you know and now we move on." The instructor said, snatching the paper out of my hands.

"Not so fast." A familiar, albeit angry, voice said. We all looked around but saw no one in sight. "In here," it said from the sitting room. When we went in, we found Mr. Todo.

"Todo, do you make a habit of teleporting into people's homes without invitation or warning?" King Moritier asked.

"Yes, yes he does," I said.

"Enough about how I got here and let's focus on why." Mr. Todo said with a serious tone.

"Instructor Kavlika, when you asked me if you could take a student into your charge for the break, you promised that you would keep said student safe and in good health."

"Y-yes." Instructor sighed.

"And yet, I have learned today that you indeed did not keep your promise and were even the reason for the student's involvement in danger. Do you know what that means?"

"Yes."

"Then, I will allow you until the end of the break to clean off your desk at the school."

"Wait!" I exclaimed. "Couldn't you allow her another chance?"

"I cannot overlook this blatant misconduct because of your personal feelings." Mr. Todo sighed.

"Then don't! Look at me!"

"Sara's right," Yama'Ori said. "You said Kavlika promised to keep Sara safe and in good health. She is definitely in good health and while she was endangered, it was something that Kavlika couldn't have possibly known or controlled."

"I disagree." Mr. Todo countered. "Councilman Bradely's stance on foreign entities and persons, especially Brexiorians, is common knowledge, as is his temper. Instructor Kavlika should have known full well that there was a possibility of him getting out of hand and took no precautions to counter it."

"W-well..." Yama'Ori sighed.

"Then there is no reason for her termination." King Moritier said. "Kavlika would not have asked Sara to bring the tea if I had not suggested it and because this is my house, it is my responsibility to make sure that all guests are safe. I knew that Kavlika was bringing a student over to spend the break here and took no precautions to ensure her safety and well-being in my house." Mr. Todo stared at him, an emotionless and stern stare, and King Moritier returned it.

After several seconds Mr. Todo finally sighed, "Very well. It is true that Instructor Kavlika cannot account for the actions or inactions that you control. I will leave her with a warning." Instructor, Yama'Ori, and I cheered and hugged each other.

"Thank you, Mr. Todo!" I said.

"Yeah yeah, just don't go thinking you're off the hook." He said to the Instructor.

"Of course! I will do my utmost from now on to ensure my student's safety," she replied.

"Good. Hm?" Mr. Todo suddenly trailed off and then said, "I'll be right back.", before disappearing. After a few minutes, he came back with my parents.

"Sara!" Mom yelled as she pounced on me, knocking me to the floor. "Oh, thank goodness you're ok."

"Why do you always seem to find the worst trouble?" Dad sighed as he joined in our hug.

"I don't know, it just seems to find me," I said, nuzzling my face into their necks. We sat on the floor hugging each other for some time.

"Aw, that's just adorable." Yama'Ori smiled. My parents' happiness towards me, quickly turned to anger towards him and

Instructor, who I think I heard yelling, "Yama'Ori you idiot!" They jumped up and were ready to pounce on them when they got stopped by a barrier.

"Now now, you promised not to rip people to shreds if I brought you here." Mr. Todo said. They continued to growl but backed down.

"Sara, why don't you take your parents to your room and talk? I'm sure it's been some months since they've seen you." King Moritier sighed.

"R-right," I said, taking both of them by the hand and going upstairs.

"Hmph, lucky bastards," Dad mumbled when we got to my room.

"Dad don't be so mean. It wasn't their fault." I said.

"Yeah yeah." Mom sighed. "Anyways, why didn't you come home for break?" Their anger was now focused on me.

"Oh, um. L-like I said, I was helping a friend." I stuttered.

"Liar," Dad said. "Tell us the truth."

"Um, well..." I stammered. After a long silence, both of them sighed.

"Did we really shelter you that much?" Mom sighed.

"What? You didn't shelter me."

"So, we let you have too much freedom?" Dad sighed.

"What? What are you talking about? No."

"Then why don't you want to come back to us?" Mom cried, rushing into Dad's arms.

"Wha- I love you guys!"

"Then why Sara, why? What did we do to make you want to stay away?" Dad sobbed, hiding his face.

"I-I-I didn't want to not come home, I just thought you wouldn't want me!"

"...What?" they said in unison.

"I wasn't doing well. I got several Cs." I started to cry. "So, I thought you'd be mad."

"S-sara. We would never be mad just because you got low grades." Mom said, quickly hugging me and Dad joined soon after.

"We miss you at home. We wouldn't let some stupid grades keep us from being happy that you're back." Dad said.

"Really?" I asked, wiping away my tears.

"Truly." Mom said.

"Ok. I lov-wait weren't you guys crying?"

"Oh, um..." Dad said. "We...might have been faking."

"...What?"

"Anyways, we love each other, that's all that matters!" Mom smiled. They wrapped me in a giant hug and squeezed me anytime I tried to protest their truthfulness. After talking for several hours, Mr. Todo came up and told us that he was leaving soon. "Well it looks like we'll have to go, but you better come home for summer break. We'll even have a special surprise."

"Special surprise? I don't need one of those." I giggled.

"Well whether you need it or not, you're getting it." Dad laughed.

"Fine. Can I at least get a hint of what to expect?" They both looked at each other and chuckled.

"Well," Mom said pulling my head on her lap. "how's this hint?"

"Mm, food?"

"Nope."

"A new house?"

"Nope."

"Moving?"

"Nah-un."

"Um, a new...toilet?"

"Are you even trying anymore?" she laughed.

"Well, I give, just tell me," I said, jumping up.

"Nope, if you want to know you'll have to come home for summer break." Dad laughed. I puffed out my cheeks in protest, but they only rubbed my head and then left with Mr. Todo. After that, the rest of the day went by as it usually did.

The next day, around noon, while I was in the main study reading spells from different countries and practicing them with King Moritier, Lord Fidelie came in and after having a silent conversation they both left, telling me to continue without him. A few minutes later I heard a commotion from downstairs and curiosity got the best of me. As I snuck my way down the stairs, guess those sneaking into the cellar lessons were useful, I could start to differentiate the voices and hear the conversation.

"General you should be in the hospital." King Moritier said.

"I've had enough of listening to doctors say this was the best they could do. If I can't be helped anymore then I'm moving on. Now where is the girl?" General Bradely said. I should have gone back to the study immediately after that, but I let my curiosity continue to outweigh my judgment even when I heard several unfamiliar voices. They were reporters, some wanting to see the General get revenge, others just asking questions and wanting to see how the story played out. Even now my instincts and common sense told me to go back upstairs, but I didn't. King Moritier managed to kick out all the reporters after some time and began just talking to the General.

"General, how many times must I tell you that she is no longer here?" he said.

"Don't give me that crap Moritier." the General said. "Your daughter's still here which means so is she." They argued back and forth and, my curiosity finally satisfied, I began to go upstairs. Unfortunately, I slipped and fell with a big thud. As I tried to get my bearings and make sure nothing was broken, the door to the kitchen swung open. "You!" General Bradely roared.

"Crap!" I thought as I threw caution to the wind and jumped up to run upstairs. Unfortunately, again, I had twisted my ankle and while my magic was healing it, it wasn't healing fast enough. The General caught me, grabbing my tail and dangling me in the air. "Let me go!" I yelled, kicking him. I was immediately dropped and heard a cry of pain followed by, "You bitch!" The stairs were no longer an option, so instead I ran to King Moritier who had been knocked out of the way by the General. He glared at me with a look that said, "You should have stayed in the study", then turned to the General. Lord Fidelie stood between us and the General, ready to strike.

"General stand down." King Moritier said.

"Why defend her! She's a spy!" the General yelled as he clutched his chest with his left, well, only arm. He turned to face us, and I wanted to hurl. His face, no, his head, had five large scars, but they looked more like open wounds, still red and swollen. One of the scars ran through his left eye, which was now just an empty socket, another ran through the center of his face, cutting through his nose, and a third clipped the edge of his right eye, exposing the veins behind it. "Do you see what she did to me!? Everything, my entire life, she destroyed in a few seconds! Do you think she can't do the same to you, to this country!?" He looked at me and I hid behind King Moritier more. "At the very least...at the very least...Fix what you did to me!"

"I-I'm sorry Sir," I said hesitantly. "I don't have any medical experience besides the basics. You'd have a better chance with an actual doctor."

"Bullshit! You did something! Something that prevented me from healing! Something that prevents the doctors from healing me! What did you do!? What did you do to me!?" He looked ready to charge us and King Moritier and Lord Fidelie braced for the attack.

"I see. So that's the issue." A familiar voice said from behind us. I turned to see who it was and could barely exclaim my confusion when I saw Grandmother walking in. "I'm fairly certain I know what has happened to you, though I will need further inspection to be sure."

"What? Who are you and how do you know about this?" General Bradely snarled.

"My aren't you ill-informed," she said as she patted me on the head. Feeling her warm hand caused the fear, anxiety, and pain I felt to vanish. "I am Seras Hollins, wife of Former General Vair Hollins and the first wolf to hold the Kofu National Heroes Award for my unbiased medical treatment that saved many during the 3000 Years War."

"You, you're that wolf that Vair married? What are you doing here?" the General asked.

"Like our grandchildren, we read what happened in the paper and were concerned, however, unlike our grandchildren, we waited until there would be the least number of eyes to come visit. It would have been fine, except you showed up with the entire press behind you."

"Hmph, so coming to check if your packmate was able to get any information in the scuffle." he scoffed.

"No. A packmate is someone who you aren't related to, but spend a lot of time with, a friend if you will. I'm coming to check on my family, my offspring since you like using Brexior terminology."

"I don't care! You're here to spy, I know you are!"

"Madame Hollins," King Moritier interjected, "can you take Sara somewhere safe?"

"Oh, there's no need to worry. Here is currently the safest place for her and besides, I came to check on the General as well."

"What do you mean?" the General asked.

"I read what happened in the newspaper and, after hearing what you said, am truly disappointed in Kofu's medical staff." Grandmother sighed. "This problem could have easily been fixed sooner if they had contacted a doctor who knows Brexior magic, but now even if I break the spell and begin healing it will still leave a major scar."

"I knew it! She did this to me on purpose!" the General bellowed.

"Yes, but also no. I'm afraid my great-grandchild doesn't have the knowledge to knowingly use Brexior magic and judging from how powerful it is, it was probably cast in self-defense."

"Like I care!" the General roared.

"Well you should, because it means that the doctors who worked on you purposely let your condition worsen." she scolded, immediately shutting him up. "Or maybe they didn't because most of the doctors that could have fixed this are half-Brexiorian, but they should have at least given you the option. Now then, your Highness, may I use your sofa? I think it would be best for the General to lay down while I perform the procedure."

"Very well." King Moritier said after a pause.

"Now hold on! I don't want a spy anywhere near me unless they're tied up for interrogation. Just because you got a national award doesn't mean you're any less a spy." the General said.

"Oh, I'm sorry." Grandmother smiled. "Did my phrasing make it sound like you had a choice? Get on the sofa, now!" She walked across the room and stood head-to-head with him. Well kind of, she's about six feet shorter than him so she was really looking up at him.

"I'd do as she says, old friend." Another familiar voice said. I guess she did say "we", but I still wasn't expecting Grandfather to be here as well. "Sorry, it took so long. The Princess was having trouble getting rid of the press, so I helped out some. Still, I'd suggest you go help her, your Highness. One already snuck in and was hiding in the kitchen trying to take pictures. I can handle Oloid." King Moritier nodded, and he and Lord Fidelie left to help Instructor.

"I'm not your friend Vair, not anymore." the General said.

"And why is that?" Grandfather asked as he picked me up and patted my head. "Because I married for love instead of for country?"

"Exactly! You gave up your soul to this she-devil spy from our enemy! You're a disgrace to your country!"

"No, you're blind and trying to continue a war that's already over, dragging the citizens of this country into the fire with you! But we're not at war anymore Oloid, you have to let it go!"

"Lies!" the General roared.

"Enough!" Grandmother snarled. "Vair I will not have you upsetting my patient or our grandchild, go upstairs! And you lay on that sofa now!"

"I don't take orders from you!" the General roared as he raised his hand to hit her. I thought Grandfather was going to have to drop me to intervene, but instead, I watched Grandmother flip the General through the air and slam him into the ground then pick him up and plop him onto the sofa.

"Let's go Cream Puff. This probably won't be pretty to watch." Grandfather sighed as he began walking upstairs. He asked me what I was doing before the General showed up and then we went to the study, and he helped me with my spell casting. King Moritier and Instructor came up after some time and began helping as well, and Lord Fidelie went home after making sure there were no more press members snooping around.

After a few hours, Grandfather went to check on Grandmother then came back and told us that she was finished. I was told to wait in the study, and it was emphasized that I stay. After another half hour, the

Instructor came and told me I could go to my room and, when I went in, I found Grandfather sitting on my bed.

"Hope you don't mind us staying in here for a little bit," he said.

"I don't mind." I smiled as I nuzzled him. Just then Grandmother came out of the bathroom, rubbing her hair with a towel.

"I hope you don't mind that I used your soap and stuff."

"No, but you're dripping water all over the floor! Back to the bathroom, I'll get the blow dryer." After blow-drying her hair and tail, we sat on the bed together. Since her clothes were being washed, I let her borrow my dress. "So, you were given the National Heroes Award? How come this is the first time I've heard about it?"

"Well, you weren't born yet, and neither were your parents when I received it and besides, I didn't think it was important."

"But it sounds so cool! You too Grandfather, you never said you were a General."

"Cool, huh? Well, I guess that's one way to look at it." Grandfather sighed. I got the feeling that I had something wrong and grew quiet. "Oh, don't be sad Cream Puff. Ignore me, I was just recalling bad memories," he said, patting my head.

"Let's change the subject. Sara, give me your hand." Grandmother said. I did as she asked, and she closed her eyes. Light poured forth as she touched my palm then faded. "Done."

"What was that?" I asked.

"I just wanted to test your magic capabilities. You're very strong, I guess that's why you were able to cast such a strong Brexior spell despite not knowing it."

"Um, about that, I know that I don't know any spells from Brexior, so how could I perform one?"

"Well because you do know them, you just don't know you know them. You've been watching me, and your parents perform Brexior magic since you were little, we just never taught you the basics to actually perform it at will."

"Oh, is there a way to learn?"

"But of course, Cream Puff!" Grandfather exclaimed. "Just like all magic, you have to feel it out, understand its rhythm, then you can use it."

"Can you teach me?" I asked as my tail moved quickly between the two.

"I can try, but it's not really something you can teach in a few hours." Grandmother giggled. "But I'm guessing you're going to want to take a nap first."

"Why?" I asked before getting hit with a wave of exhaustion.

"You've been practicing a lot of magic and dealt with a lot of stress, and the effects of the spell I used on you earlier are probably setting in," she said as she tucked me under the covers and then climbed under with me. "So, let's take a nap. It'll be nice." I soon fell fast asleep and didn't wake up until evening when the Instructor came in.

"Great you're up! Yama'Ori just got home so he's taking dinner requests, though it might be a moot point." She said.

"I don't have anything I want in particular. Where are my grandparents?" I yawned as I realized they were gone.

"They're downstairs. Your grandmother insists on making something nutritional for us so that's why Yama'Ori might not be able to cook tonight."

"Yeah, she can be pretty pushy when she wants to be." I laughed. "I'm taking a shower, let me know when dinner is ready." After my shower, I went downstairs, and we talked until dinner. I was curious where the General had gone but figured it was best not to ask. After, we went to bed, but I woke up in the middle of the night to find myself squished in a hug between my great-grandparents which would have been fine, except I had to go to the bathroom.

I wiggled and squirmed to try and get out without waking them up but failed. Just when I was going to give up, they revealed that they had been awake the whole time and were just teasing me and the next morning, they had breakfast with us before heading back home.

RECOLLECTION

Vacation

The rest of the week went by smoothly. I studied and got better at combat, which the Instructor intensified. The morning of our departure, we had breakfast while King Moritier and Lord Fidelie loaded everything onto the carriage.

"Well thank you for allowing me to stay here for so long." I bowed.

"It was a pleasure having you, Sara." Yama'Ori smiled. "Oh, and before you go, we have some farewell gifts. Mine is an encyclopedia spell book. It has every spell, forbidden and unforbidden, from all over the world and it updates itself with every new spell made."

"Here." King Moritier said. He handed me a bracelet that had clear pearl stones with pink, cherry blossom-like flower gems at the center, all on a gold string, and then put it on my right wrist before I could protest. "It helps with magic stabilization and allows its wearer to cast both attack and defense spells without using their own magic."

Lord Fidelie said nothing, just smiled as he handed me a box. I opened it and found a glass orb...well, it was a crystal ball with a cat, or maybe a foxlike creature, inside. It had a purplish-black coat, with golden-orange paws and goldish-blue eyes that stared at me before turning away again. The fur around its eyes was also golden-orange as were two rings near the end of its long slender tail.

"Thank you, but what is it?" I asked.

"It's a Keperari pup," he said.

"...And that is?"

"A foxlike cat creature that's rather shy, but loyal to the end once you befriend it. It's technically in a different dimension right now, but that crystal ball lets you two stay connected if you decide to take care of it."

"Oh! Uh-but, wait I can't accept a living creature!"

"You didn't feel you should accept everyone else's gifts but took them." Lord Fidelie used to be a politician, meaning he knew a lot about arguing and the law and would not be afraid to logic me into accepting this gift.

"A-alright, I get it. I accept your gift, thank you."

He smiled again and nodded, "Good. Besides, Kofu gave me that and said to help it, but I don't know how to take care of living things. Evident by the fact that Yama'Ori decided to teach himself cooking."

"Don't be so hard on yourself Dad...but yeah." Yama'Ori nodded.

"Ok," I said. "Wait you just admitted you gave this to me because you don't want it!" Still, it looked cute and I felt a connection with it.

Oh, by the way, Kofu is the name of the country, but also of the tree spirit who grew this entire forest for the country to be in. Her physical body is a giant tree at the center of the forest as well as the entire forest, but she has a spirit body that she uses to visit citizens as well. She's pretty mischievous, but she always protects us.

Putting on the necklace, the magic seal snapped into place. "We'll be wonderful friends." I smiled at the pup. It looked up at me and then closed its eyes again, but I think I heard a soft sigh of relief.

"Now that everything's settled, let's go." Instructor said. We left, barely making it to our train on time, and began our spring semester.

"Eh!? You stayed at the Instructor's house!?" Keri exclaimed as we caught up on what we did over the break. We had pushed the desks together and Keri, Gene, and Shota sat across from me and Instructor.

"Yeah." I nodded.

"And you got a bunch of extra training and studying while you were there!?" Gene asked.

"Yeah."

"And that General Bradely tried to hurt you," Shoyu growled.

"Umm...y-yeah. But my great-grandparents came to save me so I'm fine." Shoyu seemed displeased but accepted my answers.

"Aww so cute." Instructor swooned. "You're like the dependable, always saves the day, in the end, couples I read about in my novels. Speaking of which...has anyone noticed?"

"Noticed what?" Shoyu asked.

"Those two, they've started dating." she smiled, pointing her finger at Keri and Gene.

"What are you talking about?" Gene asked.

"Don't pretend. I can tell when an adorable couple has been made and you two are indeed adorable!"

"Tell me, on what grounds do you make this assumption?" Keri asked.

"Well, I know that you two live fairly close to each other and that you shared a booth on the train when you left and when you came back."

"Lots of friends do that. Why have separate booths when we could talk to each other?" Gene shrugged, waving his left hand.

"And that over these last few months leading up to break you two have gotten rather cozy."

"Friends spend time together all the time. What? Are Keri and I supposed to just stare off into space when Sara and Shoyu go have their "alone time"?" He snickered looking towards us.

"And I've noticed that even though you usually lean on both elbows you've decided to not only, lean solely on your left elbow, but also keep your right hand under the desk, suggesting you're holding hands with Keri who is closest on that side."

"Well...that's...I just feel more comfortable leaning on this elbow and not both and it's just a coincidence that it's my left."

"And that when I started listing all the evidence, Keri's face turned red, she's been looking down to hide it since, and just now when I pointed out your elbow, and as we speak, your face is turning a beautiful shade of red, and your guys' ears and tails are just so cute."

"I-is not!" Gene yelled as he shot up. His face was as bright as the Instructor said it was, if not brighter.

"Face it, dude, you're beat." Shoyu shrugged. With no way to hide their secret, Gene took Keri's hand, and they ran towards the exit.

"Hey, where are you two going?" Instructor asked.

"I'm taking her out to get some fresh air! It's stifling around you!" Gene barked.

"Don't make out in the hallway! Or rather, don't get caught! I'll have hell to pay if Todo finds out that I let my students wander the halls." The door closed behind them without a word. "Well, I feel great." she stretched.

"Instructor, while I do find it enjoyable that they've gotten together, I can't condone the way you went about exposing them," Shoyu said.

"I agree," I said. "They were keeping it a secret because they were waiting for the right time to tell us, and you made a complete mockery of them."

"Wait I'm the bad guy!" she exclaimed, to which we nodded. "...Fine. I'll apologize when they come back." she sighed. However, several minutes had gone by, and they still hadn't come back. "Those kids. Let's go search for them before all sympathy I had is gone." The instructor went to check the right hall and Shoyu and I went to the left. It was an old building with the only class in it being us and I have a wolf's nose, literally, so finding their hiding place should have been more than easy.

"Why Instructor trusts us, but not them I couldn't fathom a guess." Shoyu sighed.

"It's been three weeks since I've seen you, so I don't mind the alone time, maybe that's why. Besides, she knows Dad would kill you if you tried anything." I giggled.

"That's true...sadly." he chuckled. "Hey, I know you said you were fine, but are you really sure you didn't get hurt in your fight with the General? Or receive any permanent damage from that poison?"

"I told you I'm fine." I giggled. He wrapped his arm around my waist and pulled me close. In turn, I rested my head on his chest, and we walked down the silent halls. "Hey, we should start looking for those two," I said when we had done a full walk of the floor. "If we take much longer, the Instructor's going to be pretty hard on us during her lessons."

"Yeah, you're right. You have a room all to yourself, so I can just come over and hold you in my arms whenever I want."

"If you make it past Mrs. Berseria."

"Guess that's a no then."

We both chuckled then I put some space between us so we could search properly. I looked here and there but couldn't find a trace of them. On the other hand, Shoyu hadn't moved an inch and was only staring at me.

"Quit staring and help."

"Sorry, it's just...you look so cute scurrying around."

"D-don't just stand there watching me, help! The instructor will be mad if we don't hurry up." I blushed.

"Yeah," he said, finally moving from his spot.

"Good. Then why don't we check the stairwell? The instructor said she would check the most obvious places, but it couldn't hurt."

"No need," Shoyu said as he gently took my hand.

"What do you mean?"

"I'll be honest. When you asked me to search for them, I did. Mrs. Henendez taught me this spell soldiers use to locate people when they're out in battle and I wanted to use it."

"And?"

"I don't think we want to find them." He chuckled, and his face turned a slight red.

"...Oh."

"Yeah, but um...if I used the spell correctly, and I think I did, I think I know what they're doing and um, I don't want to do exactly what they're doing, but um...if we could...I was thinking maybe, um...do some of what they're doing?"

"Like?"

"Um, well, I was thinking, and you're totally free to say no, of course, but you knew that, but um...if we could do the...k-kissing part..."

"...Oh, um...yeah?"

"Um...yeah." We tentatively moved closer and looked each other in the eyes. "Um, should I...do something with my hands?"

"Um, I don't know. Should we...close our eyes?"

"I don't know." He said sheepishly. After awkwardly staring into each other's eyes for what felt like an eternity, he rubbed my cheek with the back of his hand, and I caressed his in mine. We slowly brought our faces together until our lips touched, a gentle brush at first then we pressed more heavily as we closed our eyes. I felt myself getting swept away as my ears and tail happily swished out. "I love how your ferocious wolf side comes out at the cutest moments." he chuckled when we finally pulled apart.

"W-who ever said wolves were ferocious?" I timidly asked.

"True, maybe I have an unexpectedly sweet one."

"W-we should be heading back to class. It's almost time to switch."

"Yes...let's." A familiar angry voice said. Everyone was back in class, we all wished we weren't, but we were, and there was nothing we could do except sit and listen to Mr. Todo's lecture.

"I was enjoying my first kiss too." I thought to myself.

"Sara." Mr. Todo growled.

"Ah! S-sorry." I whimpered.

"M-Mr. Todo I think you're being too hard on them. After all-!" The instructor tried to help.

"After all, it is your fault that they were left alone to roam the halls? Yes, I know that." he glared at her.

"Y-yes, Sir." The instructor slumped down.

"Even the Instructor is helpless against Mr. Todo when he's angry. We're all doomed." I thought.

"Anyone else care to speak?" he asked. I didn't look up, but I could feel his glare burning a hole in me. After several grueling hours of lecture, we were forced to endure his teachings, as he put himself in charge of the rest of our classes and had us do extra time to make up for the hours he spent lecturing. By the time our punishment was over, it was dark, and we all dragged ourselves back to our dorms and didn't even bother taking a shower. We had hoped that that was our only punishment and that we'd be free the next morning. Mr. Todo's a great teacher, but he moves faster than the Instructor and I didn't think there was anyone more aggressive than Mrs. Berseria.

Unfortunately, our hopes were in vain. When we stepped into the classroom, we found the Instructor silently crying to herself in the corner and Mr. Todo sitting at the teacher's desk. Beside it was a box labeled "Confiscated" and it was filled with different alcohols. The minute we were all seated he began class with a pop exam. As we all sat and diligently worked on the answers for the impossible questions he made, I glanced over to Instructor with the look of ever most self-pity, but she only shook her head, silently saying, "I'm in as deep as you", then I caught glimpse of glare from Mr. Todo and quickly went back to trying my hardest to scribble answers on the paper. After a few more minutes he called time, and we passed up our papers. After looking them over, he handed them back.

"A three out of a hundred." I silently groaned.

"You all seem less than pleased with your scores. Maybe now you'll pay attention so you can actually learn." Mr. Todo said sternly.

"Pay attention? We have been paying attention, your way of teaching is too hard and fast for us to learn anything!"

"Sara perhaps you would like to answer the question I put on the board." I had forgotten about his eavesdropping, but thanks to the encyclopedia Yama'Ori gave me, I think I found a spell that might be strong enough to block him from my mind. I'm just not strong enough to cast it yet.

"Yes, Sir." I sighed as I got up and looked to see what the problem was.

"Is there something wrong Sara?" he asked after several seconds of me standing there.

"You know there's a problem you eavesdropping lunatic! Are you even trying to teach us or are you just making things difficult as a way of punishment!" I shouted to myself. I knew he could hear me, but strangely, I didn't care.

"If you can't answer the question then please sit down. Would anyone else care to answer the question?" Without a second thought, I was back in my seat, and no one volunteered or even made eye contact. "Honestly." He mumbled and went to answer it for us. The rest of our week went on like this in every subject. In P.E. we were too afraid to attack him because we knew no matter what we did, the results would end in a world of hurt. Each class I felt I was getting further and further from understanding until I felt exactly the way I did, if not worse, before we went on break. I walked into class one morning and saw the Instructor sitting in her usual corner, quietly sobbing her eyes out. By this point she had become a part of the room rather than a teacher, however, today was different. I had a nightmare, though I can't remember what it was about, and woke up half an hour late. I took a shower and got dressed, but by the time I realized I was late, I was forty-five minutes late, and an hour late to class by the time I ran there. "Why Sara how nice of you to join us." Mr. Todo smiled. Well, his mouth smiled, but his eyes burned with rage.

"I'm sorry I'm late." I panted.

"Late? Oh no no, you're not late you 're-Oh my! It seems you are late...by an hour. I'd tell you to have a seat, but we were just about to head off to change into our gym clothes. After all, this is the second period."

"I know. I'm sorry I'm late, Sir." I said, placing my stuff on my desk and going to change with everyone else. In gym class, things grew worse. Mr. Todo was targeting me and everyone who tried to protect me wound up getting hit. Luckily, if you can call it that, no one was hurt thanks to a spell we use during training, just unable to move for a bit. When I did combat training at the Instructor's house, no matter who I was fighting when I went in for an attack, they would put up their arms, lean back, and twist just slightly. It was subtle so it took a while for me to notice they were doing that, but I think it helps cushion the blow and redirect the force of a punch. I also know, from trying it out during a fight with King Moritier, that it doesn't work on swords if you're barehanded, though that doesn't really matter right now. So, when I had no one else left to protect me I did just that. As usual, when fighting Mr. Todo, it hurt. If this was the pain I was going to feel by cushioning the blow, I would have preferred taking the full hit, but it did help me recover faster. Despite the clinging pain and numbness, I slowly began to hoist myself up but felt my body start to give in.

"Too slow." Mr. Todo said, coming in for another blow.

"Wait." I tried to say, but my voice refused to work. I heard a cry of confusion and a roar as I collapsed, and my vision went black. When I came to, my vision wasn't any better, but I could tell I was in the nurse's office and Mrs. Henendez was sitting across the room. I tried to speak, but my voice still refused to cooperate.

"I'll get her." I heard a voice say, then something jumped off my bed and started walking towards Mrs. Henendez who quickly came to my side.

"Sara you're awake, good. Drink this, not with your teeth though," she said putting something in my mouth. It smelled sweet and tasted like pure sugar.

"What is that?" I asked, my voice finally coming back.

"Vŭlgar. A nutritious liquid made with copious amounts of sugar. Perfect for someone who collapsed from low sugar levels." she said.

"So that's what happened?" I asked.

"Yes, and I'm quite upset. You know to come straight to me if you think you need to take your medicine before your usual time. Why did you let your levels get so low? On top of that, your body is so malnourished I'm surprised you've lasted this long."

"I'm sorry. I guess with classes getting harder, I omitted eating anything too time-consuming and forgot to watch my levels."

She scoffed and mumbled, "These students." then went back to her desk. "Are you cold? I can get you some more blankets."

"I guess I am a little cold."

"Then let me help you." the voice from before said. I felt something jump up on my bed and walked up to my pillow. "Will you feel warmer if I lay under your arm?" it asked as the Keperari pup came into view.

"I, um..."

"You don't have to talk if it's too difficult. I can use telepathy. It's probably quieter for the others as well." it said as the Keperari nestled itself under my blankets.

"You...are you the Keperari?" I asked, taking it up on its offer.

"Yes. You always tried to take good care of me, so I want to return the favor." After I had gotten back from the Instructor's house, I always made sure to talk to the Keperari and leave food and water out for it in case it wanted to come out.

"Wait what do you mean "tried"? And what others were you talking about?"

247

"By "tried" I mean you put forth maximum effort to make me feel comfortable, even though you only set out cat food for me. As for the others I mentioned, your vision is still weak due to your lack of sugar so you can't see them, but the ones you call friends and the ones you call boyfriend are also here for malnutrition purposes."

"I see. But isn't us talking, even with telepathy, still loud to them?"

"No. While I can read their thoughts, they can only hear ours if I allow them."

"So, it's like an adorable Mr. Todo."

"While that statement may be true, I'd prefer to not be compared to him. And one other thing, I'm not an it, but a he."

"Oh, sorry," I said. "By the way, what's your name?"

"I don't have one," he said. "But the poachers who caught me called me Shirantou 592."

"That's not a name, they were just labeling where they got you and how many times, they caught something there. Still, how about Shira? It may just be where you were found, but it's better than nothing."

"I... yeah. I like it," he said, rubbing his head against my chest. "Now get some rest, your body's not fully recovered. Once it is, I'll tell you about what happened."

"Rig-what do you mean?"

"Rest," he said, nuzzling into my body and going to sleep. With no options, I did the same. Mr. Marque woke me up around evening to give me more Vŭlgar then again at night to give me a proper dinner. My vision had gotten much better, and I was able to sit up. Finally, being able to see the room, I saw Shoyu, Keri, and Gene in the beds across and beside me. Mr. Marque went around the room, waking them up and setting down a tray.

"Sara, are you better?" Shoyu asked.

"Yeah, I'm feeling a lot better thanks to Mrs. Henendez's and Mr. Marque's care."

"I'm just glad you're all getting healthy again." Mr. Marque smiled.

"But from now on you're coming to see me three times a day so I can make sure you're all taking care of yourselves." Mrs. Henendez scolded as she walked in. "I'd have you visit more, but I have classes to attend to."

"Yes, Ma'am," we said. I noticed that Shira had gone back into the crystal ball and held it to my face.

"Would you like to eat dinner with us? It's not cat food this time."

"No, Marque has already fed me, so I am not in need of food," he said. After eating dinner, we discussed what had happened. Apparently, Mr. Todo was going to attack me but saw that I wasn't conscious. However, he couldn't stop his attack, which was when Shira jumped out and diverted it using a defense spell from the bracelet King Moritier gave me. After finding out we hadn't been eating from trying to keep up with his classes, Mr. Todo felt bad and ended our punishment early, so we'll go back to our normal classes tomorrow if Mrs. Henendez deems it all right. I also introduced everyone to Shira. They adored him though he seemed to hate the attention. Once everything was settled, and everyone was asleep, Shira went to my room and grabbed you so that I could do some writing before things got hectic again.

When I woke up, several hours later, everyone was gone. There was a change of clothes on the bed stand so I checked to make sure no one was coming, before quickly changing into them. I had just finished flattening out my shirt when Shoyu came in.

"Oh, Sara you scared me! How are you feeling?" he asked.

"I'm fine, thank you for worrying. Also, don't be such a scaredy cat, I'm the only other person in the room." He pouted and I couldn't help but giggle. "Actually first, can I have some coffee? From the machine is fine I just really want some."

"Mrs. Henendez has made me her helper since I used to be a doctor's assistant, so let me check your levels and then I'll tell you." He nipped my neck then wrote something in a little notebook I had never seen before and mumbled, "I guess that's normal enough. He didn't seem too concerned when he checked an hour ago." I wondered who "he" was but decided to get my other answers first.

"So?" I urged.

"Yes, you can have some coffee." I gleefully cheered and we went out to the hallway where Shoyu bought me a mocha from the machine and himself an orange soda. I immediately took several large gulps.

"That's the only one you're getting until he comes back so try not to down it," Shoyu said, casually sipping his soda as if to mock me. I told myself I would sip after my last big gulp but realized that that was the last of my coffee and looked over at Shoyu with pleading eyes. "So, you see, before you woke up, I had fallen asleep by your bedside," he said, completely ignoring me. "And don't be alarmed, but when I woke up those girls, Lust, were there. They didn't know I was with you so when they came in expecting to take, we'll underrate it and call them, embarrassing photos of you, they were pretty surprised. As usual, they tried hitting on me to get what they wanted, but I, as your diligent boyfriend, threw them out. Then after some time, I fell asleep again and before I knew it, I woke up to them all on top of me and trying to take photos. Luckily your granddad came in and saved us and Mr. Marquis took the girls away."

"I see. Thank you for being a great boyfriend." I said leaning on his arm.

"My pleasure. I just want to make sure you're safe."

"Now you said, my granddad. Which one are you talking about?"

"The ones you met this summer. Your great-grandparents are too far away to get here quickly, and your parents are even further away, as you might have expected, but your grandparents were staying close by, so they came to check on you."

"Oh? I didn't know my parents were informed, but I guess it makes sense since I did collapse. Are my grandparents still here?"

"Yeah, Mr. Todo's finding some lodgings for them right now. They said they'd come back once that was finished."

"That's good. I haven't seen them since the winery." I smiled then smoothly transitioned, "So, I was wondering, that notebook that you wrote in earlier, I've never seen it before."

"Ah, you mean this. It's my medical diary. Mrs. Henendez gave it to me and said I should use it to keep track of the medical problems patients that come my way have, how I treated them, and what the results were."

"Oh, that's a great idea."

"Yeah. There's hardly anything in it now, but I know I'll have it full one day."

"When you become a successful doctor's assistant?" I teased.

"I'll go beyond that." he laughed. We sat there for a while, enjoying the quiet.

"Hey Shoyu, you said you were my diligent boyfriend. Does your diligence also include making me happy?"

"I would say it's in the scope."

"Will you do anything to make me happy?"

"Depends, what do you want."

"Would you buy me another coffee?"

"Nope. Keeping you healthy is another part of my diligence," he said, kissing me on the nose and then laughing as I puffed my cheeks. After a while Shoyu and I heard footsteps, and my grandparents came in with Mr. Todo and Instructor.

"Sara, darling, are you sure you should be up?" Grandmom asked, coming over and checking me up and down.

"Yup, I'm totally fine now!" I said happily.

"Still, maybe a bit more rest would be better."

"Aww Grandmom you worry too much," I said as I hugged her.

"I think you're under-worrying." she sighed.

"Don't worry Ma'am. When I checked her levels a few minutes ago they were a little low, but I imagine they should have gone up by now." Shoyu said.

"Thank you for taking care of my dear granddaughter, Shota, and my look at how you've changed," she said while patting my head.

"No problem. I love taking care of Sara." Shoyu smiled. "Oh, but I should re-introduce myself. My name is Shoyu Hazimi-Martz. It's a pleasure to meet you."

"Oh, what a lovely new name you've taken. Well, it's a pleasure to meet you too. We've heard so much about you from her parents." Grandmom smiled, "Dear isn't he the sweetest." Granddad had been silently watching our exchange, or more accurately Shoyu, and continued his silence as he stared at him. "Dear," Grandmom said with a hint of a growl.

"Is something wrong Sir?" Shoyu asked.

Granddad looked Shoyu up and down then glared at him and said, "I don't like you."

"Decus!" Grandmom snarled.

"We agreed I would be honest with how I feel and, Sara, I don't like your boyfriend."

A confused, "Um...", was all I could manage to his declaration. I didn't get why he didn't like Shoyu, but when I think about it, he, like Dad and Grandfather, didn't like any boy being near me. Besides, I have no intention of breaking off my relationship just because Granddad's jealous.

"Don't "um" me, break up with him." Granddad scolded.

"Oh, don't listen to him. He's just upset that you came and hugged me first and still haven't gone to hug him." Grandmom said.

"Granddad, is that true?" I asked. He didn't answer and looked away.

"I was closer." He mumbled after a short while.

"I love you too Granddad." I giggled as I went over and gave him a big hug

"This doesn't mean I accept your boyfriend," he said as he hugged me back and glared at Shoyu who was beaming back at him.

"I know Granddad, but for now let's hug." I smiled as my tail slid out and waved from side to side.

"Fine," he said, pretending not to smile. I could hear Instructor and Grandmom whispering and giggling and soon Granddad picked me up and turned his back to them. I happily giggled and wagged my tail as I buried my face in his chest. "Silly pup," he said, putting me down and flicking me on the forehead.

"Ow! Meanie!" I pouted as I let go and covered the spot.

"Alright. Sorry," he said quickly and picked me up again.

"I bet you just want a big hug from me." I laughed as I saw his response.

"I'll drop you," he warned.

"Not if you don't want me to cry," I said holding tight to him. He was quiet and made no attempt to let me go, so I giggled and snuggled under his chin.

"Well, I'm going off to bed. See you tomorrow, Sara." Shoyu smiled as he left.

"Me too. I have to teach tomorrow. It was wonderful meeting you both." The instructor said as she caught up with Shoyu.

"Would you like me to show you back to the hotel or would you like to walk the town first?" Mr. Todo asked.

"We'll be fine on our own. Thank you very much for everything you did today." Grandmom bowed.

"Not at all." Mr. Todo smiled. "Take care. Oh and Sara, your parents want you to rest for a few more days so you'll be staying with your grandparents and if I catch you on school grounds...I'll expel you." he waved and smiled as he left.

"Hmph. Then I'll make sure you don't catch me." I puffed.

"Sara you shouldn't disobey orders." Grandmom scolded.

"Yes, Ma'am." I sighed.

"So back to the room. I'm tired." Granddad said. His feet were already on the move before he started his sentence.

"Wait! Can I have a can of coffee?" I asked cutely. They got here after I had finished the one Shoyu bought me, so I thought maybe they didn't know about it. Granddad kissed my forehead, and I thought I felt a prick. Then he pulled back and smiled at me.

"Anything for my little Cream Puff," he said.

"Hurray!" I thought as I gave him a big hug. "I've successfully gotten myself more coffee!" After my delicious coffee, we walked to the bathhouse that I, Shoyu, and Geri, the couple's name we made for Keri and Gene, had used that one time. Apparently, it had an inn attached to the bathhouse and that's where we would be staying. "Woah! The room's so big!" I exclaimed. It was as big as a living room and there was another room right next door. There was a huge outdoor bath in the back that overlooked the mountains and fields.

"Mr. Todo really outdid himself buying us this room." Grandmom giggled as I explored here and there, having a wonderful time.

"Alright alright, sit down," Granddad said as he sat on the tatami and grabbed me as I scuttled past.

"What are we going to do?" I asked excitedly.

"We are going to" There was a knock on the door and the proprietress came in.

"Sir, I have your dinner ready," she said.

"Eat dinner." Granddad finished as the food was brought in.

"Everything looks so good. I can't wait to eat it." I said as my mouth watered. There was an assortment of Vampire and Brexior foods as well as a few I hadn't seen before. I reached out my hand to take a lobster tail, but it was hit away by Granddad.

"No. You eat when I say so." He came over and kissed me on the cheek while rubbing my head. Just like the last time, I felt a pinch. Sitting back down, he picked up a lobster, soaked it in butter, sprinkled it with garlic, and held it out to me. I happily closed my eyes and opened my mouth, but after several seconds didn't taste a thing. I opened my eyes and saw that Granddad was just staring at me holding out the lobster. I leaned in to eat it, but he pulled it away. "No," he said and then ate it. I sat back and watched in disappointment.

"Dear don't tease her like you did the kids, let her eat," Grandmom said. She held out a dumpling to me, but Granddad ate it before I could even get near. "Decus!" she scolded.

"She doesn't eat until I say so," he said while chewing.

"Why!?" I protested.

"For thinking you tricked us into buying you a coffee. You didn't think we'd notice the coffee can in the trash or the coffee smell on your breath, so this is payback."

"In other words, he's just having his fun." Grandmom sighed.

"Fine. I'm sorry for trying to trick you, so can I please eat?" I asked.

"No," he said.

"Meanie!" I said, puffing out my cheeks.

"But I will let you sit with your eyes closed and mouth open. Then when I decide you should eat, I'll put a piece of food in." The idea sucked, but I did as he said. After several minutes something was put in my mouth. As I chewed it, I realized it was a dumpling and wagged my tail. "Good girl," he said. Dinner was long and tedious, but by the end, I had gotten a whole lobster to eat by myself, so I was pleased. After dinner, we went to the bath outside. The shadows that stood tall and seemed to pierce the sky were the mountains and they cast a darkness over the fields, but in spite of that, all was bright because of the full moon.

"This bath is so nice." I sighed as I sunk in.

"It is isn't it?" Grandmom smiled.

"And you can see the mountains and fields, they're so pretty."

"You just want to run to them, don't you?"

"I do! What about you Granddad? Don't you want to run in those fields for hours?"

"Mm," he grunted. I swam over and snuggled my head against his collarbone.

"Aww, don't be mad Granddad. You can have the lobster tomorrow." When I said, "I got a whole lobster", it was more of a Grandmom telling him to give me the lobster, so he wasn't too happy.

"Hmph!" he pouted.

"Promise!" I said as I hugged him.

"Alright fine I believe you, now get off," he said pushing me away.

"Waa! Meanie! I pouted. He scoffed and turned away.

"Decus dear, won't you apologize to our granddaughter?" Grandmom asked as she wrapped her arms around his back, and he tensed up.

"I'm...sorry Sara," he said.

"Yay! That's what a granddad should do." Grandmom said as she kissed his cheek. Granddad sunk into the tub, and I thought I heard him mumble, "Teasing hag." After the bath, we dressed in yukatas and shared a futon. "Would you like to watch some TV?"

"But I don't see a TV in here...and I don't think TVs exist here," I said.

"They don't, but we have a portable TV," Granddad said, waving his hand and making a TV appear.

"Woah! That's so cool!" I exclaimed.

"What do you want to watch?"

"Let's watch movies!" He flipped to the movies section, and we watched movies until I fell asleep. When I woke up Grandmom and Granddad were already gone and there was a knock at the door.

"Good morning esteemed guest." The proprietress bowed.

"Good morning," I said rubbing my eyes. "Do you know where my grandparents went?"

"Yes. They're downstairs. They asked me to show you to the bathroom to get washed up." After following her and getting ready, I went downstairs for breakfast. The minute I walked into the food hall I was wrapped in a giant hug.

"Good morning, Cream Puff! How are you? Do you feel ill? Do you want to rest?" A familiar voice asked frantically. My mouth was covered so my words were muffled. "What was that?" he asked.

"I said I would like to breathe Grandfather!" I managed to exclaim. He quickly let me go and began searching my body for any issues. "Stop it. Stop it!" I yelled as I heard giggles from the staff and other patrons.

"Vair knock it off." Grandmother said as she pulled him away. She looked at me and I could tell she wanted to check as well.

"Go ahead." I sighed and she immediately smelled and circled me like Granddad did when we first met.

"Ok. She's totally fine." she sighed, relieved.

"Now can I have breakfast?"

"No," Granddad said from the table, not even looking up from his plate.

"Then...then you can't eat either!"

"Oh? You think you can take my food?" he asked as he put a waffle in his mouth. We stared each other down and I made one attempt. He grabbed me and held me a hug hold.

"Ngh! Lemme go!"

"Nope."

"Alright, Decus let go." Grandmother said after listening to our banter for a short time. He sat me down in the seat next to him with a dissatisfied look.

"It was fun teasing her." He mumbled, eating another waffle. Then he looked at his plate full of food with a disgusted look, but then he got an idea. He put a piece of bacon on his fork and held it out to me.

"I'm not playing that game anymore! You barely fed me." I said. Saying nothing, he pushed the bacon on my lips. Hesitantly, I opened my mouth and ate it. He did this several times until I decided I could trust him and would happily eat.

"Decus if you were full, why'd you get more?" Grandmom sighed.

"The same reason you got a new plate and haven't even touched it yet," he mumbled.

"Hmm?" she glared at him and he quickly fed me another piece of bacon. After his plate was cleared, I licked off the syrup, so it was sparkling clean then Grandmom offered me her plate. Grandmother and Grandfather smiled as they watched us and went to get plates of their own.

"We probably shouldn't have fed her so much," Grandmom said as I was lying in our room with a stomachache.

"It hurts!" I whined.

"It's not completely our fault. If she didn't keep eating, she wouldn't have a stomachache." Granddad mumbled.

"Hurts!" I whimpered.

"I'll go downstairs and see if they have any medicine." Grandfather said. Just as he was about to open the door, it was slammed open.

"My baby!" Mom yelled as she burst in and wrapped me in a choke hug. "I'm so sorry for leaving you! Please tell me you're alright."

"It hurts."

"What? Your head? Your legs? Your arms?"

"No, my spine! You're breaking me in two!"

"Oh, sorry," she said putting me down. My stomach still hurt and being moved around just made it worse, so I whined as she put me down. At that moment a terrible feeling washed over me. It was like being swallowed in endless anger. I looked towards the door and saw Dad slowly walking in. He looked pissed.

"Good morning, Sara. We visited Todo and he told us what happened. Looks like because of your malnutrition, the stress of his teaching style was too much. That's why-" he growled.

"You're mad at me?" I whimpered.

"I'm going to kill him."

".... I.... what....?"

"I'm going to kill the horrible man who did this to you," he said sitting beside my bed. I was completely dumbfounded and lost for words. Mom was behind him shaking her head to silently say, "Don't worry. I'll stop him". He continued, "Now are you hurt anywhere? You whimpered not too long ago."

"She has a stomachache," Granddad said.

"What? Just another tummy ache? And here I was worried sick about you." He picked me up and wrapped me in his arms, hugging me close. Immediately my stomach stopped hurting and I felt better.

"Thanks, Daddy. I'm better now." I said, but he didn't let me go. "Dad?"

"Just a little longer," he whispered. I smiled and snuggled my head into the side of his neck. His arms wrapped tighter as if I would vanish into the air after those words. Finally, after a heartfelt and warm eternity, he let me go.

"Dad, you were joking about killing Mr. Todo, right?" He said nothing. "Dad?"

"No comment."

"Don't worry Sara, Mommy's going to make sure you can always visit Daddy without a prison guard." Mom smiled. Dad scoffed and she added, "Even if it means I have to kill him myself."

"But then I won't have either of my parents," I said. Dad threatens a lot, like a lot a lot, but he'd never actually kill anyone.

"Sara, I think it's time you know," Granddad said. "Our son, your father, used to get into fights."

"Wait really?"

267

"Yes, we've had to bail him out of jail too many times to count." Grandfather sighed. "At one time I thought all the fortune I made during my life would be depleted by a single grandchild."

"But everything got better once he met your mother." Grandmom giggled.

"Oh, remember when she stopped him from picking a fight with those nobles?" Grandmother laughed.

"Though he ended up fighting them all anyway when they insulted me for it." Mom sighed. "But I still love this knucklehead and I won't ever stop." We all laughed except for Dad who had slowly begun to turn red and was trying to hide it.

"So, trouble finding us runs in the family, huh?" I giggled.

"Sara!" Dad said in a booming voice, "The only thing you need to know is that I will protect and love you forever!" Then, realizing he was yelling, he took a deep breath and patted me on the head. "I don't know what I would ever do if I lost you, so just try to stay safe." I smiled and nodded, giving him a big hug to help reassure him. That afternoon we played cards, shogi, and other fun games while watching TV and I introduced them to Shira, who they immediately loved. Dad or someone would check my sugar levels periodically and eventually, we took a nap. It wasn't until around dinner that I woke up or really, was awakened. Before

I had fallen asleep, I was trapped in my parent's hug, which wasn't so bad since I loved when we slept together like that but was alone when I woke up.

"Sara. Sara wake up." I heard a voice.

"Mm," I grumbled.

"Sara dinners here. Don't you want to eat?"

"A million more minutes," I grumbled as I turned on my stomach and pulled the covers over my head, only letting my face out to breathe.

"What a handful." Someone said.

"Aww, but it's quite adorable. We haven't gotten to see this for a long time."

"Six months. Maybe seven."

"Mmm," I grumbled to let them know of my dissatisfaction.

"What I don't understand, is how a girl with the metabolism of a hummingbird and who slept through lunch, isn't going to get up for dinner." When I thought about it, I was hungry, but I was also comfortable. I had forgotten how nice it was to be able to sleep during the day. I heard a sigh and then felt the presence of someone's face in front of mine. I got a kiss on the forehead and then a squirt of blood in my mouth. It was sweet, but also salty.

"Ok, I'm up." I sighed as I slowly sat up.

"I knew that would wake you up," Dad said as he patted my head.

"Meanie." I yawned and stretched.

"Oh? How so?" he asked poking my cheeks. I slinked over to Mom and laid on her lap.

"What do you mean "how so"?" she scolded. "Not once have you ever let her go hunting. You always bring the blood back for her. It's only natural that a young vampire who gets an inconsistent amount of blood would get excited when she tastes it."

"Well…I…"

"You know blood is an important part of a growing vampire's diet," I said, still half asleep.

"That's right. And a vampire who doesn't get enough blood when they're young has to face a crushing bloodthirst when they get older. You're basically setting up our child to go to jail!" Mom continued.

"Alright, I get your point!" Dad said. "I'll stop being so protective...kind of...and take you out to learn hunting on your next break."

"Yay," I said as I drifted back to sleep.

"Yay! We finally convinced him. Now wake up, they brought us a delicious salmon." Mom said. I immediately got up and began nomming away on the fish, much to Dad's, and Granddad's displeasure.

The next day I was feeling great so I decided I would go to school. Everything was going well. I had snuck out from under my parents' arms, taken a bath, and gotten dressed in my school uniform, but as I was on my way out the door my stomach growled. At first, no one woke up, so I continued getting ready, but it continued making louder noises, and before I noticed Mom and Dad were awake and pounced on me.

"Thought you could escape huh?" Dad said.

"Patients need to stay in bed until released by the doctors." Mom giggled.

"Gak! Ok ok I get it now get off!" I pleaded. They got off and dragged me back into the room.

"Of course, if you're able enough to try and make a break for it, then I guess you're able to go to school." Mom said.

"So..."

"So... you can stay here for today and we'll send you back tomorrow." I sighed in disbelief. "Aw don't be like that. We didn't get to see you much during break, we just want to spend time with our little girl."

"Well...ok. And I did miss you guys."

"Great. Now that that's settled, let's go get some breakfast." Dad said. We went downstairs and had omelets before returning to our room.

"By the way, where's everyone? I haven't seen them since we took that nap yesterday." I asked.

"They left." Mom said.

"My parents were actually visiting my sister and came to see you since they were closest," Dad said.

"Aww, so they all went home?" I whimpered.

"Yeah, but they told us to spend tons of time with you to make up for it." Mom said, hugging me.

"Mm, so what do you want to do today?" I asked as I tried to find a way out.

"We're going to have you show us around," Dad said.

"Ok, but I've only come to town once. I can't really say I'm an expert." I giggled as Mom tickled my feet. So, we walked around visiting different stores and at the end of the day, we decided to eat at one of the restaurants. "Today was so fun! I just wish my friends could have been here with us!"

"I never heard of any friends," Dad said.

"Dad don't be like that. I told you in one of my letters that I had friends."

"We thought they were imaginary." Mom said.

"Mean!" I shouted.

"Sara we're at a restaurant." Dad scolded. I puffed out my cheeks in a silent pout.

"Aww, we were just kidding. Of course, we would love to meet your friends." Mom laughed as she tugged on my cheek.

"Stop it!" I giggled.

"Oh, so cute. I'm glad she takes after me." she sighed.

"Yeah," Dad said. "Even though she obviously takes after me."

"No, I'm sure-"

"Stop!" I interrupted before it got any more embarrassing. The waitresses were already looking and giggling at our banter.

"So cute. Well before we head back to the inn, I'm going to use the bathroom." Mom said as she got up. "Oh and...she takes after me!" Then she ran off.

"Don't worry Sara, we'll take her to the hospital eventually." Dad nodded. I sighed in dismay, but I couldn't help but giggle too. Dad and I were sitting in the restaurant, talking and giggling as we waited for Mom. I heard the door open, and a waitress said, "Welcome", but I didn't pay much attention to who came in until she walked up and slammed her hands on the table.

"Well, well, what have we got here." Hadesia snickered.

"Look what's snuck through our defenses." Satania laughed.

"Oh dear me." Lucia mocked.

"What do you want?" I glared.

"We were just coming by to have some dinner, but it looks like this restaurant's not good because we found a filthy, dirty rat," Hadesia said.

"Go away."

"Shoyu said he wouldn't leave you no matter what, and here you are cheating on him."

"And with an older man no less." Lucia sneered.

"He's my father!"

"Oh? I'm sure you have many "fathers". Which one do you like the most?" Hadesia asked.

"I'm not joking, he is my father!"

"Mmhmm," she said as she snatched my cup. "So, Mr. Father, instead of playing with Sara why don't you come play with us?" Satania asked. She and Lucia were swarming around him and touching him.

"We promise you'll have a good time," Lucia said.

"A much better time than you would with her," Hadesia said as she lay on his lap. "Oh, and Sara we'll be sure to tell Shoyu about how you cheated on him."

"Get off him!" I snarled. I had readied my claws and teeth to rip them to shreds. The waitresses were all panicking, trying to figure out what to do, and there was no help in calming my agitation.

"Hadesia I just thought of something good." Lucia giggled, stroking Dad's oddly calm face. "Do you get a lot of clients from the school?"

"Oh, if you do, we would love it if you introduced us to them," Hadesia said. She went to kiss him, and my rage boiled over at the thought of her lips even touching him and I lunged forward. There were shrill screams from the waitresses and before I knew what happened, I was slammed to the floor and pinned down.

"Get off-" I had tried to jump to my feet but was slammed back to the floor. Someone was sitting on my chest and pinned me down, knocking the wind knocked out of me. After a short moment they moved to my stomach and relieved some of the pressure, but I still couldn't get up.

"Sara." they barked.

"What!" I snarled, finally looking at my attacker. "Huh? Dad?" He had transformed into his wolf form and pinned me down.

"It's alright Sara. Calm down," he said through a series of ear twitches and whimpers. He gave me a big lick across my face, and I felt my anger subside. "Good." he sighed as he transformed back into a humanoid. He helped me up and immediately drew me close and began patting my head. "It's alright now. Just calm down," he repeated soothingly. I closed my eyes and tried to calm down.

"Dad," I asked, "were you the one who flipped me over?"

"No. That was..." he trailed off looking across the room behind him. I heard a glass break and peeked around him toward the sound. Mom was in the corner with all three girls pinned against the wall with one arm.

"I'm sorry sweetie that was me. I didn't want you to get in trouble." she smiled, sending a chill down my spine, before turning her burning icy gaze back to the girls. "Now listen," she said to them, "I know teenagers like to have their fun and do things they shouldn't, but if you ever come near my husband or daughter again, I can promise that you will be screaming and not in the fun way you enjoy. Understood?"

"Y-yes, Ma'am!" they nodded. She let them go and they scrambled out of the restaurant. It's been a long time since I've seen that gaze, and I wouldn't hold it against them if they had wet their pants. Just glad it wasn't directed at me.

"Sara." Mom said turning around and I thought maybe I spoke too soon as she walked up to me, and I shuddered. She bent down to be at eye level then patted me on the head. "Thank you for sticking up for your father while I was away." She smiled with kind eyes. I was surprised, I thought she was angry, but I soon smiled and nodded. After apologizing to the waitresses and manager, and giving them a check to cover the funds, we went back to the inn and found Shoyu and Geri waiting for us in the lobby. They tried to pretend that they had been there the whole time, but it was obvious that they had seen the fight, or at least the aftermath. Still, we went to our room, and I told them what happened then everything proceeded normally. I got to introduce Keri and Gene to my parents, and they went back to the dorms after we talked for hours, and they gave me the classwork and homework that our teachers had assigned. Mom and Dad helped me with most of it, but Mrs. Berseria's work was to do exercises and no matter how much they cheered me on to do that final sit-up, I couldn't do it. I never thought much about it before, but I was glad we had a room with a private bath for me to soak my weeping muscles.

I refused to move so Dad carried me out and dried me off and Mom dressed me. Then we lay on the futon and I went to sleep, having sweet dreams of dancing candy where I was the princess, and my husband was a delicious coffee. The best part was I could eat as many of my subjects as I wanted and my husband was from a big family all trying to court me, each a different coffee flavor, so when one husband fell ill because I drank all of him, I could get another. I was so happy until I woke up. Not only because it was only a dream, but also because no one was in the room. Feeling bummed and wondering where my parents were, I got up, and just as I did the door slammed open, and in came my first husband.

"Mocha!" I laughed as I jumped up and immediately began drinking him. I heard a laugh and looked up.

"You really love your coffee." Dad chuckled. "So much so that you talk about it in your sleep."

"Mocha," I said going back to it.

"I know you love your husband, but don't you want your royal subjects?" Mom asked. I looked over and she was holding two huge bags of candy.

279

"Citizens!" I smiled. They came in and sat across from me. Dad had brought every one of my husbands and Mom brought my subjects.

"Now Sara even though we bought all of these, you are not to-hey!" Before Mom could finish, I had already started. Both of them tried to stop me, but I ate as much as I could before they took it away. Eventually, they gave up and I finished off the coffees, both regular and iced, and bags of candy. Mom and Dad fell asleep in front of the TV, so I decided to snuggle under their arms and go to sleep with them. After I had settled down and started to drift off, they jumped up and began tickling me. "This is payback for not listening!" Mom laughed.

"But you were the ones who brought it all at once!" I giggled.

"Don't point out our parenting flaws!" Dad laughed. When they stopped to take a short break, I jumped up and began tickling them. After a fun tickle fight, we spread out on the floor and laughed.

"Oh, I guess you can go to school tomorrow." Mom giggled.

"Mm! I'll go to bed early today so I can get up early tomorrow!" I laughed.

"Then again there is only one day left in the school week," Dad said.

"So, I don't see any problem with giving you a doctor's note to recuperate." Mom continued his logic.

"Really? Great!" I said. We laughed and rolled around on the floor, played games, and had tons of fun. Shoyu came by and gave me more work, but after I finished that we had a great time just messing around.

After a fun weekend, I finally went back to school. It had been a while since Mom and Dad went on a long vacation, so they decided to take one since they were already off. The instructor welcomed me back with a quiz, Geri gave me a box of assorted rice, and Shoyu greeted me with a kiss.

"So class, now that we have our esteemed ace student back, let us take a quick test." Instructor said.

"What do you mean ace? And you just gave me a quiz." I said.

"Well after Shoyu brought me the papers you finished the day before, I graded them and you have the highest score on all of them, bringing you to the top of the class. Plus, that was a welcome-back quiz."

"What? But Keri works harder than me, how did I pass her?"

"I've kind of let my grades slip with all the work I have to do." Keri giggled.

"So that's it. You're our class's Valedictorian." Instructor smiled. After that, we took our test and I got the highest score out of everyone, though it was only three people. The rest of the school day went by without incident, and we went to the school cafe to study. While we were there, we heard the other students talking about Lust and how they had run back to the school terrified about something. Looks like Shoyu and Geri weren't the only students who were passing by the restaurant at that time and pictures got out. They were too blurry to see me or my parents, but you could definitely see Lust's faces soaked in tears. There were also pictures from when they returned to school, apparently someone had tipped off the News club.

"Shady, Mr. Todo." I sighed in my head.

"I thought it would be a good lesson for them." I heard his voice say.

"I thought Shira put a protective spell!"

"Ouch! Not so loud I'll go deaf."

"Good then you won't be able to eavesdrop...but how did you get in here?"

"My spell is weak," Shira said. "I'm not strong enough to create ones that can stop him forever yet."

"One day I'm going to block you, Mr. Todo," I said.

"Yeah right-I mean, of course you will!" Mr. Todo exclaimed.

"One of these days."

"Yeah yeah anyways, could you come down to my office?"

"How come? Did I think something?" I asked sneeringly.

"Don't be snippy. I sent Marque to get you, stop being a brat and come along."

"What! Why you-"

"Earth to Sara!" Shoyu shouted, snapping me back.

"What?" I immediately realized that while I had been talking to Mr. Todo, I had forgotten to keep an eye on my actual surroundings.

"You were so zoned out. Is everything alright?"

"It was probably the headmaster," Keri said.

"For shame. Your woman is being stolen by an immortal dragon." Gene shook his head.

"He's not immortal just a half-vamp-wait that's not important!"

"Now now, what could all this commotion be?" Mr. Marque chuckled.

"Mr. Marque, good evening," Shoyu said.

"Good evening to you too, Master Shoyu. I have come for Lady Sara. Master has asked for her presence."

"Oh yeah, he did say he sent you." I sighed. "See you later guys."

"Ok!" They all said cheerfully.

"Sara! I'm so glad you're okay!" Mr. Todo exclaimed as he gave me a huge hug.

"This is why you wanted me in your office so desperately!" I asked as I struggled to break free.

"I'm sorry! I'm so sorry! If I hadn't been such a meanie, you wouldn't have been stressed and I'm sorry!" he sobbed.

"Let me go! Your tears are getting me soaked!"

"Master Todo. We passed Lady Berseria on the way here. She was talking to a student but should be on the way to her office soon." Mr. Marque said.

Mr. Todo immediately retreated and sat whimpering on a sofa in his office.

I walked up to him and sighed, "Listen, I don't blame you for anything that happened. Besides that, I'm fine. I'll make sure to check my levels and eat healthy and regularly every day, so stop worrying." Then I smiled and calmly gave him a hug and patted his head. "Ok? So, don't worry about me anymore." I let him go and started walking to the door. "Now if that's all you wanted, I have to get back to my room and start studying."

"True that is all I wanted," he said, grabbing my hand to stop me. "But now there's something I need."

"What?"

"Food."

"Huh?"

"I'm going to put you on a diet. One to help make sure you stay nourished, and your levels stay regular, so this doesn't happen again. The others are already on it."

"...What?"

"That means not a lot of coffee. Not a lot of candy. And no late-night snacks."

"Nope. Pleasure doing business with you." I tried to walk out, but he had a tight grip on my hand.

"Sara I'm being serious. I know I joke a lot, but I want you to stay healthy."

"Well, I'm ok with how I am! That was a freak accident, it won't happen again! ...And how did you know I have late-night snacks!"

"Sara the reason your levels were so all over the place is because you had only sugar and no nutrients, causing your insulin to constantly spike. That's why, for your sake, I'm going to put you on a diet. This doesn't mean you can't have any coffee or candy. It just means you have to take it in moderation."

"One question. I'm grateful that I get to have candy and drink coffee, but how come you don't want me to stop it altogether?"

"If you stopped completely, whenever your levels got low, you'd run the risk of going into a coma. At least if you're taking in sugar, that risk is lowered."

"Ok. Final question."

"Anything." Mr. Todo smiled.

"How'd you know I had late-night snacks?" He smiled at me but stayed silent. "Are you the one who's been sneaking in and taking them!?"

"Sara, please. How would I know where in the dorm you hide your stashes of snacks?"

"I never said I hid them in the dorm," I growled.

"...Um....look a bird!"

"Thief!" I yelled as I pounced on him. "Those dumplings and lobster were my favorite!"

"I didn't know those were your dango dumplings and buttered lobster hiding in the corner!"

"I didn't say what type of snack they were either!" I yelled as I pulled his ears.

"I-! Uh-! Ow! Don't hit me! Ow!"

"If I may intervene," Mr. Marque calmly said, ignoring our exchange. "Lady Sara it was wrong of Master Todo to take things that he knew were not his and I will have him apologize immediately."

"I'm very sorry!" Mr. Todo bowed.

"Humph." I scoffed and turned the other way.

"However," Mr. Marque continued, "I do recall there being a rule that no open food or drinks are to be in the dorms except for medical purposes, which is to be on file. We only have one snack on file for you and it is neither of the ones specified in this fight, meaning you have been breaking the rules."

".... I guess I can forgive him." I pouted.

"And I guess I can replace the food I took and overlook this transgression." Mr. Todo said. We shook hands and made up.

"Good. Now then Lady Sara, there's a bit of a surprise waiting for you outside. Please have a good day." Mr. Marque nodded. I wondered what he meant as I left and was surprised and happy when I found out.

"Hello, Sweetie." Mom laughed as she and Dad walked up the stairs.

"Mom, Dad, what are you doing here?" I asked.

"That's the first thing you say when you see us." Dad sighed.

"Sorry. I'm glad you're here, but aren't you on vacation? And what about work?" I giggled.

"True I do have quite a lot of meetings when we get back." Mom sighed.

"And I have some follow-ups, but they're all in good hands," Dad said.

"So, since this is the first vacation we've had for a few months..." Mom said. They looked at each other and chuckled, "We decided to stay here!" At first, I just looked at them. I couldn't believe they were finishing each other's sentences like that, then I realized what they had said.

"Wait so you're taking a vacation here?" I asked with sparkling eyes.

"Yup." They nodded.

"Hurray!" I jumped.

"Does Sara care to give us a hug?" Mom asked, stretching out her arms.

"Sara does!" I laughed as I rushed into them, and she squeezed me as much as she could.

"So, Sara, we asked Mr. Todo and he said it was your choice," Dad said after he gave us a hug. "Do you want to stay with us in the inn or stay in your dorm?"

"Stay with you!" I giggled.

"Well, then it's decided. With us, you'll stay!" Mom said. We were walking out of the main building when I heard a pop sound and confetti fell gently in front of me.

"Aww, it was supposed to be more amazing, but I guess this is all I can expect from a party favor," Shoyu said as he stood in front of us. "Oh well, I guess I'll just-Mr. And Mrs. Hollins! You were still here!" he exclaimed when he noticed Mom and Dad beside me.

"Yes. We decided to take our long overdue vacation." Mom smiled.

"Well, that's great. I'm glad you're getting some rest."

"Shoyu what are you doing here? And why did you have a party favor?" I asked.

"Oh well, I wanted to surprise you with a gift, but a cherry bomb seemed over the top and I couldn't afford any of those drop-down balls."

"Shoyu, I swear you'd celebrate anything as long as I'm involved, wouldn't you?" I sighed.

"Maybe." he blushed.

"So? Where's my gift? You brought it didn't you?"

"Why is it that you act all modest when someone else gives you a gift, but when I do, you act all greedy?"

"Think of it as you being someone special to me." Taken by surprise he blushed again. I was having a wonderful time teasing him. "Now." I smiled holding out my hand. Shoyu didn't enjoy being mercilessly teased in front of my parents and started to walk away.

"I don't have it with me. Come by my room later and I'll give it to you." he pouted.

"Oh, alright don't be mad." I giggled as I skipped into his path. "I don't care what you got me. Would you like to come have dinner with us at the inn?"

"Sure," he said, smiling instantly. "As long as I'm not intruding."

"Of course not! You're always welcome, right Mom!" I called, to which she smiled and nodded. Dad grumbled, but Mom quickly elbowed him, and he stayed silent as we made our way back to the inn and had dinner. It was kind of awkward since Dad glared at Shoyu the whole time, but we had a fun conversation. Eventually, though, he asked something I never expected.

"Shoyu," Dad growled, "what are your feelings for Sara?"

Shoyu was surprised and stuttered, "Um, ah...what?"

"Your feelings for my daughter, what are they?"

"Um...well I...you know..." He stammered, not even looking Dad in the eyes. I tried to protest and help Shoyu put, but Mom quickly silenced me.

"Spit it out!" Dad snarled.

"W-well, Sara makes me...h-happy and...is confident a-and fun to be around and I l-like that...about...her." The room fell silent and, even though I wasn't looking up, I knew both our faces were bright red.

"Hmph." Was all Dad said as Mom quietly sipped her tea?

"Well, I suppose we'll go take a bath." She stretched, grabbing my arm and dragging me with her.

"I um, I guess Mr. Todo told you guys why we were in trouble," I mumbled as we soaked in the public bath.

"He did." She sighed. "We're not mad Sara, it was just a kiss, we just don't want you two to go too far. You're still young with centuries of life ahead of you. Don't feel like you have to rush, ok."

"I know Mom. Aside from Lust trying to force themselves on Shoyu, we haven't been thinking of doing anything... baby-related."

"Pfft, the first time I've it referred to like that."

"W-well I was trying to not make it embarrassing!" I blushed. She teased me mercilessly and I decided to get out of the bath first.

"Sara!" Shoyu called. He had been sitting on the bench by the stairs waiting for me.

"Shoyu! You escaped my Dad." I teased.

"It was no easy task. Your mom coming out too?" He asked as he held up a fruit milk.

"Thank you and no. She's staying in a while longer." I said taking the milk. We sat quietly on the benches sipping our milk. The front desk was empty, and no one was in the dining hall.

"So, Sara..." he said, breaking the silence.

"Y-yeah."

"Here." He held out a small, badly wrapped thing.

"Um...thank you." He had turned away so I couldn't see his face, but his ears were bright red. I unwrapped the object and found a necklace chain with a base for a jewel.

"It's so you can wear Shira's habitat around your neck rather than in your pocket. This way he can see what's going on." I smiled and, after affixing Shira's crystal ball to the base, put it on and let it hang just below my collarbone. Then I wrapped my arms around Shoyu, leaning on his back.

"Thank you, Shoyu. It's a wonderful gift." He flinched when I kissed him on the cheek, then I got up and started heading back to the room.

"S-Sara!" he exclaimed. He grabbed my hand and when I turned around, he kissed me. "I just...wanted to kiss you," he said with his head hung low. I smiled and snuggled up to him.

"That reminds me, I never said it back."

"Said what back?"

I looked up into his blushing red face and smiled, "I love you too."

He blushed brighter and mumbled, "I said I like you", and I giggled, giving him another peck before we headed back to the room. Mom had somehow snuck out of the bath and was asleep with Dad on the futon, so, out of habit, I jumped on them yelling, "Wake Up! Wake Up!"

"Alright! Alright, we're awake!" Dad yelled, pushing me off. He sighed, then started playing Tickle Monster. Mom crawled out from under the covers and went to stand and wait near the door with Shoyu and once we finally settled down, we all watched some TV. "Shoyu don't you have to get back to the dorms? I recall Mr. Todo only permitting Sara to stay off campus."

"Huh? Oh, that's right." Shoyu sighed.

"Don't be so mean." Mom scolded. "Shoyu you can spend the night with us. We won't mind."

"Thank you, Ma'am." Shoyu smiled as he crawled under the covers with us. He snuggled next to Dad and quickly fell asleep.

"I guess it is late and I have to go to school tomorrow. Guess I'll sleep too." I said.

"Goodnight." Mom said.

"Goodnight," Dad grumbled. Mom turned off the TV and I heard a, "I'm still watching that."

"They're going to sleep just watch TV tomorrow." Mom said. Dad grumbled and turned over and I giggled before drifting to sleep. The next day, Shoyu and I got ready for school and headed out.

"Remember when we used to walk to school together every day," he said.

"Yeah. It was always nice, even on a rainy day." I giggled. We said good morning to Mr. Marque, who greeted students who only lived a train ride away, at the gate, and went off to start class. The school was the same as always.

"Alright everyone before you head out, I have an announcement." Instructor said. "As you all know your next break isn't until summer and then we'll be starting a whole new year. So, we're going to introduce what this school is famous for...Abroad Studies!"

"Abroad studies? I thought that was only for high schoolers." I said.

"Nope. It's for everyone, but high schoolers don't have to get permission from their parents."

"I see. So basically, Sara and Keri just have to ask their parents if they can go." Gene said.

"Yup. As well as get the necessary vaccines for traveling to that country."

"So how do we sign up?" I asked.

"Just fill out this paper and get it back to me, Marque, or Mr. Todo and we'll send the necessary forms to your parents to sign," she said giving each of us a form. The bell rang to signal the end of school and Shoyu and I quickly rushed back to the inn.

"Can I use your cell, pretty please?" Shoyu bowed.

"Can you pretty please sign this?" I bowed alongside him as we busted open the door.

"Um...what is this about?" Mom asked.

"We just got the forms for the abroad program. Since I'm in middle school I need a parent or guardian's consent." I said.

"So, you want us to sign this form?" Dad asked, tapping the paper I put in front of him.

"Well, I wanted to call my parents and ask them if it's ok," Shoyu said.

"Did either of you even look at the options?" Mom asked. We stared at each other and then quickly looked at the form. There were plenty of options for us to choose from. I looked down the list and checked off Brexior.

"Done," I said handing the paper to Mom.

"Did you look at requirements and listings?"

"I'll be spending one year at the Brexior Boarding School in the capital under the care of their royal family."

"Good. Shoyu?" Dad said.

"Same," Shoyu said. They nodded and signed both our papers.

"Yes!" we both jumped up and yelled. After several months, it was finally time for summer break, and I got an even better surprise going home.

RECOLLECTION

Travel Arc

I expected to see Mom and Dad when I got off the train, but instead, the Hazimis were the only ones there to greet me.

"Mr. and Mrs. Hazimi! How are you?" I said as I hugged them.

"Wonderful Sara! I heard you had a hectic winter break." Mrs. Hazimi smiled.

"Why are you the first one to hug my parents?" Shoyu chuckled.

"Oh, don't be like that, but where are my parents? I don't see them." I said. The Hazimis looked at each other and then giggled.

"They have a very special surprise for you." Mrs. Hazimi smiled.

"They brought it home a few days ago. Your father told us to bring you home with us and he'll come get you when he's ready." Mr. Hazimi said. Shoyu and I had a great time seeing the town again. He showed me a new taco place that had opened up and the new games they added at the arcade. We ran into a few students and teachers from before and while it was awkward, nothing bad happened. After, we went and played games at Shoyu's house until my dad came over to pick me up.

"So, what's my surprise?" I asked.

"Oh, you know. Something special." Dad said.

"How special?"

"Super special."

"Will you tell me?"

"No."

"Please?"

"No."

"Come on."

"Sara," he sighed, "you'll get to see it soon, ok."

"Fine." I giggled. We got home and I happily pranced into the house and yelled, "I'm home!" It was kind of quiet, but I soon heard rustling from upstairs and ran to find its source. "Hello!" I said, tracking it to my parent's room.

"Long time no see." Mom laughed. She was holding something to her chest and rocking back and forth.

"Is that my surprise? What is it?" I asked, moving closer and she moved so that I could see it better.

"This is your new baby sister."

"I-what?" I said looking at the small child in her arms. She had brown hair like Mom's, but bluish-grey eyes like Dad's.

"Her name is Fiore," Dad said as he came in.

"Toast."

"...What?" they both asked.

"Her name is Toast because her hair looks like you got a perfect slice of toast." They both looked at me and then laughed.

"Fine. You can call her Toast, but that's just a nickname." Dad said.

"Can I hold her?"

"Of course." Mom said, handing her to me. She was so small, and she looked at me with big eyes.

"Hi Toast, I'm your big sister." I smiled. She giggled and reached out towards me. "She's mine now," I said as I began walking to my room. That was quickly over as she began crying a few minutes later. "How do I make her stop?" I asked, bringing her back.

"She's probably hungry." Mom giggled, taking her back and holding her to her chest. Toast immediately stopped crying and began suckling. The rest of my day was helping Dad make sure the house was in order and Mom was comfortable. I had so much fun playing with Toast, Shoyu did as well when he came over, and I hated that break was over so soon.

"Ugh. I can't take it anymore!" Shoyu complained as he collapsed and laid his head on my lap. We were back on campus, a week early, to pack for our trips and make sure everything was in order.

"I asked if you wanted me to come with you," I said.

"I know, but still." he pouted. We were sitting in Gene and Shoyu's dorm. I had been studying about Brexior and its language. Keri and Shoyu had left for an appointment, and as you could tell, Shoyu was back and in a sour mood. Turns out only a limited number of people can go to the same country, and the Instructor gave us the announcement late. So, while I was going to Brexior, Shoyu had to go to its neighboring country, Grebior.

"I get where Shoyu's coming from. Why do we have to get so many shots just to visit another country? I got all my shots when I came here!" Gene said.

"Oh, that's right. Gene, you're from Brexior." Shoyu said.

"Yup. That's why I asked him to help me learn the language. I already know most of it though, so it's pretty easy. The culture is still a bit hard for me." I said.

"Yeah, I figured learning the language would be hard, but it's been easy for me so far." Shoyu sighed, sitting up.

"Well, you're a Dimensional, it'd be strange if you didn't pick up a language quickly," Gene said.

"I guess you're right." Shoyu sighed.

"Sorry to butt in, but Gene could you help me with this," I asked.

"The Matsukchi Festival? Sure, what do you need help with?"

"Well, I get that it's to honor someone, but who exactly?"

"Dead people," Shoyu said.

"Dead people?"

"The Matsukchi Festival is when everyone climbs up Mt. Moore and places offerings that remind them of their loved ones, like their favorite flower or food, into the Moon Cauldron. The King and the Yukijin light the Blue Moon Flame, and then everyone howls to let the spirits know that they're still loved and remembered so they can move on to be helpers of the moon." Gene said.

"Oh, I see, but why do we have to wear black, white, or blue clothing?"

"Wearing those colors is a means of respect and they're also the country colors."

"Hmm, I think I get it now."

"Hard at work, are we?" Keri chimed as she came in.

"Keri! How was it?"

"Horrible. Just absolutely horrible. Gene, hold me." Gene wrapped his arms around her and kissed her on the forehead.

"You two are so cute together. It's too bad your parents are making you go to separate places." I said.

"I know. My parents were pissed when Mr. Todo called and told them what we did, but it's not our fault."

"Yeah, we can't help if we love each other," Gene said as they began kissing. Shoyu and I looked at each other...then at the ceiling...then at the floor. Finally, they stopped. Soon it was time for Gene and I's appointment. I hated being inspected and prodded and especially hated the shots, which I would have to come to get more of in a few days since they can't give them all at once, but I endured it. Finally, it was time to go on our trips. Shoyu, like I said, was going to Grebior, the snake country, and Keri was forced to go to the country of arms: Deraha. Gene's parents were sending him across the ocean to the country Hael, a country known for their strict belief in morals. After bidding everyone farewell, I was waiting on the platform for the train with Shoyu. Quite a few other students were going to Brexior and Grebior, all of different ages. Everyone was in their own little groups, talking about what we expected to learn, when I felt a tug on my skirt and, looking down, saw a cute little girl. She looked to have just graduated from kindergarten.

"Neri, Nori," The Brexrior words for big sister and big brother, "are you going to Brexior too?" she asked.

"Yes, we are. What's your name?" I bent down and asked.

"My name's Berri. Can I ride with you? I'm afraid I'll get lost if I go alone."

"My name's Sara, and he is Shoyu, and of course, you can ride with us Berri, but where are your parents?"

"My parents live far away. They offered to come see me off, but I didn't want to bother them and now I'm afraid."

"Well don't worry Berri, you're in good hands." Shoyu smiled.

"Yay! Thank you, Neri, Nori." she smiled. "Um...is it alright if I hold your hand?"

"Of course." I smiled. We held each other's hands, with Berri in between me and Shoyu, and got a seat together when the train came. We would have to take a bullet train to Kiori, a three-hour carriage ride to a different train station, half a day by smoke train to Brexior, and finally, a day and a half to get to Nügdleger, the capital. After playing games for an hour on our second train, as well as talking and eating, Berri and I fell asleep. Even though I'd been going to this school for a while, I only just now learned that Adestria starts at first grade as Berri was attending her first year here. There is a kindergarten and daycare, but it's mostly for staff's children. Anyway, Shoyu had gotten one of the attendants to bring a blanket for us.

When I woke up it was night and I could hear the attendant's voice over the speakers, "We will be arriving at the Brexior border in an hour. A visa check will be starting so please have yours ready. Please make sure to have all your belongings and thank you for your patronage. Again, we will-"

"Ah, Berri, Shoyu, it's time to wake up." I yawned.

Shoyu didn't hear a thing, but Berri stretched and yawned, "Are we there already?"

"An hour."

"Please wake me then." She snuggled up to me and immediately went back to sleep. I giggled and looked out the window. It was dark, but you could see lights dotting the hillside here and there.

"Hmm? Oh, good you're up." An attendant said as she walked by. "I hate to bother you all while your little sister is still sleeping, but I just need to check your visas."

"Of course," Shoyu said, immediately popping awake to hand her our visas.

"Alright, all set. Make sure to take care of each other while you're studying." she smiled as she waved goodbye.

"Little sister? I guess it does seem that way. But how did she know we were going to study?" I smiled.

"Come on Berri look. It's so pretty. Besides if you sleep right now you won't be able to sleep later." Shoyu said.

"Yes I will." she yawned. She popped her head up to protest and then saw the beautiful mountains and hills dotted with lights out the window. "Woah! So pretty." she gasped.

"Right. And you wanted to sleep." I chuckled.

"Ok, I'll stay up. Promise." she giggled as she searched out the window. Shoyu and I chuckled again and watched the scenery pass by.

"We probably won't get to see this in the morning. We'll have to come back here sometime during the day." Shoyu said.

"Huh!? Why!?" Berri exclaimed.

"This is near the border, the countryside of Brexior. We're going to the capital, Nügdleger, to attend the school there." I said.

"How far is the capital from here?"

"We still have a day and a half left for our trip once we get off the train and onto the next one." She puffed out her cheeks and made a sour face.

"That's too long! I want to be there now!" she yelled.

"Hey, keep your voice down." Shoyu scolded. We rode for another half hour, falling back asleep, and the attendant woke us up twenty minutes before our stop. After, we got off and started the final leg of our journey. This was where Shoyu parted ways with us, getting on a separate carriage to continue to Grebior. It was late when we arrived in the capital so I guess I shouldn't have expected a lot of people to be there, but they could have at least left some lights on. Still, the high schoolers, who I assumed had been to Brexior before, just began walking and talking as if it was no big deal, so I guess this was normal. In fact, even the other middle schoolers had friends waiting for them, so I guess Berri and I were the only newcomers.

"Neri I'm scared," Berri said.

"Don't worry just hold my hand. I can see in the dark, so I'll lead us." I said. She latched onto my hand and stuck to me like glue. "Don't worry. I don't see anything that would scare you in the least." I giggled as we carried our bags through the dark town.

"Still..." she whimpered, "Neri how come you can see in the dark? Is it magic? Can you teach me? I want to see so I'm not afraid."

"Unfortunately, it's not magic."

I let my tail gently rest on her shoulder and she screamed, "Ah!? Oh, it's Neri's tail. Don't scare me!"

"Sorry, that wasn't my intention." I giggled. "But this is how I can see. I'm half-Brexiorian."

"Oh. So, the other half is a vampire?"

"Yup."

"I wish I was half-Brexiorian."

I began to ask her what she was but saw something moving ahead of us. And growled, "Who's there?"

"Humph. Even for a half-Brex, you're slow." Someone, in wolf form, said from behind us. Berri and I, cautiously, eyed the wolves who had shown up. I had transformed into wolf form and carried Berri and our bags on my back so I could run if anything seemed suspicious. There were about four other wolves that came with the male, Hajiel. "Those bags would be easier to carry if you transformed back," Hajiel said. He was back to a humanoid and was looking down on me and Berri. He annoys me. Always condescending and thinks he's better than everyone. "Well if you don't want to that's fine. I'll just take a few." he reached down, but I jumped away and growled a warning at him. "What the hell! I'm just trying to help!"

"Ha! Sure, you were. Just like you were "helping" us when you snuck up behind us and surrounded us." I growled.

"I really am just trying to"

"Hajiel." An older wolf cut him off. "This is what you get for your little prank. Leave her be."

"Tch!" Hajiel snorted as he continued walking. He transformed into a wolf and ran off ahead of us. The rest of the trip was made in intense silence. Maybe I was being too serious. I mean, it probably was just a prank, but that was still no excuse for his actions and besides we're in a foreign country we know nothing about! I know Gene said that everyone in Brexior is super nice, but I still couldn't trust him. After walking through the main square and passing by a huge fir tree, from which the town gets its name, we arrived at some steps. Berri yawned and began falling asleep on my back.

"Don't worry. We're almost there." The female said as we began walking up the stairs. I couldn't tell what exactly it was. It looked like a building, but what type I couldn't see.

"Please, won't you forgive our brother, and us?" Another wolf from the pack asked.

"If I thought I could actually trust you then maybe," I said. "But I don't so no." The wolf whimpered and fell back behind me. We reached the building at the top of the stairs, but all I could tell from it in the dark was that it was huge. "We're not going to be ambushed when we go inside are we?"

"N-no. Well, not ambushed in the way you're thinking." one of the wolves said. I growled and began to back up. "No! We're definitely not bad people, really! Damn that Hajiel, he'll definitely pay for this." he said.

"Berri, hand on tight ok," I said.

"Yes Neri." she yawned, and I cautiously went inside. Once in a lit area, it was clear that this was indeed a palace.

"Yo." Hajiel scoffed as he leaned on the wall.

"Berri, come on now it's time to get off," I said. She slowly slid to the floor, and I transformed back and picked her up. She immediately fell asleep in my arms, and I couldn't help but giggle. I heard Hajiel scoff and then a swatting sound and him yelling, "Ow!" I bent down to pick up our bags, but then Hajiel came and swiped them out of nowhere. "Hey give those back!" I yelled. He ran off and I chased after him. He kept running despite my yelling and went into a room. I followed after him and the second I stepped into the room, he slammed the door behind me. "W-what do you want!" I yelled, realizing I just took the bait and was led into this situation, but he said nothing. He simply walked past me and put our bags in the corner. "I said what do you want!" I repeated.

"She must be very tired to sleep through your yelling," Hajiel said. I started to ask what he meant, but he put his finger to his lips. "Quiet. Don't you know how to use your inside voice? Or maybe low-born blood isn't taught that."

"You-How dare you! My family is very prominent!"

"Maybe in the vampire's country, but here you're nothing, but a citizen. The only social class we use is Pack Law and new members to the pack are always Omegas." Then he sighed, "No, that's not what I meant." He sighed again and ruffled his hair. "What I meant is...um...ugh, forget it!" He stormed out, but before he slammed the door he said, just barely loud enough, "Sorry." I wanted to follow up and figure out if he was actually trying to apologize, but I was exhausted and fell asleep on the bed as soon as I sat down.

"Solumnus stop. Nori said not to bother them." someone said.

"I'm only looking. I won't wake them up." someone else said.

"Solumnus stop!" a third voice yelled. I opened my eyes and saw four little kids, about Berri's age, arguing.

"...Um...good morning..." I said. They turned to me and froze, then tried to make a beeline for the door, but I pounced on all of them. "Who might you cutie pies be?" I giggled.

"Wha-! I'm a guy, I'm not cute or a pie!" One in a blue yukata said.

"Sorry sorry. So, who are you all?" I laughed as I got up.

"Huh? Oh, um I'm Solumnus."

"My name is Cherri." A girl in a yellow yukata said.

"My name is Lacus and this shy girl hiding behind me is our youngest sister, Helen." A boy dressed in a green yukata said.

"N-nice to meet you..." A cute little girl in a white yukata said.

"Nice to meet you all." I smiled. "So, what compelled you all to come into a girl's room uninvited?"

"I-it was Solumnus' idea! He's the oldest out of our litter!" Cherri said.

"H-hey!" Solumnus yelled and they began fighting.

"Hey, stop that you're scaring Helen!" Lacus yelled as he joined the fray.

"Heh, guess it doesn't take much for littermates to turn on each other," I said.

"Um...m-may I sit with y-you while they f-fight?" Helen whimpered. I smiled and gently picked her up.

"Of course, I don't mind." She gasped, as if expecting me to yell at her, then snuggled against my stomach.

"Excuse us Ms. Hol-" The male from before, now in human form and in a red knight-like suit, came in, saw the fighting kids, then blew up. "What are you all doing in here? I told you not to enter this room and that we had a guest staying here! And why are you fighting!" he stormed in and separated them. "Solumnus you're the oldest in your litter, in line to inherit the throne, act like it!"

"Ah, we just-!" Solumnus whimpered.

"Enough! Time out! All of you to your rooms! Solumnus, you come with me!"

"No!" Solumnus yelled. He broke free of the grip on his wrist, and they all ran behind me.

"We won't let you punish only Solumnus!" Lacus yelled.

"That's right! One for all and all for one!" Cherri yelled.

"Um...equal punishment under the law..." Helen whispered.

"Aww, they're so cute! So, you all can work together. Wait why are you hiding behind me!?" I exclaimed.

"Nori would never do something to us with guests protecting us," Solumnus said.

"At least not if he doesn't want Daddy to scold him!" Cherri laughed. The man had a twisted face of anger and frustration.

After thinking it over he relaxed and sighed, "Fine I get it. It's just that I want you all to grow up with the right attitudes."

"If you ask me, I'd say they already have the right attitudes," I said.

"They came into your room uninvited and began fighting."

"But they stuck together when exploring instead of sending one person to check it out and when you were scolding them, they stuck together to protect each other. Sure, they fight amongst themselves, but isn't that just a part of being siblings." The man was speechless, which made me think I overstepped a boundary. "Um...I'm sorry. I came off too strong. I was an only child until recently, and my sister is only a month or so old, so I'm sure I don't know entirely where you're coming from if I do at all and-"

"No." he smiled. "You're right. That is everything I want to teach them. Thank you."

"N-no problem. So, what did you want from me?"

"Oh right. First and foremost, I want to apologize to you for last night."

"No worries. Hajiel apologized to me last night. I'm the one who should be saying sorry."

"No no, but we'd go in circles all day if we continued so I'll just go on. I came to get you and Ms. Neum sized for your uniforms."

"Oh right. I guess the measurements are different for each country." I giggled. "I'll wake Berri and get ready."

"I'll send someone to come get you two for breakfast after." he nodded. "Come on you guys let's leave Ms. Hollins and Ms. Neum alone."

"Aww, ok. We'll see you later Neri." The pups said as they left, and I got up and went to bed. Berri really must have been tired because she slept through everything.

"Berri wake up. It's time to get ready." I said gently.

"I don't wanna," she said.

I giggled, "Are you sure? The tickle monster might get you if you don't."

"Tickle Monster?" she yawned. I pounced and the sheets flew in the air as we laughed and rolled around. After, we took a shower together and I combed and dried her hair. The seamstress came in and took our measurements and then we got dressed and were taken to a large dining room.

"Neri, Berri! Sit next to me!" Solumnus yelled. He and his siblings were already seated.

"I will!" Berri cheered running over.

"Hm, there aren't assigned seats are there?" I asked.

"What does it matter, if all my older siblings pronounce their right to the throne, I get it! So that means whatever I say goes!" Solumnus said, puffing out his chest.

"That's not until we renounce it, stupid." I heard from behind as something hit my head and I spun around. "And you, don't stand in the way like an idiot," Hajiel said.

"Well sorry!" I puffed.

"And I'm not stupid!" Solumnus yelled.

"Yeah yeah sorry. So, what are you discussing, other than pointless crap?" Hajiel asked.

"I was wondering if there were assigned seats," I said.

"Hmph." he scoffed looking around. He then grabbed my wrist and pulled me to the table, pushing me into a chair by the head of the table and sitting in the chair next to me.

"Hey, we wanted her to sit near us!" Cherri yelled.

"Shut up! She can't sit next to all of you anyway!" Hajiel yelled back. They started arguing and eventually, his littermates and siblings came in.

"Jeez shut up all of you!" A girl yelled.

"You're yelling too!" Hajiel replied.

"Only because you-"

"Quiet!" The man from before boomed. Everyone stopped and quickly sat down. The man sighed and sat down across from me. "Why do you always...Ms. Hollins, Ms. Neum, please excuse our siblings."

"It's alright, really," I said. Though I could have done without being pushed in a chair.

"It was fun!" Berri laughed.

"More importantly, brother why are you sitting over there?" Hajiel asked.

"Because I want to," he said.

"But-but that means..." Hajiel murmured.

"Did you want her to yourself?" he laughed.

"No! I don't, but fine, we'll move somewhere else!" Hajiel said, grabbing my hand.

"Enough of this ruckus!" An even boomer voice rang. The doors swung open and in walked a man and woman with extravagant clothes. "Hajiel unhand our guest and sit quietly!" The man sat at the end of the table nearest to me and the woman sat next to me, with a polite smile.

"Y-yes, Sir," Hajiel said and reluctantly sat down. These two were in the pamphlet for the school, the ones who would be taking care of me, King and Queen Goligius.

"Now then, it is a pleasure to meet you Ms. Hollins, and you as well Ms. Neum. My name is Arthur Goligius the Third." the King said.

"And my name is Mary Goligius. Pleased to meet you as well." the Queen said.

"It's a pleasure to meet you both as well." I smiled.

"Oh, me too! It's a pleasure!" Berri waved.

"Yes, quite a pleasure young one." Mrs. Goligius laughed.

"My goodness that reminds me!" the man in the knight suit said. "Between Hajiel's prank and my younger siblings' antics, we never did tell you our names. Mine is Christopher, eldest of the first litter, and these are our youngest siblings Solumnus, Cherri, Lacus, and Helen of the third litter."

"My name is Sherri, second born of the first litter." The girl who had talked to me before said.

"Not that you'll see much of us, but I'm Madius and this is my twin Karius, youngest of the first litter." The man next to her and his twin said, "Nice to meet you."

"Oh, me next, me next!" The girl I talked to last night jumped up. "My name's Sissy, second born of the second litter, and these are my twins Maxus and Noire, we're triplets even though I'm the only girl! You already know the oldest, Hajiel, and how much of a pain in the ass he can be, and these last two are our litter sisters Hama and Tama, youngest of the second litter! They're not twins, but they look so alike, isn't it cool! Also, I'm really sorry about scaring you guys yesterday, we just wanted to have some fun! Please don't hate us for it! Anyway, our litter is only two years older than you so I hope we can be friends! Oh! And we'll definitely show you around today! I'll take you to my favorite sweets shop!" she rambled.

"As always you say so much in one breath." Christopher sighed.

"And who the hell's a pain in the ass!" Hajiel yelled.

"You are of course. I said that." Sis smiled. "Oh, by the way, Sara, hope you don't mind me calling you by your first name, but you can call me Sis."

"Don't change the subject, you're more of a pain than I am!" Hajiel yelled.

"Shut up! You're yelling is annoying!" Sis yelled.

"Sis, you're yelling too," Noire said.

"You want to fight!" Hajiel jumped up.

"So, you can lose like you always do!" Sis laughed.

"You little don't always lose, I let you win! Dad can testify to that!" Hajiel turned to King Goligius who sat quietly.

"Actually, I would like to hear more about this "scare" you gave our guests last night," he said. The entire litter fell silent just as breakfast was brought in. "Sissy, Noire, Maxus, since you are kind enough to take our guest to sightsee before they start school tomorrow, I will hear your testimony after."

"Yes, Father." Sis, Noire, and Maxus said together.

"I-I'm going with them," Hajiel said.

"You, Hama, and Tama will stay here and give us your side of the story." Queen Goligius said.

"Yes, Ma'am." they sighed and so breakfast went on with a tense atmosphere.

"So that's Nügdleger!" Sis smiled. After breakfast, Sis, Noire, and Maxus took Berri and me on a tour of the town as promised.

"Wow, it's more amazing than I thought. Especially the sweets." I said.

"Hehe, I see you liked my favorite store. Listen, if you ever want pastries when I'm not around just mention my name to the owner."

"Sis stop it." Noire sighed.

"Quit using your influence to get what you want." Maxus joined in.

"Shut up! I can do what I want!" Sis yelled. They started arguing and getting into a fight. This was about the fifth time since we had started the tour.

"Do siblings always fight?" Berri asked.

"We're not siblings, we're littermates!" Sis yelled as Noire shoved her head to the ground and she kicked Maxus.

"I don't get it," Berri said.

"Get off! Listen," Sis said as she kicked off her littermates and crawled from under the fray, "littermates are pups born at the same time, in the same litter. Siblings are part of a different litter and can even have different moms or dads."

"But then how are you, Maxus, and Noire triplets if you're all littermates?" Berri asked.

"Because we shared the same umbilical cord!" Maxus said as he pounced on Noire.

"That probably explains Sis' lack of boobs!" Noire said as he head-butted Sis in the back.

"You're dead for that comment!" Sis yelled and it became an all-out brawl. In the end, it took several adults to break them up before injuries got too serious and we were escorted back to the castle by the guard. The triplets were called away to go see their parents, so I decided to study with Berri more on the Brexior language and culture. Soon we heard a knock on the door and Hajiel came in with a clothing rack.

"Your uniforms are done. Try them on and make sure they fit correctly," he said.

"Yay!" Berri yelled as she took hers and ran into the bathroom.

"You could have waited till I said come in," I said.

"It's my castle, I didn't have to knock." he scoffed. As usual, we don't see eye to eye. I sighed and took the uniform designated for me.

"Neri will you come help me!" Berri called.

"Yes, I'm coming!" I replied. "No peeking." I glared at Hajiel who scoffed and rolled his eyes before turning his back and sitting on the bed.

It took a while for me to help Berri try on hers because she kept squirming and jumping around.

"Hey! What's taking so long!" he called.

"Just a minute! Wait, why are you still here!?"

"Shut up! I'm here so you can let me know if I should tell the seamstress to make it bigger!"

"Fine fine!" I finished putting mine on and called, "It fits fine now get out!"

"Wee!" Berri yelled as she burst out of the bathroom.

"Berri wait!" I yelled as I chased after her.

"Don't I look pretty!" she said standing in front of Hajiel.

"Sure. I bet the boys will be all over you." he chuckled. Berri giggled and ran back into the bathroom.

"Jeez Berri. Can't you chill for one second?" I sighed.

"You too." He mumbled.

"What?"

"You...look nice too," he said, turning away.

"Are you blushing?"

"S-shut up! I was just giving you a compliment!"

"Well thank you." I smiled and he glanced over and then quickly turned back.

"N-no problem. By the way, your ribbon's crooked."

"Huh? Ah, you're right! Maybe I should have Sis teach me how to tie it tomorrow."

"If you want, I can teach you now," he mumbled.

"What?"

"Nothing! Never mind! Anyways if it fits then I don't need to be here anymore, bye!" He jumped and ran towards the door.

"Um, Hajiel!"

"W-what!"

"Forgive me if I'm wrong, but I get the feeling that you like me, so before things get too serious just know that I already have a boyfriend. He's just studying abroad in a different country right now." He didn't say anything, just stared at me. "Um, Hajiel?" I said.

"Please excuse me?" he said and left. I thought maybe I hurt his feelings, but I would prefer to tell him now than for him to find out later.

I went into the bathroom and changed back into my clothes, helping Berri out of her uniform as well.

"Good morning, Sara! You're certainly up early!" Sis giggled.

"Ah good morning, Sis. I actually got up earlier, so I just wandered around and helped out the staff until it was time to wake up Berri. Do you think you could help me tie the ribbon?" I said.

"Wow, you got up before the maids! That's amazing! Aren't you tired?" she asked as she helped me.

"No, I'm used to it. At Adestria we always get up early and do exercises."

"Ehh!? Sounds like a military school! I think I would die if I went there!"

"I feel like it'd be the exact opposite."

"We agree." Noire and Maxus said.

"Ehh!?" she exclaimed. We laughed and went into the dining room for breakfast. School wasn't much different from Adestria, my classes were chosen for me, but students at Brexior usually get to pick their own classes and can choose to go to morning, afternoon, or night classes or all of them. There were a few classes that really threw me off, like the hunting class where we had to hunt as a pack, which I've never really done. I sometimes hunted with Mom and Dad, but for the most part, they only taught me how to hunt alone. Surprisingly though, Sis or one of the other siblings were always in my class to help me. We were only scheduled for morning classes, so school was over at twelve for us.

"Ah! What a day! I wish I could throw myself on the bed and go to sleep." I exclaimed. While the royal family was taking care of us, we were still supposed to be staying at the school, so Berri and I were going to our rooms and the second litter decided to show us the way. "Oh, thanks for helping me with my classes."

"No problem. If you want, we can go to one of the meeting rooms in the castle and study together." Sis said.

"Yeah, I think that'd be a good idea," Hama said.

"From what I saw during our hunting class, you could brush up on pack order and signals," Hajiel said.

"I've only ever learned to hunt alone or with my parents and they've only ever let me chase it to their hiding spot," I said.

"Wow talk about untrusted."

"T-they trust me! Just...not enough to let me catch dinner with them."

"You're not trusted." The litter said in unison.

"...A-anyways, Berri how was your day?"

"Fun! Cherri, Helen, and I made cute origami animals! Then we made kites, then played outside!" she smiled happily.

"Really? That's great. I'm glad you had fun."

"She tried to change the subject," Hajiel said with disappointment.

"Such a fail. I wouldn't have her catch dinner either." The rest said.

"Shut up! I can't help it!" I yelled. "I think I'll go study by myself. Bye." I took off and quickly found the room number on my key. "Humph forget them. My parents trust me, they're just overprotective. I could hunt by myself if I had to." I mumbled.

"Then prove it." I heard Hajiel say.

"Ah! What? Where are you!?" I yelled as I turned around but didn't see him.

"Boo," he said as he hung down from the ceiling. Out of habit and fright I sucker punched him to the floor then healed his face cause I used more vampiric strength than I meant to. "Ow! What the hell!"

"You're the one who just came out of nowhere! How'd you follow me!"

"It's your own damn fault for not noticing!" We stopped and glared silently at each other. "Anyways," Hajiel said, getting up, "Prove that you can hunt by yourself. You do that and I'll get the litter to stop making fun of you."

"And you. I want you to stop too." I demanded.

"...No can do."

"Why!"

"I...have my own reasons." He turned away and walked around the room. "A-anyways! There's a whole forest full of both small and large prey surrounding the capital. We'll go to the outskirts so that you aren't disturbing anyone, and I'll watch you hunt from the trees."

"Fine challenge accepted!" I said. We went out to the outskirts, avoiding the litter. "So maybe I should have asked before I accepted, but what exactly do you want me to hunt?" I asked as we stood at the edge of a huge pine forest.

"Well since you talk a big game, how about you catch one? Of course, if that's too much then a small game is fine. If you can't catch anything by nightfall, however, you admit defeat."

"As if! I'll definitely catch something! Just you wait!" I declared.

"Humph, I won't hold my breath." he scoffed and jumped into the trees. Vowing to prove him wrong, I transformed and ran off into the woods. It sucked. I had been prowling for hours and hadn't come across one prey and it was going to be dark soon. Well, I guess I did come across a rabbit, but after I killed it, it rolled down a steep cliff and I couldn't get it. I had no idea where Hajiel was or if he saw it and actually wondered if he was still there or if I had been roaming for hours alone.

I stalked around the mountain forest as the sky turned bright orange wondering to myself, "Where the heck are the rabbits, or coyotes, or anything edible." I heard twigs snap from behind some bushes and quietly stalked over. A full-grown Elk buck was leisurely eating grass. He had a coat of pure white, covered in scars, and huge blue antlers. Its hooves sparkled as if made of galaxies. "A herd leader? Just my luck. He looks big enough to feed a family of ten for three weeks." I thought to myself. I slowly circled behind it and crept up. Slowly...slowly...slowly...and pounce! I think I heard Hajiel yell something as I jumped up and bit into the back of the buck's neck. He bellowed loudly and ran into a mad sprint. He darted here and there trying to shake me off and I tightened my grip, but if it had kept up, I would have fallen off. I needed to stop him, to puncture the main vein, or snap his neck. Remembering that I was part vampire though, I used my vampiric strength to bite down as hard as I could. The buck bellowed louder and went crazy. I dug my claws into his body and refused to let go. Still, this guy's neck was unnecessarily strong. I knew it was cracking, I could feel it, but even with my strength, it was still taking an insanely long time. I pressed down as hard as I could, to the point where my jaws hurt. Finally, after one final mad dash and a bellow that seemed to echo throughout the mountains, the bone crunched under my teeth and the buck fell over, hitting the ground as I jumped off and crushed its windpipe.

"I...I did it." I panted.

"Sara!" Hajiel yelled as he ran up to me. He looked at the dead buck and then at my blood-covered fur. "Did you...do this?"

"I did. I took down this buck." I said. "I took down this buck! How do you like that!"

"You...you could have died, you idiot! Bucks are known for stabbing wolves with their horns and this buck is notorious! No matter how many wolves go after him or how skilled they are, he crushes them with his hooves or stabs them with his antlers, and you...you're happy!"

"Well...I didn't know about that. I was just trying to kill him." He sighed and looked at the elk again.

"You really killed this bastard. Eat him."

"Huh?"

"You've been roaming around the mountain for most of the day. You deserve to eat your kill." Hajiel said as he walked behind some bushes.

"Where are you going?"

"To leave you to eat your hunt and..."

"And?"

"And...to take care of some business."

"What business could you have, except to spread the news of my glory?" I scoffed.

"Shut up and don't mock your elders!" he yelled and ran off.

"Well, whatever." I sighed and then looked at the elk. Since he said it was mine, I decided to eat it. Before, though, I had to perform Barguel, a ceremony to commemorate your prey's life by looking into their eyes and accepting their flesh. Once that was done, I ate for about half an hour, finishing what I could before deciding to take a nap while I waited for Hajiel to come back.

Something didn't feel right and woke me up, so I looked around. It was fully dark now, but seeing nothing, I figured it was just my imagination, however, the nagging feeling wouldn't leave. Suddenly a red wolf jumped out of the bushes and looked from me to the elk.

"Did you kill this?" he asked.

"Yes, I did."

"Who helped you?" he growled.

"No one."

"Liar!" he snarled.

"I'm not lying," I growled.

"Many wolves have died trying to take down this buck, many extremely skilled wolves, and you expect me to believe that you, a novice child, did this by yourself!"

"I'm sorry that many have lost their lives, but I took this elk down by myself!"

"Enough!" The wolf lunged and knocked me down. He held me down by the throat and, no matter how much I kicked and clawed, refused to let go. Still, I continued trying as I gagged and choked.

"What are you doing!" I heard Hajiel yell, and the wolf flew off. I rolled onto my feet as I tried to catch my breath. "Sara are you alright!"

"Y-yeah...for the most part." I choked.

"Guard! What did you think you were doing?!"

"I'm sorry my prince. But this girl. She is a liar! She claims to have taken down this buck alone, the very elk that has taken so many of our brethren!" he pleaded.

"She is not lying. The buck was felled by her fangs and her fangs alone." Hajiel growled.

"My prince," I heard a woman's voice say and several wolves came from the bushes around us. "I mean no disrespect, but how can you possibly know that." the old she-wolf asked.

"Because I've been watching her hunt since we got out of school and I saw her sneak up behind this buck, that I myself didn't even notice, without a hint of presence," Hajiel replied.

"Impossible! No matter how skilled, this buck was always able to detect a presence! How was she able to sneak up on something that generations have been unable to do!" The red wolf protested.

"Um...Commander, we saw them." A young she-wolf said.

"What?!" The commander yelled.

"When?!" Hajiel asked.

"You see Commander," her scouting partner said, "we were doing our rounds and noticed the two come into the forest. It didn't seem like the two would cause trouble, so we let them be but kept a close watch on them. When it started getting dark, we were going to tell them to go home, but we noticed this she-wolf stalking something."

"By the time we realized it was this notorious buck," the she-wolf said, "she had already jumped on his back and bit into his neck. The prince chased after her and we decided to try going around to cut the buck's route off from the front, but he kept zigzagging and we couldn't tell which way he would storm next, so the situation became too dangerous and eventually, we lost sight of them and decided to regroup."

The red wolf was silent then said, "...I guess I owe you an apology."

"Eh? Um...no it's fine," I said.

"It's not. You're not only the only wolf to take down this buck, but you did it alone. Treating you with the utmost respect is what I'll do from now on."

"Good." Hajiel nodded. "Sara I'll have someone bring your kill back to the dorms and talk with the principal, so it'll be fine."

"Eh? Really?" I asked.

"You are now the most famous person in the entire country. An exception can be made." The commander said. "Now, let's get to our second problem."

"What second problem?" Hajiel asked.

"These two only let you go because your presence wouldn't have caused a problem, but seeing as you have no business this far out, prince or not, you are children who have just snuck away from home. To add on that, you hunted an elk, a prey that children aren't supposed to hunt without parent consent, and a pack. Finally, we're the Border Guards, meaning we guard the border from the intruders, which means you're too close to the border." The old she-wolf said.

"Oh," Hajiel said. "Any chance, you'll overlook it since she killed the notorious buck elk?"

"No." the pack said.

"Geh! Didn't think so." he sighed. And so, we were escorted back to the castle where we were interrogated, or really lectured, by the King and Queen. The buck was then cooked and sent to the families of the wolves that it had killed, but I was allowed to keep the antlers, eyes, pelt, and hoof which I decided to send to Mom and Dad. After, I went back to my dorm, took a shower, and was greeted by a sleeping Berri. She was wrapped up in her blankets sleeping with a huge smile. I giggled and properly tucked her in, and then I went and got in bed. I'm starting to not feel well, maybe I shouldn't have eaten so much.

The night after I killed the deer was really strange, though I understand it now.

"Your name." A voice said, waking me from my sleep.

"What?" I mumbled.

"I would like to know the name of the one who has killed me."

"What are you talking about?" I asked as I turned over. In a glowing light, the buck stood beside my bed. "W-what!?"

"I'm the buck you killed and ate. My name is Yuon. Please tell me your name."

"...S-Sara."

"Sara. I have lived for more than 2,000 years. Many wolves have tried to take me down, but you're the first to succeed. As a reward, I give you, my powers." The elk spirit glowed and I woke up in my bed with Berri sleeping snuggled against me.

"Sara why're you awake?" she asked when I moved to get up.

"What do you mean "why"?"

"It's so early. Not even the stars are up. Let's go back to sleep."

"Berri, you had a bad dream?" I asked and she nodded. "I'm going to the bathroom, then we can go to sleep."

"I'll go too," she said, getting up and following me. "Sara," Berri said while we were washing our hands. "I like how you have blue antlers holding the orb for your necklace. It's pretty."

"Antlers?" I asked. I looked in the mirror and saw that the base for the necklace Shoyu had given me, was now blue antlers and held the entire orb rather than just the top.

"Just an extra thank you." I heard a voice whisper. I looked around but saw no one.

"Guess I'll treasure this even more." I giggled. Berri looked up at me with a confused, tired look and I picked her up and went back to the room to sleep. The rest of the school year I was famous, and people found my necklace to be especially pretty. For the year I was there, I created crystalizing spells by mismatching parts from the Brexior and vampiric spells I learned and turned different things into crystal versions of themselves. The easiest thing to turn into crystals were eyeballs, and I eventually had a whole collection of crystal eyes from prey I had hunted, including Yuon's.

We went to school year-round and didn't have more than a two-day holiday, so I was never able to visit my parents or little sister, but I was able to meet my grandparents on my Mom's side. It was nice and I got to spend a lot of time with them since they lived in the country. Hajiel never told me his feelings, but when the train doors were about to close, he ran up and kissed me on the cheek, then ran off yelling, "I'll find a way to make you love me!", much to his family's embarrassment. After we got back, we were given the choice to stay in the program we were in, go to another program, or stay at school. Berri decided to stay, but I wanted to explore the world, so I decided to go to all the different countries Adestria offered. So, for the last year of middle school and the first three years of high school, I was abroad and didn't really get to see my friends and family. Even so, I enjoyed it and had tons of fun learning new languages, cultures, and spells.

RECOLLECTION

Graduation

My final year of high school was about to start, and it felt thrilling. I technically didn't need to take classes and since I had already been to every country in the program, I decided that I would stay at Adestria. A few things changed over the years, the old building the Instructor taught us in was torn down and a new building was made, but Adestria was still Adestria, surrounded by lush green valleys and mountains. I was coming back from Duraha, the arms country Keri had to go to during her first abroad year. Even though it was a strict military country, the people were really nice and helped me with everything they could. Because they believe in knowing your enemies, they made sure to teach as many languages, cultures, and battle styles as possible and if they hadn't been kind enough to provide different tutors and learning facilities, I might not have done so well. I had gone to Hael earlier, which was similar, but I just couldn't get used to it because they required girls to learn etiquette. Oh, after Brexior I went to Grebior, the snake country Shoyu went to, it was interesting. They don't have an actual school system, but instead have home tutors and outdoor classes that anyone can show up to and the culture is...interesting to say the least. Anyway, I had to take a train from the Kofuian port to the school and found Mr. Marque waiting for me.

"Good afternoon Mr. Marque! Has the school changed any more since I left?" I called. He gave me a puzzled look, then smiled and bowed.

"Not at all, Ms. Hollins."

"Aww, that's too bad, I was hoping Mr. Todo put in a sweets shop on campus."

"...But then the kind couple in town would be out of business." he chuckled.

"Oh yeah, we wouldn't want that." I was curious why he was delayed in answering me but didn't think much about it. We went to the school, and I skipped up to Mr. Todo's office. "Good afternoon Mr. Todo, how have you been?"

"...Um...good..." he said.

"I brought you a souvenir!" I said holding out a figurine of Duraha's mascot.

"...Thank you..." he said, slowly taking it.

"Mr. Todo what's wrong?"

"...Well...um...Sara, I was just wondering what language you're trying to speak."

"Huh?"

"Ms. Hollins I was wondering as well." Mr. Marque said. "You haven't noticed that you're speaking a mix of several different languages?"

"No! I thought I was speaking vampiric!" I exclaimed. "I learned so many languages in Duraha that they all sound natural to me! What do I do?"

"...Sara calm down. Here." Mr. Todo said and popped a candy in my mouth.

"What is this? Medicine to fix me?"

"...No, a candy. You always calm down when you eat sugar."

"Now Ms. Hollins there is no need to be so upset about mixing up the languages." Mr. Maque said. "It's an easy fix, you just need to calm down and relay what you want to say in a single language."

"Ok," I said.

"Ah, there we go. Keep doing that and you won't have to worry." Mr. Todo said.

"Thanks."

"Anything for my little students. And thank you for the souvenir. Ah, that's right! Your uniform came in. Though I suspect you'll only be staying for a semester."

"Why is that?"

"Well Ms. Hollins, remember when you asked me if anything new had happened at the school?" Mr. Marque asked. "Well, we're not building anything new, but we do have a new program being added to the abroad program."

"Really!?"

"We're still working out a few things, but if we're able to make a deal, would you want to be one of the first to go?" Mr. Todo asked.

"Definitely!"

"Then it's settled." he smiled. "Now then, I'm not certain where Keri and Gene are, but Shoyu is in his room." Oh yeah, Shoyu graduated two years earlier, but since he had been a doctor's assistant for so long, he graduated college pretty quickly and took a job as Mrs. Henendez's assistant. Since he was only required to be there when she was not, though, he spent most of his time with me, when I was on campus, or studying for his PhD and since he was no longer a student, he got his own room in the boy's dorm.

"Really? Then I'll go say hi!" I was super happy a new program would be available and skipped towards the door.

"Sara!" he called.

"Yes!" I smiled.

"...No never mind. I know you're a good girl. Just try not to give students the wrong impression that it's ok to date a teacher." I nodded, though I didn't know what the "good girl" part implied, and gleefully left.

"One minute!" Shoyu called when I knocked on the door. I'm going to totally surprise him. He knows I come back around now, but depending on how far away the country is, I'm sometimes not able to see him before I leave again. When he opened the door, I jumped into his arms.

"I'm back Shoyu! Hope you didn't miss me too much!" I yelled as I wrapped my arms around his neck, and he toppled over.

"Wha-what the-Sara!?" he exclaimed as we crashed on the floor. I snuggled my face into his neck and smelled forestry and meadows.

"I came all the way here to tell you that I was back," I sat up and leaned my forearms on his chest. "And all I get is a, "What, Sara"? Cruel!"

"I-I'm sorry it's just that..." I looked at him and realized that all he had on were pants and his hair was still wet.

"Did you just come from the shower?"

"Yeah," he said with a blush. Then I smelled his hair and chest. "S-Sara?"

"Your shampoo smells like forest and your body soap smells like meadows. It's a nice combination to attract bees."

"Eh? Oh, the couple at the general store gave it to me. It's something new they made, and they wanted me to test it. It's supposed to attract females."

"Well, I guess I do like the smell. But I like the person wearing it more. Now let's dry your hair before you catch a cold." Getting up and turning my back, I went to pick up the towel that had fallen to the floor. Soon after, his arms wrapped around me while he rested his chin on my head. In my time away, he had grown several feet taller than me and used that to his advantage. "Let me go."

"Hmm, don't want to. Break free," he said as he held me tighter. I tried to squirm out but utterly failed. "Give up?"

"Fine." This always happened when I came back, but I swear one day I'll break free. I looked up at him and saw his smug face. His hair had droplets of water in it, and one dropped onto my nose. Suddenly he let me go and sneezed. "Told you you'd catch a cold!" I scolded as I grabbed the towel and began furiously drying his hair.

"Ah, ok, I get it, Ok! You're drying my hair not ripping it out!"

"Humph. I think you could use a little discomfort." He silently sat on the floor and hid his face with the towel. "...ok sorry. I'll be gentler." Still nothing. "Shoyu is your hair dry?" I peeked under the towel and the second I did, he gave me a kiss.

"Heh heh, I win."

"Not fair!"

"Well, I tricked you." he laughed. "But I wasn't satisfied with that kiss."

"Well too bad. I don't kiss people who tease and trick me."

"Not even a little one?" We silently stared at each other without making a move. "Please, Sara. I really missed you this past year." he whimpered. Pulling a puppy dog stunt like that, of course, I couldn't resist.

"I've really missed you too Shoyu," I said, sitting on his lap and wrapping my arms around his neck. After several kisses, we parted. "Happy now?" I giggled as my tail happily swished from side to side.

"One more," he said. We kissed once more then Shoyu fell back, and we nuzzled our noses together and relaxed in each other's embrace.

"Aww!" I heard Keri squeal. I bolted up and saw Geri standing in the doorway along with a few of the students.

"She's so cute. Wonder what class she teaches." The students mumbled.

"Gene! When-how long have you guys been standing there!?" Shoyu asked.

"Long enough." Gene laughed. "And good job on not locking the door or even closing it all the way." We quickly jumped up and Shoyu went to put on his shirt while Geri shooed the students away and came inside.

"How much did you see?" I asked.

"Don't worry Sara," Keri said as she took my hands and smiled. "We only saw everything from the super passionate kissing to the most passionate final kiss to the nose nuzzle."

"Meanies!" I yelled, breaking away and running to Shoyu. After making an escape from the boy's dorm, we made our way to the café, but I refused to talk to Geri.

"Aww come on Sara, we said we were sorry," Keri said.

"We're sorry we didn't knock, but we were just so happy," Gene said.

"Shoyu did you feel a breeze?" I asked.

"Ah alright alright! We're sorry! Really and truly!" Keri said. "Now please listen. We have something very important to tell you."

"Hmm...ok, what is it?" They looked at each other and smiled then turned gleefully to us and said, "I'm pregnant!"

"Eh?" They looked at us with a big smile.

"Again!?" Shoyu and I yelled. Something I forgot to mention, Keri had a kid at some point between graduating middle school and starting high school. It was a baby boy named Geb, who currently takes classes here at Adestria.

"We just found out a day or two ago when we were on break," Gene said.

"I wasn't feeling well and went to a doctor. Isn't it great!" Keri smiled.

"Um...I mean I'm happy for you, but..." I said.

"I know I know. I'm still in high school and this is our second child, but we've done wonderfully with Geb. I think we can handle another." Keri said.

"Well, I see no reason for us to object," Shoyu said.

"He's right, we hope you find lasting happiness." I agreed.

"Thanks, you guys. To be honest, our parents aren't too happy, so we were really looking for the support." Keri said.

"I understand. My parents would probably throw me out of the house if I got pregnant."

"Yeah. We only told our parents over the phone, since we didn't want to talk to them face to face, but I'm sure they would tell me to never come back."

"My parents would be angry, but they'd come find me after a while."

"Ah, lucky! My parents would never do that."

"Enough about our parents. Let's be overjoyed at the fact that Keri and I will be having another child!" Gene cheered.

"Yes, let's over be joyed." A woman's voice said. We turned around and saw Instructor standing with a smile and Mr. Todo behind her, not with a smile. "Since you're all high schoolers now, I bought you all beer!" she said holding up a plastic bag.

"Encouraging underage drinking in front of your boss is, a good idea." Mr. Todo growled.

"O-of course I was just joking! Right guys, you knew that! No drinking until you're the legal age! See Mr. Todo, Mr. Boss Man, I don't encourage underage drinking, look! There's not even alcohol in this bag, it's juice! Juice and coffee and-" Several cold cans of beer fell from the bag and rolled on the table with a clang.

"Not encouraging at all." Mr. Todo sighed. Instructor Kavlika didn't make eye contact, just slowly picked up her cans, placed the coffee and juice on the table, and sat down. "Getting to the point." Mr. Todo sighed again. "Your parents gave me a call."

"Eh?" Keri said.

"Not just your parents, all of your parents...well bye." And he disappeared.

"Wha-Todo get back here! Why did they call?" Shoyu yelled.

"Oh, thank goodness he's finally gone!" The instructor said as she cracked open a can of beer and took several chugs. When she finished, she slammed the empty can down and opened another. "Yeah, that definitely hit the spot. Even more so after being glared at."

"I'd still like to know why our parents called. I mean for Geri it's probably because of this pregnancy thing, but why Sara and my parents?" Shoyu sighed.

"You're loved."

"Does that mean you know why?" I asked. She took several more chugs then chucked the empty can into the trash and opened a third one.

"I can't say." she giggled.

"Well, if she's giggling, I guess it means that it's nothing bad."

"Or that she's drunk," Gene said.

"Are you kidding? I can't get drunk that fast." Instructor laughed. "Anyway, Sara you seem to be taking the incident quite well."

"What incident?" I asked.

"Um...Shoyu you haven't told her?"

"I thought it wouldn't be right when Geri had something so amazing to tell!" Shoyu exclaimed.

"Shoyu, what happened while I was abroad?" I demanded. He gave me a look of complete despair.

"Fine, I'll tell you, but...let's talk in my room." he sighed. We bid Instructor and Geri farewell and returned to his room.

"Now, we're alone. Start talking." I said.

"Um...isn't it a surprise? Keri and Gene having another child?" Shoyu laughed.

"Talk," I growled. He sat on the bed with a dejected look.

"Well, you see, while you were away Hadesia, Satania, and Lucia tried making moves on me as usual." he said, "But as usual I turned them down and left! But they became more persistent and then one day, Mr. Hordruml, you know the one you said was creepy, he told me to come back when school was over. When I did, he was doing it with Hadesia. She invited me, but I declined and immediately tried to leave, but then Lucia and Satania closed and locked the door and pushed me to the ground. E-even though I tried to break free, I couldn't get them off me and...eventually they pulled my pants off. They didn't get any further though because Mr. Todo broke the door down and saved me! But...um...yeah..." Once he was done talking, we sat in silence. I sat on the bed next to him and pulled his head to my chest.

"I'm sorry." I said, "Sorry for leaving you alone to deal with these feelings and for forcing you to relive them instead of listening." I felt my chest grow wet as he cried. After a while, he moved back and wiped his face.

"Thanks, Sara. I've been beating myself up for it for a while, but I feel better now that you're here." He then pulled me to his chest and began nibbling my ears. "After that incident, Mr. Todo sent them back home. He also fired Mr. Humdruml, so you don't have to worry."

"Good. I'm glad you're safe." I sighed as I let him lick my ears. We fell back on the bed and snuggled together, eventually falling asleep. After we woke up, we texted the group and went back to the cafe to talk with Geri and the Instructor about how our talk went.

"So that's what happened," Shoyu said.

"I should have bought Shochu." Instructor pouted.

"Well, at least Sara was able to resist the urge to make her partner hers." Keri giggled.

"Um...thank you, I guess. I really hadn't meant to snap like that though, I'm sorry if I put any pressure on you Shoyu." I said.

"Don't worry about it. If something like that ever happened to you, I'd probably do the same."

"It just shows how much you both love each other," Gene said, tickling Keri. "I, on the other hand, can't suppress that urge at all."

"Which is why Keri is pregnant again." The instructor said as she sipped her beer.

"It's better than losing her." Gene protested.

"You'd never lose me," Keri said as she snuggled his arm.

"Except if I steal her." Instructor said.

"I'll definitely protect you from that," Gene said as he picked up Keri and walked away.

"Sara I'll protect you t-hey wait to get back here, she's drunk!" Shoyu shouted at them.

"Sorry. Taking Instructor back to her room is your job now." Keri giggled as Gene bolted into a sprint, laughing.

"Ah, we got tricked." I sighed.

"Totally," Shoyu said.

"Don't worry. I'm going to buy Shochu and then I can make it back to my room by myself." The instructor said as she tipped here and there.

"No, we'll take you back to your room." I sighed. Shoyu and I each took a side and helped her stumble back to the girl's dorm. Mrs. Berseria saw us and, after a stern talk reminding Shoyu that he was no longer a student, took Instructor the rest of the way to her room. Shoyu brought me to mine and kissed me goodnight before heading back to his dorm and I stood in my room and looked around. "Nothing's changed." I sighed to myself. The books that Yama'Ori sent me, or more gave to Instructor, but she was too drunk to want to read them and gave them to me, were still strewn across the floor waiting to be read again. My bed was quickly made and had wrinkles all over the blanket. Even the trash from late-night studying that I said I'd get to later was still tossed all across the room. I took a deep breath and got the smell of paper and ink. "Yup this is my room, and it hasn't changed at all." I sighed. I wonder if I'll have the same reaction when I go home. Come to think of it, what do I want to do after high school? Continue travelling maybe?

Adestria hasn't changed at all over the years. There are a few new teachers, and the freshmen are just adorable, but nothing else. It was still just me and Keri in the Instructor's class, who for now was a permanent instructor, but Gene often hung out with us on his days off from farming. Instructor came with a hangover as usual, a habit Shoyu told me she started after the first year. The only thing different was that we were in the new building instead of the old one we had gotten used to.

"Today, my adorable seniors, we are going to be quietly reading while I take a nap." The instructor said as she laid her head on her desk.

"Mrs. Drunkard, does that mean we can go to the library like usual?" Gene asked.

"Gene, I have a splitting headache. I don't want to hear your snark comments." Instructor glared. Gene laughed and we left the Instructor to take her nap.

"Well see you guys later!" Gene called as he and Keri walked to the cafe.

"You're not going to the library?" I asked.

"Of course not. We're going to spend time together." He said as they disappeared down the stairwell.

"Jeez, those two." I texted Shoyu and we met at the library and checked out a few quick reads, then went back to his room, as mine still wasn't clean, and laid on the bed together while we read. When it was time for me to switch classes, we gave back the books and I went to Mrs. Berseria's class. The skills I learned in Duraha helped a lot and I was the first to stagger her. The rest of my first day back at Adestria was just as fun. After school, we met Geri at the cafe and were talking over snacks and coffee when Mr. Marque and Mr. Todo came up to us.

"Hey Todo, how's it going?" Gene waved.

"I've told you countless times not to call me in such a casual manner." Mr. Todo glared. "Otherwise, I might be inclined to leave you out of this juicy tidbit."

"What? What?" I said excitedly.

"Well, as the others know, Adestria offers a program where underclassmen get to speak with their uppers and local graduates. So, do any of you want to do it? Know that you'll be assigned to any underclassman, including kindergarteners, that need you."

"I'll do it!"

"I knew you would Sara, that's why I already signed you up. I already signed all of you up, actually, so this is just a courtesy."

"Sir, I think the children, and I as well, would appreciate it if you didn't do such things before telling us." Mr. Marque said.

"Ah, children love you Marque. I'm sure you can take care of them."

"I assure you I can. The problem is I've been taking care of children my whole life. Even now I'm taking care of an incredibly large one." Mr. Marque said, and we couldn't help but giggle.

"I think I'll take that as an insult." Mr. Todo said as they began to leave.

"Good because it was."

"Then I'll take it as a compliment."

"You're unbearable." Mr. Marque sighed until they were finally out of earshot.

"So, I guess we don't really have a choice." Gene chuckled.

"Oh well, sounds like it'll be fun," I said.

"I deal with underclassmen all the time as Student Council President, but dealing with smaller children will definitely help us raise Geb and our new child." Keri giggled.

"Then it's settled. We'll try our best and take on this challenge seriously!" Gene said to which we all agreed. Shoyu and Gene were walking us back to the girl's dorm when someone called Keri. We turned around and saw a woman and man walking towards us.

"Crap, we forgot!" Keri panicked.

"Keri let's go to your room! They won't be allowed in" Gene said, but then a greenish-black blur struck him down.

"Failure! How do you expect to protect a girl if you can't even tell when you're being hunted!" The greenish-black blur, which I saw was a wolf, yelled as it sat on Gene.

"Ack! Dad get off!"

"Why don't you make me?"

"Um excuse me, Sir, please get off my friend," I said. The wolf glared at me then got off Gene and transformed.

"You must be Shoyu which means you must be Sara." the man laughed as he purposely mixed up our names and ruffled my hair. "It's a pleasure to meet you both after hearing so many stories from my son."

"Guys this is my father, and my mother is hiding in the trees over there," Gene said as he got up.

"Wrong! I'm behind you." A woman said as she wrapped her arms around his head and pulled him to her chest.

"Mom let go!"

"Sara, Shoyu, I'd like you to meet my parents as well," Keri said with the most desperate look for help I've ever seen.

"Pleasure to meet you." The woman from before said.

"It's nice to meet all of you." Shoyu and I bowed.

"Now I do hope you won't mind, but we have to talk to your dear friends about their decisions." Gene's dad bowed. They were gone before we could say anything, along with Gene and Keri.

"I guess...we'll just sit in my room until lights out," I said.

"Y-yeah," Shoyu said. As we got to my floor, he asked, "Come to think of it. Do you think our parents are coming?"

"They live too far away," I said as I opened the door. "There's no way they're-"

"Hi, Sara!" Mr. Hazimi said as he stood next to Mom, Dad, Toast, and Mrs. Hazimi.

"Wha-how! How are you here!" I exclaimed as Toast ran headfirst into me.

"And why?" Shoyu asked.

"Well instead of taking a long trip from town like you guys, we decided to use the trans-dimensional component on the house and take a bullet train from the capital. It cut our trip by a day and a half." Dad said.

"And we're here because, for the past several years, you both have refused to come home to see us. So, we decided to come to you." Mrs. Hazimi giggled.

"Mom, Dad I'm really sorry I haven't been home recently. I just wanted to wait for Sara." Shoyu said.

"And I never know at what time during the break my exchange will end. Sometimes I get back only to leave for the next school year." I added.

"A call would be nice though." Mom said.

"But-"

"And a souvenir!" Toast exclaimed.

"Ma'am, Sir-" Shoyu said.

"You don't even have an excuse!" Mrs. Hazimi scolded.

"Eh!? But I was waiting for"

"You still could have come home." Mr. Hazimi said. We hung our heads, utterly defeated.

I heard a laugh and then Dad's hand stuck to my head and ruffled my hair as he said, "Ah, we're not angry", and he pulled me in for a hug.

"Just messing with our delightful children." Mr. Hazimi laughed as he grabbed Shoyu in a headlock-like hug.

"Dad let go, let go!" Shoyu yelled.

"Let the boy go!" Mrs. Hazimi scolded. "I can't hug him if he's flailing about like that!"

"Same!" Mom scolded Dad as she took me from him and hugged me to herself.

"Mom let go. I can't breathe." I said.

"Huh! Oh, I'm sorry Sara dear!" she said as she released me.

"My turn!" Toast said as she jumped into my arms.

"Anyways, you're here. Now let's spend time together." Dad said as he snuggled us and toppled onto the bed. "I know. Let's take a nap together. You love those."

"Dad let me go. I have to study and-hey! Wake up!"

"A nap sounds quite nice." Mom said as she joined us and made escape impossible.

"Nap! Nap!" Toast yelled.

"Hey! I need to study! Are you listening!"

"Oh, just let them be Sara darling." Mrs. Hazimi giggled. "They won't say it, but they pulled quite a few all-nighters, or maybe all-weekers, to be able to come see you today and they were so excited they didn't get a wink of sleep on the train."

"Really?" She nodded then they took Toast, who was too excited to sleep, and left. "I guess, I can take a little nap," I mumbled as I pulled the covers over us and snuggled into a comfortable position between them. I woke up to the gentle, soothing voice of Mom and her soft touch as she ran her fingers through my hair.

"Good morning sleepy head." she giggled.

"Morning?"

"Well, it's not really morning. It's actually night so don't worry."

"Night...of the same day, right?"

"Of course, silly."

"Sara, we have a surprise gift for you," Dad said as he came over from my desk.

"What is it?" I yawned and felt a warm and salty-sweet liquid pour into my mouth. "Tell me before you give me blood," I said as I wiped my mouth. "What if I had leaned forward? Then we would have kissed! I'm grossed out just thinking about it."

"You used to always say you were going to marry me and shower me with kisses. Now you say it's gross, I'm hurt."

"I was only three back then!"

"So, you're saying it was all a lie."

"Of course, it was!" He dropped his ears and gave me a long sad face. "...M-maybe it wasn't a complete lie...and it's not like I think kissing you is gross, but only on the cheek."

"That's my precious girl," he said as he gave me a hug. As I saw Mom laugh, I realized I had been wrapped in a hoax. We laughed together until Dad finally put me down. "Anyways, it's time we go start your surprise."

"Eh? The blood, wasn't it?"

"Nope. The blood was a prerequisite for the actual surprise." Mom said.

"Are we going out?"

"Yes, but make sure to wear something you can easily run in," Dad said.

"Hm, then I might have to change."

"Don't worry. Your mom and I figured you might need something, so we brought it along." Dad said as he gave me an outfit.

"Um...you are going to leave for me to put it on, right?"

"I used to dress you all the time. You would take bathes with me, now you don't want me in the room to change your clothes." He pouted.

"Just turn around." Mom laughed and he continued to pout as he turned his back.

"No peeking," I said.

"I can peek if I want," he grumbled.

"Not if you want to remain the father of the year." Mom said to which Dad scoffed. I hadn't realized it earlier, but my room was completely clean.

"Did you guys clean my room while you waited for us?" I asked.

"Of course! We couldn't very well stay in a room as horrifyingly unkempt as it was."

"W-well I only spent a few days to two weeks in here at most and I was usually studying, so I never really got around to cleaning it."

"That's still no excuse," Dad said. "We even found a chocolate bar that had melted and refrozen over and over until it got mold."

"Honey that was a rat." Mom said.

"W-what? No, it wasn't, it was just a fuzzy chocolate bar."

"It only seemed like a fuzzy chocolate bar because it was fat when you picked it up."

"W-was it dead?"

"After it jumped at me and I chopped its head off, yes." Dad hated unclean things, but particularly hated rats, though Mom said he got better after I was born, and I even had several pet mice...mostly for blood-sucking training. His clean addiction is part of the reason why I was surprised by Mrs. Berseria's comment all those years ago. I thought everyone kept their houses that clean.

"Maybe, we should re-teach Sara how to clean instead. I thought I did a good enough job, but I obviously need to teach her more and try harder with Fiore, so this isn't repeated."

"So, you're going to teach me something?" I asked.

"Yes, and it's not going to be cleaning." Mom glared. "Now, we are leaving, and do not say anything else that would tip her off about the surprise." She pointed at Dad who was too busy checking his hands, and everything he touched, for diseases to notice. So, after Mom reassured Dad that he didn't catch anything, we caught a train to the nearest non-vampire town.

"Wow, it's so pretty!" I exclaimed as I looked at the lights that decorated the trees like blossoms.

"Don't get too enamored, we're not staying here," Dad said.

"Aw, but the trees."

"We have a much better surprise than trees for you." Mom said.

"What is it? Will you tell me? What is it?" They took me over to a part of town where only the moon's light glowed. "What are we-" I began to ask but stopped when Dad put a finger to his lips. We hid in an alley and stood there for some time while Mom peeked out every once in a while. She looked like she spotted something and signaled Dad.

"Ok so we're going to tell you your surprise now," he said. "We're going to let you hunt for blood." At first, I couldn't believe what I heard, but Mom and Dad's expressions told me they weren't lying, and I would have jumped for joy had Dad not stopped me. "So, you know the basics.

A young male is coming down the sidewalk and, as much as I hate it, you're going to take his blood." I nodded and honestly, couldn't be happier, but I had to calm down. Too much excitement could lead to accidental damage to the blood vessels in the prey and I don't want to mess up on my first try and give Dad an excuse to never let me hunt again. I carefully snuck to the edge and waited for the person to walk by. They got closer...closer...and right as they passed, I jumped out and bit into the person's neck. Like I've said before, vampire teeth are always coated with a numbing poison that makes prey numb the second they puncture the skin. The blood was so warm and salty and sweet! It made me want to drink till my stomach exploded, but since there are only about five liters of blood in a humanoid, we can only take one or two pints, so I would have to take blood from several other people to be full. I released my catch, licked the wound to help close it up, and was running back to the alley when the man grabbed my arm, which scared me half to death.

"But it's alright." I thought, "Mom and Dad will definitely save-" When I looked over at the alley, there was no one there. They had abandoned me.

I was beginning to panic when a familiar voice said, "Sara relax, it's me", and I turned to see Shoyu smiling at me.

"S-Shoyu! What are you doing here!?"

"Well, my parents wanted to get to know the area so we came here. I had to use the bathroom, but the closest one was a mile away. Still to think you were the one hunting me. I guess that means your dad finally let you go on your own." he chuckled and rubbed the spot where I had bitten him.

"Y-yeah...sort of. D-did I hurt you or tip you off that I was here?"

"Not at all. If I were a normal humanoid, then I definitely wouldn't have known you were there, and your poison would have worked completely."

"Y-you're not lying just to protect my feelings, are you?"

"He's not lying. We could clearly tell that you did everything correctly." Dad said.

"Dad! Mom! Where did you two come from? No, more importantly, where did you run off to!?"

"Well, we thought about saving you in case it was a vampire, angry that you had used them as prey, but then we thought it'd be a good experience for you to learn what to do in these types of situations, so we jumped to the rooftops to watch." Mom smiled.

"Then we saw it was Shoyu. And then we had to hold off a rising urge to kill." Dad said as he glared at Shoyu.

"He had to, but I thought you two were cute. Anyways, Shoyu, I'm sure your parents are waiting for you. Thank you for your feedback and try not to leave your parents alone for too long." He nodded and we bid Shoyu farewell and continued hunting until I had a full stomach and I fell asleep on the train ride back to the school.

"Aww! I didn't study at all!" I whined when I woke up the next morning between Mom and Dad, in my dorm room.

"Hm? Oh, good morning, dear." Mom yawned.

"I didn't say good morning! I have a test and-" Dad covered my mouth and pulled my head back to his chest.

"Shh. It's ok. Daddy will fight off the nightmares and kill your mean boyfriend."

"I didn't say that!" I yelled as I pulled his hand away. "Wake up! Wake up both of you!"

"What?" Mom asked as she finally woke up.

"We were finally asleep." Dad groaned.

"I'm grateful that you guys trusted me enough to let me go hunting alone, kind of, but I didn't get any studying done because of it. Couldn't we have gone somewhere closer for my first hunt?"

"Sara, sweety, you have the day off today." Mom said as she wrapped me in a hug and began going back to sleep.

"Wake up! What do you mean?"

"Mr. Todo caught the flu. Whenever he's sick, he closes down anything that would make him worry, and making sure everyone is paying attention and doing their jobs correctly and professionally is too much worry." Dad mumbled as he wrapped both of us in a hug and nuzzled his head next to Mom's.

"So, my test is tomorrow?"

"Or whenever he gets better." Mom said.

"Yay! That means I get an entire day to study and..." I realized I was trapped between Mom and Dad. "Um, could you possibly, let me go?"

"Adorable little Sara," they mumbled in their sleep. I guessed this was the exhaustion from doing all those all-nighters and my only option was to sleep with them. Then a thought popped into my mind.

"Hey, Dad," I said casually.

"Yeah?" He mumbled.

"You've really grown up."

"How so?"

"Well, you knew Mr. Todo had the flu. That means that whenever you went in to talk to him, he was already sick, but hadn't shown symptoms yet. But you haven't freaked out or anything. That's why I said you've grown-" Dad jumped out of the bed, ran to his bag, and took several pills then took out a spray and began spraying the entire room.

"You just had to...mention that..." Mom coughed. Deprived from sleep, Mom and Dad reluctantly were up and decided to help me study for my test, though as revenge they didn't make it easy and by the end, I found the test far easier than studying for it.

Mom, Dad, and Toast were set to leave the day after next so after they woke up from their "naps", we went to a restaurant to have one final meal together.

"Sara, I'm really glad you're doing ok and happy that you've gotten to explore the world in your time here," Dad said as we ate dessert.

"I know. It's been so fun and next semester I get to go on another exploration because they're adding another country." I said.

"That's great Sara." Mom said. "Guess that means we won't see you this break either."

"Aw I'm sorry Mom, but I really want to do it."

"It's fine Sara, she's just pouting," Dad said. "But it couldn't hurt to send us a letter."

"Ok, I get it. You miss me and want to know I'm doing ok."

"Yes, and while a letter isn't you in person, at least it's not nothing at all." We laughed and he wiped some chocolate syrup off my and Toast's mouth. "But there is one more thing. You're a senior now, almost an adult, and I heard about your friend, Keri, so I want you to know that if you get pregnant, I will spank you until just thinking about sitting hurts your butt."

"O-ok." I whimpered.

"Then," he said, "we'll help you in any way we can."

"But that doesn't mean you just go out and do it!" Mom said.

"I know." I giggled.

"Do what! I want children!" Toast asked gleefully. We avoided her question with more dessert and the rest of the night we laughed and had fun. They left around noon while I was in school, and I excitedly waited for the closing months that would signal the start of my abroad program by helping underclassmen and kindergartners with their questions and tutoring them. I became the "Ultimate Neri", as they called me thanks to Berri, and they loathed the idea that I was going to be spending the final part of the year away.

Still, the day of the decision came, and the country was added to the list. I waved goodbye to the children and my friends and told Keri to send me a picture of their new child, then I was off. I was going to the country of Hitoris, the country of indulgent pleasures. I'm not exactly sure what "indulgent pleasures" are there, but it's probably nothing too out there since Mr. Todo made a contract with them. It's also the last country Mr. Todo can add for now since no other countries have a school system or good enough foreign relations to warrant a safe and educational trip. I wish they did though, then I could visit more places. The instructor told me to think about what I want to do in the future, but my family's so rich, I don't really know what I can do so I decided to go ask Mr. Todo before leaving completely. I was waiting outside his office when he popped up out of nowhere and scared me into clocking him, then we went into his office.

"Sara you're so mean! When you see me jump out at you, the first thing you do is hit me?" he whined.

"Yes! Why'd you jump out?"

"So, mean." he pouted. "So, what is it that you want? I already have a rough idea-"

"From listening to my thoughts."

"Now now, the method's not important. Though I must admit, Shira has gotten exceptionally better at creating barriers."

"...I need help figuring out what I want to do after graduation."

"I already have an answer."

"That's because you've been listening to my thoughts and had time to think about it."

"Anyways," he said, completely ignoring the comment, "why don't you go here." He handed me a pamphlet to Friea College. It was a small college on its own little island.

"Not that I don't enjoy an island vacation, but, why here?"

"It's an ambassador college, among other things."

"Ambassador?"

"You don't have to go. If you have other plans in mind that's fine. I just thought this would be a great path for you."

"Really? But I don't know the first thing about being an ambassador."

"That's what the college is for. Sara, I only suggest this because you have the makings for it. You can solve disputes, wherever you go people like you, you want to expand the world, and best of all, you have a curiosity to explore." I looked at the pamphlet and read through a bit of it. Ambassador doesn't sound so bad, it actually sounded pretty fun, until I read through the entire pamphlet.

"Mr. Todo, what is this about learning assassination?"

"I have no idea."

"Mr. Todo."

"...Oh alright! It's so you know how to protect yourself. Trouble does seem to always follow you so sending you to a school run by the Hydra Guild sounds like a good idea. You'll learn the Assassin Guild's techniques for protection and the Adventurer Guild's techniques for surviving."

"...Fine. Aside from that, I don't see why I shouldn't go."

"Oh, and Sara," he said as I got up to leave.

"Yes?"

"Be safe on this final trip. I set up everything to make sure you'd be safe but can only trust that the queen kept her side of the contract, and can't be there to save you so please, be safe." I wasn't sure what he meant, but he seemed serious. I nodded, bid him farewell, and went to get ready for my final abroad trip.

After a three-week boat ride from Grebior, Hitoris was not what I expected. The area where the school was had a garden and a fountain, but the surrounding areas looked like slums, with small square houses made of metal, stacked onto other square houses. The worst part was that there were no dorms. I was used to having to stay in an apartment from staying in Duraha, though I was with a foster family, and Grebior gave me an entire house but neither was filthy like this. The "indulgent pleasures" they spoke about in the pamphlet, were nothing I wanted to take part in, and aside from being slums, every other house was a prostitution club and I had to walk around ten orgies just to get off the dock. As I tried to find a path to the school that didn't involve walking past people having sex, three men dressed in black walked up to me.

"Excuse me. Are you Sara Hollins from Adestria?" The short one asked.

"Y-yes."

"Please don't be alarmed. I apologize that you had to see the state of our country, but at Vagis we promise protection for all our abroad students. I am the Principal, Mr. Tintama, and these two are just guards. It's a pleasure to meet you." Mr. Tintama held out his hand and I cautiously gave him mine and shook hands. When he let go, he and the guards eyed each other suspiciously. "We prepared a car for you right over there. Please get in." The car was a fancy limousine with fruit, wine, and vials of bright liquids. Several of the vials had fallen and caused the car to have a sweet smell. "P-please ignore those! I'm very sorry about that, the car must not have been cleaned out like we had asked." Mr. Tintama glared at the driver, who shrugged. The windows were blackened so it was impossible to see outside...but when I thought about it, I didn't really want to. Mr. Tintama and one of the guards sat on each side of me and the other sat across from me. "S-Sara please excuse my brazen questions, but at Vagis we like to make sure everything is...as it should be, so please bear with me," he said.

"Alright," I said and he took out a clipboard with a questionnaire.

"First have you ever had sex?"

"No! Of course not!" I know he said brazen, but that's just too private and he and his guards had the most disgusting looks on their faces, it creeped me out.

"So, you are a virgin?" Mr. Tintama asked enthusiastically.

"Y-yes."

"The school asks that you inform us when-I mean if you lose it while you are here."

"I understand, but my boyfriend isn't here so I don't think it's necessary."

"Of course. Your boyfriend's not here so there wouldn't be any need." he chuckled disturbingly.

"Don't worry Sara, I'll protect you," Shira said telepathically.

"Thanks. It makes me feel better knowing I have you." I replied.

"Now then," Mr. Tintama said, pulling me back, "we would usually require that you schedule a GYN appointment every month while you're here, but seeing as you're a virgin that won't be necessary. Neither is the monthly pregnancy test, nor the daily STI test, though that one usually isn't necessary anyway, so with everything out of the way we'll just drop you off at your home. Here is your schedule for your classes and your house and bathroom key."

"Bathroom key?"

"Yes. The queen stated that Mr. Vicer asked us to prepare a special bathroom just for you." The car stopped and they dropped me off in front of the student apartments.

"By the way, is there a library here?" I asked as I got out.

"Yes, it's on the basement floor of the school." Mr. Tintama said. I thanked him and went inside. I quickly found my room, running past the boys and girls who called me over while they were doing it with three other people, and locked myself inside. My room was on the third floor and the library was all the way in the basement of a different building. I decided to take a look at my schedule. Since I had completed all my core credits, except one, it was mostly elective classes, but all of them had something to do with sex. After preparing myself, I ran out of my room to the school library. Because of how the buildings were set up, there was no elevator, not that it'd be safe in this rusted, rickety mess. There were only shabby stairs on the side of the houses and platforms to make up a front porch. I went inside the school building and down to the lower level. It was time to see what the heck is up with this country.

I found a history book and went to sit at one of the tables, but quickly jumped up as someone licked my leg, and hid behind a bookshelf instead. They're called the Sekkusu race and have a strong lust to mate with everyone they find, often never getting married. Because of their sex drive, children are often held for twelve years before giving birth to them and are already ready to copulate and take care of themselves. I also learned that there were two halves of the country, the rich side, and the poor side. The rich side sounded nice and was where most of the country's revenue came from, as it was a great vacation spot. The poor side was where the dock was, and the school acted as a buffer between the two sides. I don't know what deal Mr. Todo made with the queen, whose name is never mentioned, but I suspect she didn't keep her end of it, and I have no way to tell him. This is going to be a long senior year.

The next morning, I walked onto the beautiful campus, but all I could think about was that I wanted to leave. I got no sleep as harassers kept knocking on my door and asking if I wanted to have "fun". I'm glad Mr. Todo asked for me to have a separate bathroom because I found out the next morning, that there's no separate one for boys and girls. Still, this led to many more harassers trying to break in that Shira tried to chase off, but eventually ran away from as they tried to rope him in as well. So, my first day at this abroad school was not at all going to be fun.

I also hated my uniform, if it could be called that, as it consisted of a small black bikini top and a short skirt that just barely covered my underwear. I decided to wear a shirt underneath the bikini and, since I was up most of the night, I took some fabric that I got when I visited Girda and added it to the skirt to make it longer and even added some embroidery with gold glitter to the end to make it sparkle. I had to check before leaving to make sure it was clear and, to my surprise, they actually held back their lust to get ready for school. It was a quiet morning as walked to the campus, with only one house that had a lot of noise coming from inside, but there was no one on the streets. "Lucky! I found the time I can explore." I thought to myself, though it was possible that since this was the first day of school, no one wanted to be out. I'd have to hope this was an everyday occurrence. Still, I was happy I wouldn't have to see anything, at least for right now, and made it to the wonderful campus untouched.

"Sara! What are you doing here so early and in such an outfit?" Mr. Tintama greeted me.

"Early? School starts in fifteen minutes, and I took advantage of the school's policy to allow us to customize our uniforms."

"It is true school starts in a few minutes, but, as you might have guessed, none of our people are the morning type. So, it'll be another hour or so until anyone shows up."

"Well then, I guess I can just explore the school until it actually starts."

"I-I see. Yes, you can do that," he said, getting that weird look on his face. "Yes, that'll be perfect! I'll take you around the school and show you the facilities we offer."

"Yeah," I said, feeling I should have stayed at the dorm. He held my hand while showing me where all of my classes and the bathrooms were, saying it was a big school and he didn't want me getting lost. I loathed it but couldn't find a good enough reason to get him to let go.

"So that's the entire school. We still have forty-five minutes in our schedule before anyone else shows up. What would you like to fill it with?" he asked as we finished the tour.

"Thank you for taking me on a tour, it'll be easier to find my classes now. Since we still have forty-five minutes, I think I'll go to the library."

"The library is a wonderful idea. Shall I accompany you?"

"No. I'll be fine on my own." I politely smiled.

"Come now, what kind of host would I be to leave you," he said as he pulled me along to the library. After we got there, I walked around and looked at the selection.

"Sara, what are you doing?"

"Looking at books. I figured I'd read until school starts."

"Oh? O-oh! Yes! Of course, what else would you do in a library?" he exclaimed with a look of disappointment. I sat down at one of the tables after finding a book about Hitoris' culture and fairytales and Mr. Tintama disappeared somewhere after a while. As expected of this country, all their tales had lewd plots and characters and their most worshipped and favored holiday was Orj Day, a holiday where everything shuts down and everyone comes together to create one big, giant orgy. It happens during their winter break so at least I found out when I should stay inside. I finished the book just as the bell to open the school rang and went to my first class. No one came in until right before the last bell except for the teacher, Mrs. Chitsu, and when she came in, she looked at me and then started hitting on me. I was saved by some students coming in, but they kept looking at me and smiling.

Throughout the school day, people kept passing me notes telling me to take off my clothes or threatening me if I refused and teachers would come and lean uncomfortably close to help me with work, I didn't need help with. The worst and most horrifying thing I learned...Hadesia, Satania, and Lucia are in all of my classes and want revenge for getting kicked out of Adestria. Surprisingly though, aside from glares and mouthed words, they haven't done anything to me, but they always whisper with other people and giggle in my direction, so I feel like they're up to something. I'd hoped that at the very least in my last class, Human Studies, things would be better, but even that light was blotted out. The seating chart the teacher put on the board had me sitting in the front row, so everyone behind me kept pulling my skirt and asking to see if I had a wolf tail and if it was sensitive to touch. The teacher was also late, writing that he had something to do, and the school has a policy that the last class of the day doesn't end unless the teacher says so, so I really wished he'd hurry up.

Fifteen minutes into class and he still hadn't shown up and the kids had gotten tired of me ignoring them and surrounded my desk trying to pull my clothes off as Lust laughed. Shira clawed and nipped at them, but with everyone surrounding me, it was hard for him to keep everyone away. No matter how hard I tried the stress was just too much and I couldn't hide my tail and ears anymore. They loved this and tried to grab at them causing me even more stress. Suddenly the door flew off its hinges as a foot kicked it in. I couldn't see who kicked it, but I didn't care. Seeing the open door, I jumped over the crowd and tried to run out but slammed into a tall red-haired man. He wasn't Sekkusu, I could tell that by his magic, but I couldn't tell anything more than that. It was familiar though. He looked down at me, with glaring red eyes, then at the hooting kids. As they came to surround me again, I instinctively grabbed onto him and tried to find some way to hide in his presence.

Suddenly a booming voice that shook the room yelled, "Sit down you ingrates!" I thought for sure my ears would explode and tried to cover them.

Everyone was dazed then one kid stepped out of the crowd and said, "M-make us!" The man sent a chilling glare at him, and all the kids immediately ran to their seats. I was relieved that for the time being, I would get some peace.

"You." I heard him say in a low growl and looked up to meet his ice-cold gaze. "You're still standing and you're clinging to me. I suggest you stop both those things if you don't want to be punished."

"I-I'm sorry!" I whimpered as I quickly let go and ran back to my seat. I heard Hadesia snicker, but she stopped immediately when the man glared at her.

"My name is Roan Martz, but you all are going to call me Mr. Martz," he said as he wrote his name on the board. "I'm your Human English and Mathematics teacher. I apologize for being late, I got caught up in a meeting. As many of you know, I've been teaching here for sixteen years. Now, let's get started. First, I want you all to introduce yourselves. Tell me your name, what you like and dislike, and anything interesting you'd like for us to know." He went around the room clockwise so I would be the last person to talk, but before the second person had even started, I felt people tugging on my skirt. I tried to ignore it, then to brush their hand away, but by the time the third person had finished, it had become unbearable, and I turned to tell them to stop. "Why aren't you a social butterfly? Since it seems you like to play and be the center of attention, why don't you stand up by the board."

"But Mr. Martz I-"

"I know that sounded like a question, but it wasn't." I quietly sulked next to the board as the kids looked and snickered at me. Mr. Martz ended class on time only on account that he was late but said that next class we should expect to stay late. Feeling humiliated, I grabbed my stuff and ran back to my dorm, ignoring all the shouts and tugs that I got. "I hate this! This sucks! I want to go home!" I cried as I slammed the door to my room and faceplanted onto my bed. The first day of school and I've already been humiliated several times. I want to go home, but I still have several months of this to endure.

"Sara," I heard someone knock, but I didn't want to talk to anyone, so I tried to ignore them, but they kept knocking. I heard snickering so it was probably Lust, "you forgot your notebook." It was obvious they weren't going to leave so I wiped my face and went to the door.

"Yes," I said as I cracked it open. Lust and a gaggle of other people were outside.

"Here you go. Your notebook." Hadesia smiled as she handed it to me through the crack.

"Thanks," I said as I took it and closed the door.

"Wait. We were kind enough to bring it to you, couldn't you at least invite us in as thank you?" Satania asked.

"Sorry, I don't feel like having company." I heard them snicker and laugh on the other side of the door. The next morning, I reluctantly went to school. I bypassed Mr. Tintama and went straight to the library since it was the best place to sit and wait for school to start. Again, I was harassed by teachers and students, and again Mr. Martz thought I was flirting and made me stand in the front of the classroom. On the third day, I couldn't take it anymore. Mr.Martz was writing a probability formula on the board for our homework even though school ended fifteen minutes ago when someone raised their hand. They asked if the formula could be used to decide when I was going to take my clothes off, another asked if it could decide when I'd lose my virginity, and a third asked if it could decide who I would sleep with first. I ran out of the room, and to my apartment when I felt myself start to cry. A few minutes later, Lust came asking what was wrong and why I had run out of the room while sneering and snickering. Eventually, they left, but others stayed at my door asking if I wanted them to comfort me. I wanted to be left alone, to shrink into the space and hide until everything was over and I could go home. Shira hopped out and tried to comfort me as I cried myself to sleep, and I refused to get up in the morning. I woke up to someone petting my tail and bolting up.

"It's ok Sara it's just me." Mr. Tintama said while sitting on my bed. Shira must have gone back inside the crystal to make sure that he wasn't kicked out, since pets aren't technically allowed, but since he didn't try to wake me, Mr. Tintama probably didn't even knock before letting himself in. "I heard what happened yesterday and your other teachers tell me it happens quite often. Sara, why didn't you say you were getting bullied?"

"I didn't think anything would change." I sniffled.

"Of course, it'll change Sara. We won't let you continue to suffer," he said as he patted my head.

"Really? Because no one did anything while it was happening."

"I know and on behalf of all your teachers, we're sorry," he said as he put his arm around my shoulder. "Do you forgive us?" I wiped my face again and nodded. "Thank you, Sara. Would you like me to stay and comfort you and make sure no one comes to bother you?"

"No, I should be fine."

"Ok. Ah, and I should tell you, we're looking into having your room changed since people keep coming here so you should start packing your things."

"Ok. By the way, Mr. Tintama, how did you get in?"

"I have the spare keys in case of emergency."

"Oh." I had started thinking he was a better person than I gave him credit for, but as I was thinking that his hand started moving from my shoulder to my chest and he began kissing my face and neck. "What are you doing!?" I yelled as I pushed away.

"I'm comforting you."

"No! I don't want this!"

"Come now Sara it will be fun, and you'll feel better after." He had lust in his eyes, and I doubt he was even listening. I tried to run out of the room, but he grabbed my arm and pushed me down on the bed. "Don't worry I'll be gentle," he said, putting his hand up my shirt and kissing my neck.

"No!"

"It'll be fun." He began to put his hand in my underwear. I bit his throat, just missing the main artery, and ran out of the room as he recoiled in pain.

I had no idea where to go, everywhere I ran people tried to grab my skirt or push me down, but I finally found a place where no one could reach me. It was a small hole that was between the roots of an old tree and blocked by a giant boulder. Leaves from the tree had fallen in and created a soft bedding. Even though people were hooting and calling for me to come out, I felt calm here and eventually, I fell asleep. When I woke up it was afternoon so I couldn't leave since there would be a lot of people out plus...I didn't want to go back to my dorm. I shuffled around a bit to toss some leaves on my head and noticed something soft. I brushed off some leaves and saw a sandwich wrapped in plastic wrap. There was a note that said, "I don't know if you like fried bacon and sautéed lettuce sandwiches, but I thought you'd be hungry." I was hungry, but I worried who gave it to me and how. It was impossible for anyone who wasn't extremely slender-bodied or a small child to get in and Shira hadn't left me since I came, but he didn't see who left it. I looked up at the branches above, but they would make it difficult to come from above. Besides this nation is full of sex-crazed lunatics who would do anything for sex, not leave a sandwich...unless it was laced with aphrodisiacs. I eyed the sandwich suspiciously, hit it with my hand, then smelled it. If they could drop a sandwich down here then they would be here, but even after convincing myself of this, I kept the sandwich at a very far distance. I poked the sandwich and fled then after it didn't do anything, was about to hit it again when my stomach made a loud growl sound, and a voice in my head said to eat it.

So, very cautiously, I unwrapped the sandwich, smelled it, then licked the bread. It had fried bacon, lettuce fried in the oil from the bacon, and bread that soaked up whatever oil was left. I took the sandwich apart, put the bacon on the plastic to save for last, and ate the lettuce and bread. It all tasted like bacon and fried lettuce, but the bacon tasted the best. Happy, I curled up and fell back asleep, waking up again around evening. I wiped my face with my hand and yawned, I didn't really feel like getting up, but I had this strange feeling I was being watched. I was facing the tree and didn't see anything, not that I really would, so I turned over to see if someone had figured out how to climb the tree. Instead of a person, I saw a snake. It was some kind of red viper snake with red eyes glaring at me. I contemplated what to do. It was only a few inches from my face so a strike would be impossible to dodge, but it didn't seem threatened. It definitely came while I was asleep, maybe it didn't think I was a threat. It didn't even attack when I turned over and I would figure someone suddenly moving would startle a snake. Maybe, it wasn't real? I reached out my hand to poke it and it immediately hissed at me so I quickly withdrew my hand and moved back as best I could. I hoped that if I didn't panic and waited, it would go away, but as I started to panic more and more, a rough, but gentle voice called me.

"Hey." the voice said and I looked around to see where it came from. Aside from the people, who were enjoying themselves outside, it was only me and the snake in the hole. "I'm right here." I looked at the snake. "Yes me. I'm the snake."

"The snake...is talking..."

400

"Why is it a surprise? You're a wolf and you can talk and even transform into the shape of a human."

"T-that's true, but I can't talk like a human in wolf form, and neither could any of the snakes I met in Grebior." It dawned on me that the voice sounded familiar.

"Whatever, I'm glad you ate the sandwich. I wasn't sure if you would like it. Sorry, I forgot to bring you a drink."

"That's alright, but if you don't mind my asking, who are you?"

The snake looked at me then sighed, "First we need to leave. It's not safe to be out at night."

"But I'll be fine here so long as no one knows."

"I found you because they know where you are now and since these people completely change at night, we need to go. A door and four walls are the minimum needed to survive once it gets dark. Now let's go before the sun sets completely." I got up, brushed off the leaves, and followed the snake out between the tight space where it transformed into a human shape.

"Mr. Martz! You're a snake!" I exclaimed. "And more importantly, you came for me?"

"Yes, I'm a snake, in a way. I'll explain it later, but first, where are your things? That hole is too small to fit them, so I assume you have them hidden somewhere."

"N-no. Mr. Tintama came into my room after hearing what happened, but then he tried to "comfort" me, so I bit him and ran without any of my things."

"... I see." Mr. Martz said, turning away. A couple or two fell over and knocked me over.

"Eh! What happened? Oh, what a cutie." The two men said as they looked at me. Mr. Martz rushed over and grabbed my hand. "Huh? Where'd she go?" they said before getting back to what they were doing.

"Sorry. I cast a spell that will hide us for a little while, but you have to stay close to me." Mr. Martz said as we started walking.

"Ok. Um, so where are we going?"

"To get your things."

"Um, I don't want to stay at my dorm."

"I know. We're only going to get your things."

"And after?"

"I'm taking you to where I'm staying. I put in all the locks myself so no one, but me has the key."

"Your place..."

"I promise I won't try anything with you." he said then mumbled, "I would never betray Lia or him like that."

"Lia?" I asked, but instead of answering he said, "Close your eyes". "Huh? Why?"

"There are quite a few people here. I don't think a young girl like you should have to see something like this."

"It's ok Mr. Martz. I just do my best to ignore it and make sure I don't get dragged in." It's not really alright, I don't want to be subject to see or hear any of this, but until I go back there's nothing I can do. Mr. Martz glanced at me and then pulled me onto his back.

"Hold on tight. I don't want you falling off." He transformed into a wolf and started running and within a minute, we reached my dorm.

"Mr. Martz, I didn't know you were a wolf too."

"Like I said, I'll tell you later. Do you have your key?"

"Yes." I hesitated to unlock the door and cautiously opened it. There was no one there, just a trail of dried blood that led from my bed to the door.

"Let's get your things quickly. The sun is nearly set." Mr. Martz said, completely ignoring the trail.

"...You aren't going to ask?" I hesitated.

"Early today I saw Tintama rushing to the hospital after he said he was going to go check on you," he said, picking up one of my bags.

"I-I see." Mr. Martz took the key to the bathroom to see if I left anything important in there while I checked to make sure all my things were in place. I heard someone walking up the metal grate stairs to my room and thought it was him, but when I turned around it was Mr. Tintama.

"Good evening, Sara. How are you?" he asked with a smile. He had bandages wrapped around his neck and dried blood from this morning on his clothes. The smile he wore was only a weak attempt to deceive me and it quickly vanished from his face and was replaced by a grotesque look of rage. "Sara, might I ask why you bit me and ran off? I was only trying to comfort you, but you rejected me completely."

"I didn't want your "comfort". Now please let me leave."

"But Sara I only want to make you happy. Now, I would understand if you enjoyed it a little rough. Just let me know that beforehand." I backed up but was stuck between him and the bed. "Now let's continue where we left off." He reached for my hair, but I jumped back before he grabbed it. I grabbed the bag and turned to run, but Mr. Tintama grabbed my head and shoved me to the floor. "Don't worry Sara everything will be fun and enjoyable." He said as he pulled me up by my hair. Shira jumped out to try and protect me, but was quickly flung against the wall and knocked out cold, returning to the crystal ball. I tried clawing Mr. Tintama, but he would slam my head down into the floor repeatedly and I had lost most of my energy after several hits. The pain from his grip was excruciating and as I looked at him through the blood that covered my eyes, I realized just how insane he was. It was dark out now and I could hear others coming to see, or maybe partake in, what was going on and knew if I didn't do something soon, I would die.

I glanced at Mr. Tintama once more and saw he had the crazed look of a serial killer. No amount of talking would bring him back and I felt a throbbing urge to survive so I grabbed Mr. Tintama's arm and crushed it. He screamed in agony and fell back. Once he let go, my vampiric magic began healing my wounds and I went into my True Wolf form. I'd grown since the last time with General Bradely and broke through the ceiling and back wall while the floor caved under me.

"A-amazing." Mr. Tintama trembled. "What a beautiful coat. It's-it's perfect." He crawled over and grasped some fur on my toe. "Sara please have my children, at least a daughter. Then, when she gets as beautiful as you I can- I can-" I wanted no part of whatever he was thinking. I could feel the building leaning under my weight and knew that it was about to fall. I shook off my paw, which sent him flying off into a wall, nipped my bag, and jumped to the street. The stacked square houses looked like one small ledge in this form, and I saw barren beaches and fields behind them. I also spotted Mr. Martz running back from the crumbling bathroom. He jumped from the ledge onto my head and signaled which direction to go. We ran off, past the school and into the rich part of Hitoris. We ran off the marble path and through the rainforest and, even though it was dark, I could make out marble buildings in the distance thanks to the streetlamps, something the poor side didn't have. A short while after we had crossed over, he signaled me to stop.

"Sara, can you transform to a smaller size?" he asked.

"Huh? Oh, I guess this form is kind of large." I said as he jumped off and I went to my humanoid form.

"And your vampire strength isn't exactly adding to the solution." We continued walking until we reached a house. It was made of wood instead of marble and stood out like a sore thumb since it was the only house around.

"Why's your house in the middle of a rainforest?" I asked.

"Because I didn't like having roommates. I built it by myself from the ground up, which is why I wasn't going to let you run over here and ruin it."

"Sorry, was I really causing that much damage?" He pointed to where we had come from, and I saw the school's roof had collapsed from the impact of my jumping over it. "Oh."

"I built my house with a sturdy foundation, but if you had gotten any closer it wouldn't have lasted a second."

"I guess it is a good-" I began before the world started swirling and getting dark, and Mr. Martz's voice began to sound very far away. When I woke up, my head was throbbing as if it were being beaten like a drum, then I remembered it was beaten against the floor. There was something on top of it and when I touched it, I felt something cold and wet.

"You're awake now?" I heard Mr. Martz say. I tried to get up to see where he was, but moving made the throbbing worse. "Here," he said as he handed me a glass of cold water with a straw.

"Mr. Martz, what happened?" I asked as I took sips.

"You remember what you learned about the delay time for spells and magic?"

"Sometimes if you don't feel the effects of a spell right away, it'll hit you like a wave of exhaustion later."

"Exactly. I contacted your school, and they apparently figured something was wrong since they couldn't contact you and the queen was refusing to check why, so someone is already on their way and should be here in a day. In the meantime, get some rest." I nodded and fell back asleep while hiding under the covers and woke up to the sound of yelling. Most of the delay had worn off, but I still had a slight headache. Because of it, whether I strained to hear what was being said or to ignore it, my head only hurt more. Suddenly I vaguely heard my name and decided to try and listen further.

"We demand that that monster pay for the damages!" someone shouted.

"No! She's a young girl who was scared for her life because one of your citizens tried to rape and kill her!" Mr. Martz argued. It sounded like they were in a pretty heated argument about me paying for the damage to the city, so I guess that means Mr. Martz is arguing with an official.

"I understand that she was scared, but destroying a country is a call for reimbursement!"

"Then let me ask you, is the reimbursement you're looking for in the form of money?"

"No. She destroyed the country because she was afraid, and that is our fault. What the queen wants is for her to help the wounded by giving simple medical aid."

"And what type of medical aid?"

"Like I said it's simple! Giving water, food, and favors."

"Exactly! The reimbursement you want is for her to give people sex! I refuse to allow such a thing both as her teacher and as a person!"

"What, does it matter how she helps them? It is a necessity for our people so she should give it to them!" I had thrown a pillow over my head when the door slammed open and Mr. Martz yelled for them to stop before yelling in agony. I bolted up, but before I could run, a tall shadow towered over me. "So, you're the girl? Hmm, you do have a certain air to you that could drive someone insane." I looked over at the door and saw Mr. Martz keeled over in pain and clutching his stomach as blood soaked his shirt. "Don't worry about him, more importantly, we have a request for you, but I think it may have changed now."

"I refuse!" I yelled as I rushed past him and began using healing magic on Mr. Martz.

"I see you overheard us, but perhaps you misunderstood me. My, or should I say the queen's, request is not something you can refuse, so I suggest you come with us." the official said, grabbing my arm.

"I still refuse, and you can't force me to go!" He looked shocked then a grin spread across his face.

"That fire in your eyes, we definitely can't give that to those filthy wounded peasants. You will be given to the nobles to help them cope with the destruction. Now, you said I couldn't force you, but-" He began pulling me away from Mr. Martz, "What if I told you that unless you agree to come with me, your friend will die."

"No!" I yelled as he commanded some soldiers to start kicking and beating Mr. Martz.

"Will you do as I say?"

"Fine! I'll do as you say! Just let me heal him!" I pleaded. He signaled the soldiers to stop, and I rushed over to begin the medical treatment. After I finished, I was taken to the castle and thrown into a dungeon to wait for the queen, who arrived shortly. She had on a pink bikini and loincloth, which barely covered anything, and a paper-thin veil as she looked me up and down.

"Well, you're certainly pretty. I'm glad Todo sent you." She smiled. "As queen, you should know my name, but it's no surprise if you don't, considering most peasants don't get that luxury. So, for your knowledge, I am Queen Ovastes and you are subject to my every whim."

"Is this for wounding Mr. Tintama or because I caused the school roof to collapse?" I asked.

"Oh neither. I could hardly care about such unimportant things. You are here because you're my pawn."

"Pawn for what?"

"For Todo of course. He came here some years ago, saying he was making some abroad program and wanted to see if Hitoris was a safe enough learning environment. I agreed, of course, on account of his stunning face and chiseled abs. I told him his students could stay in the dock town, whatever it was called since it was closest to the school, but he demanded that we build dorms here. I could understand why he wouldn't want his students near the peasants, they're disgusting, but it was a big ask. He visited our country several times to check on the progress of the dorms and got fed up with the lack of any."

"So, this is to get revenge for him asking you to build safe housing?"

"No silly." She laughed, kissing my cheek. "In all his visits, not once did he take me into his big muscular arms. It was insulting and frustrating. So, when he wanted to call off our collaboration, I sent him my three daughters, Hadesia, Satania, and Lucia. Those of us with noble blood aren't as affected by our urges, but since those three, their fathers were of lesser origin, I wanted to prove that the peasants weren't as bad as he thought, while also having them seduce him for the next time he visited." Figures those three would be the queen's daughters. Her kind face warped into a twisted bevy of rage as she continued, "But those three utterly useless girls not only failed to seduce him but caused enough trouble that he sent them back! Their failure allowed him to gain the upper hand and gave him reason to demand the dorms be built lest he end contact, so I sent them to dock town as punishment!" Blood dripped from her clenched hands and onto the floor as I backed away. Seeing this, she regained composure and smiled at me again. "Sorry about that young one, I get a bit energetic sometimes."

"N-no problem."

"Good. So then, do not worry about your safety while you are here. You are my pawn to draw Todo back here so, so long as your demands are not to the extreme, I will ensure to accommodate you. Is there anything you need at this moment?"

"Um, well, I could use some sugary food." She called in a slave, who was bound in chains, and told her to bring me something sugary to eat. Once I was done, she had that slave take me to a nice lavish room, which I was to stay in unless I got permission. The slave left, but I could tell she was standing right outside the door so escaping there would be difficult. I considered the window, but even a Wolf-Vampire wouldn't survive that fall. There was a house I could try to jump to, but I likely wouldn't have made it. Then I noticed the man standing on the roof. He had a black cloak on and waved at me. I couldn't tell who he was, I didn't know anyone with his build but waved back. He nodded then, after looking around, he began walking on the air towards me! Don't get me wrong, I know there are some creatures that can just do that, like Lyconians, but I had never seen it before. He was mere steps from the window when the door opened, and I spun around.

"Lady Sara, Queen Ovastes asked me to deliver your bags. Is something wrong? You look like you've seen a ghost."

"Not at all! I'm fine!" I smiled.

She gave me a puzzled look, then set my bags on the floor near my bed saying, "We made sure to wash all clothing articles within. Please make sure to check you have everything." As she walked back to the door, she turned to me and said, "And please get rid of any notions you have of escaping. Our queen is being kind to you. Don't make her change her mind." After she left, I stood, frozen, by the window. The man was gone, seeming to have vanished, if he was ever there at all.

Eventually, I checked my bags and then waited around. The slave came into the room to check on me at random, so making a plan was difficult. The bathroom looked promising at first, but the window was far too small for me to fit through. By nightfall, dinner had been brought to me and I fell asleep soon after. I woke up to fireworks and people cheering. The slave mentioned that a festival would be happening earlier, so at first, I thought nothing of it, but there was a particular light that seemed to not fade like usual fireworks, and I turned over to see the man in the black cloak standing over me. My first instinct was to punch, but my hand went through him then I realized he wasn't a man, but a fire.

"Glad to know you're ok." An unfamiliar voice said from the flames. "Now get up. I already grabbed your stuff, but I can't grab you."

"I-ok," I said, jumping up and following him to the window. I had so much I wanted to ask but now was not the time.

"Quickly, out the window." He ushered me.

"But how?" I asked as I climbed on the sill. "There's no way I can make that-" Suddenly, the cloak was wrapped around me, and I was pushed out the window. Actually, that's incorrect. I fell out the window as the entire room was picked up and turned on its side by a giant golden dragon. I landed roughly on his hand, but the cloak cushioned the fall, and then he threw the building at a set of archers taking aim.

"Todo get back here!" Queen Ovastes yelled from a different part of the castle rooftop.

"I'd rather get my student and these people home safe." Mr. Todo's voice boomed out of the dragon's mouth. I knew he was half-dragon and that dragons could be big, but he was almost the size of a large mountain and his voice echoed louder than the fireworks happening right above us.

"You'll regret this Todo! I'll make sure of it!"

Mr. Todo held me up to his shoulder where I hopped on and found Mr. Martz and a mix of slaves and non-Sekkusu people. Then in a low growl, he replied, "If you follow through with what you're thinking of doing, it will be your country that pays the price." They glared at each other, probably talking using telepathy, and then Mr. Todo sighed and began flapping his wings as we flew toward the ocean. He had to dodge a few arrows, I guess Queen Ovastes wasn't giving up that easily, but eventually, we got far enough away.

"Once we were smooth flying and didn't need to hold on for dear life, I admired the view and the wind blowing through my hair and thought, "I wonder if I could go into my True Wolf form and just stand here and feel the wind through my fur?"

"You could, it'd be like having a small pup on my back, but I'd rather not risk you falling." Mr. Todo said telepathically.

"I'd only be a small pup 'cause you're so huge! You know I managed to cause Vagis' roof to collapse just from jumping over it."

"Ha, child's play! I could have torn the whole building down just from sneezing."

"Well, I also knocked over a whole stack of buildings...also from jumping."

"I could have taken out the whole neighbor with a yawn."

"Well I...I...argh fine you win, but only because you're freaking huge!" We laughed as he landed on a small island with a boat waiting in the water. As per my request, Mr. Todo let anyone who wanted to, which was everyone, slide down his wing onto the boat before transforming back to humanoid and hopping on himself. We were introduced to some crewmembers who seemed more like pirates than staff from Adestria and I learned that was because they were. We were shown to our rooms on the boat and began sailing off. I got a room to myself and was writing everything that happened over these few days in you, when Mr. Todo knocked on the door, and guess what, he actually waited for a response before coming in and sat on my bed after asking if it was ok.

"I just wanted to continue our conversation." Mr. Todo said after sitting down.

"Oh, the one we were having when you flying? I already said you won."

I laughed, but Mr. Todo remained somber before saying, "Sara, I truly apologize for allowing all of this to happen to you. I should have done a better job at ensuring safe conditions for you and never should have let you go, knowing that woman's plan."

"So you knew she'd try to keep me there as a bargaining chip?"

"I didn't know her plan exactly. She's cunning and knows how to keep me from her mind unless she wants me to hear it, but yes. I had an inkling."

"...Wel nothing you can do about it," I said after a brief pause.

"What?"

"It's not your fault. She seems hellbent on you sleeping with her, but there's nothing you can do about that. As for everything else, it's not your fault either. Like Dad says, trouble follows me wherever I go, so don't beat yourself up over it. Besides, I got to see you in your dragon form so that's cool."

He stared at me for a bit then chuckled, "It's not easy being half-dragon you know. It requires a lot of energy." We laughed and talked for a bit more then he left, and I went to bed.

The next day, I woke up and was blinded by the sun as I went on top deck. Once I got used to it though, everything looked amazing. The sky was cloudless, the ocean was crystal clear, and the wood frame of the boat finalized that pirate feel.

"Sara you're up!" Mr. Martz called. "I'll get you a change of clothes." He walked off, but when he came back, he looked like a messenger about to deliver bad news. He handed me a sailor outfit with a white shirt and a navy blue skirt.

What is this?" I asked as I held it up.

"Sorry," He whispered, "When I told Mr. Todo, you were up he said, "Perfect! I needed someone to test out the new uniform...ah who am I kidding! I just want to know what Sara would do if I gave this to her."

"Sara would find him and give him a swift punch in the gut."

"I figured that."

"So, what's for breakfast? I'm starving." We went and ate breakfast under the deck. While we ate, he told me that he was Shoyu's father. His mother, Lia, had died during childbirth and he found it difficult to take care of Shoyu while dealing with his grief, so he sent him to Mrs. Mari. They frequently exchanged letters, and he did occasionally get pictures of Shoyu from her, but they've never actually met. After breakfast, we went back on top deck and talked until he had to go help with cleanup duty.

"Good morning, Sara! Do you like the sailor uniform I got you?" Mr. Todo asked as he walked over.

"Yes of course I do. Come closer."

"That glare in your eyes tells me to keep a safe distance, plus I heard you say you were going to punch me, and I'd rather not get punched."

"Hmph, eavesdropping dragon," I mumbled, leaning on the side.

"I prefer crafty."

"So, um, whose boat is this?"

"A friend's."

"...What's the name of this friend?"

"You'll find out." I stared at his goofy face for several seconds before returning my gaze to the sea. "When he shows up, say thanks for me, ok."

"Will do Mr. Todo," I replied as he walked off.

The day after that, Mr. Martz had more cleaning duties after lunch, so I went back out to the deck. The afternoon sun was warm and with the swaying of the ship, I couldn't help but yawn.

"The beautiful sun reflecting off the ocean's glass-like surface makes you want to sleep, doesn't it?" someone giggled. I turned and saw a woman walking towards me. She was gorgeous and had beautiful pink hair. Behind her was a man with maroon-red hair, with a dejected expression as he looked out to the ocean. "Mr. Todo said your name was Sara, right? I'm Arisu Kaiba, but you can call me Arisu, and this man behind me is my husband, Tsubasa Kaiba."

"Yes, nice to meet you Mrs. Arisu." I smiled though a little concerned that I might be the reason for Tsubasa's dejection.

Maybe noticing, Arisu came to my left, furthest from Tsubasa, and whispered, "Listen, I know Tsu-tsu doesn't look happy right now, but that's because he just woke up from his 18-hour nap."

"What are you whispering to her about?" Tsubasa asked as he came and stood on my right.

"Nothing nothing!" Arisu giggled. "And Sara, call me Arisu. The "Mrs." isn't necessary."

"Ok." I smiled.

"I wouldn't mind if you called me Tsubasa," Tsubasa mumbled just barely enough for me to hear him.

"Ah ok," Tsubasa grunted then looked back out to the ocean.

"So, you're doing better now?" he said after glancing at me.

"Ah yes. Thank you very much Tsubasa for-um...what are you doing?" Immediately after hearing my answer, nine tails materialized and began to wrap around me. "Hey stop!" I yelled as they quickly picked me into the air and made their way under my clothes.

"Tsu-tsu stop! Put her down!" Arisu yelled.

"I'm checking for infection. We won't be nearing any ports anytime soon, so if she has one it's better to find it now," he said in a monotone voice.

"I already checked when she was asleep, stop before she thinks you're a pervert!" He promptly put me down, though only after a long pause in which he considered a retort, then considered against it. "Please don't think bad of him," Arisu said as she fixed my clothes. "He means well, he just doesn't always know the correct way to do things."

"I know the correct way," Tsubasa mumbled, much like a child who doesn't want to admit they don't know. By the way, I'm sure you may have figured this out, but Arisu and Tsubasa are kitsune and the one important thing to remember about kitsune is that one trillion years for them is equivalent to one year for us. So, a ten-year-old kitsune is ten trillion years old. They still act like a ten-year old though and the Kaiba name is really important, but I don't feel like going into it now.

"It's ok," I said. I knew he didn't mean any harm, so I didn't feel there was any reason to be angry. Tsubasa looked back out onto the ocean, but I could tell that he was relieved I forgave him. Then his ears twitched, his tails moved like the waves in the ocean, and he walked off.

"Jeez, that husband of mine. Oh well, at least now we can talk." Arisu said. "So, by now you might like to know where we are and where we're headed right? Well, you're right if you're thinking that this ship is going to your school, though it'll take at least two weeks so there'll be a few stops."

"I see. So where are we now?"

"Right now, we're near an uninhabited island called Hu." She said, her six tails waving excitedly.

"Hu? What type of name is that?"

"It's part of the Ogre language. Translated it means Fire. The reason it's called that is because of that mountain in the center." she said pointing to a large jet-black cone-like lump.

"What is that?"

"A volcano. Its eruptions frequently engulf everything on the mountainside in flames. Only a few plants and birds seem to make it."

"That's...kind of sad."

"Oh, don't worry, because it erupts so much, nothing's there so nothing dies."

"I guess that's better." She laughed and we looked out over the ocean. The two weeks went by quickly and we eventually made it back to Hali, the port town of Kofu. As soon as I got off the ship, I was greeted by a giant wolf pouncing on and licking me.

"Are you ok? Let me check you!" Mom asked frantically.

"Mom I'm fine!" I laughed as her tongue slid all over my face.

"Yeah right! Strip, right now, so I can check!"

"Now now, honey. Don't embarrass our grandbaby in public. Let's get her in the carriage first." Grandmother said. Before I could protest, I was picked up and placed into a carriage.

"See you later!" Mr. Todo called, not the least bit concerned about me. After much struggle, we made it to a hospital where I was checked out.

RECOLLECTION

I Miss You

Wow, it's been a long time since you've been written in. I guess you'd like to know what happened after the hospital. The rest of the year went by quickly. Geri had a baby girl, which they decided to name Geri, and everything was fun. Dad got his PhD and Granddad became a teacher at Adestria. The Ambassador College was really nice too and Auntie is rambunctious as always. One day, we went to Brexior. We had gotten an invitation from the royal family to visit, and we were sitting outside at a local cafe having dinner. Solumnus was as energetic as ever and was the first to hop into the carriage when they were getting ready to leave. That's when it happened. A wolf, a former soldier during the war who suffered from PTSD, showed up. He had earned a name for himself as a serial killer and before I could do anything, I blacked out. When I woke up, I was in the hospital with Grandma and Grandpa at my bedside. I was unscathed, but Mom and Dad had died. It's almost the two-year anniversary of their deaths. I miss them. Everyone does. Shira doesn't talk much, but he told me Mom kept a diary, so here I am. Reading about the life she had. It's comforting with you around. If it's alright with you, maybe I can write here too. I'm Erin Hollins-Martz. I'm ten years old and the daughter of Sara Hollins and Shoyu Hazimi-Martz. There's a weird glow in the sky and everyone was freaking out about it downstairs, but now I think I'm being called for dinner, so I'll talk to you later.